LOST IN PLAIN SIGHT

LOST IN PLAIN SIGHT
BY
David Gerard

Copyright © 2010 by David Gerard

All rights reserved. No part of this book may be reproduced, stored, or transmitted by any means—whether auditory, graphic, mechanical, or electronic—without written permission of both publisher and author, except in the case of brief excerpts used in critical articles and reviews. Unauthorized reproduction of any part of this work is illegal and is punishable by law.

This is a work of fiction and, as such, it is a product of the author's creative imagination. All names of characters appearing in these pages are fictitious except for those of public figures. Any similarities of characters to real persons, whether living or dead, excepting public figures, is coincidental. Any resemblance of incidents portrayed in this book to actual events, other than public events, is likewise coincidental.

ISBN 978-0-557-35408-5

To Tammy ... who always believed in me
Emily & Gregory ... who have shown me the meaning of love
... and Julian M Gerard, your legacy continues ...

"A genius sees through reality to the truth on the other side"
Maxim

CONTENTS

One	1
Two	9
Three	21
Four	33
Five	39
Six	43
Seven	51
Eight	55
Nine	63
Ten	69
Eleven	73
Twelve	81
Thirteen	89
Fourteen	97
Fifteen	103
Sixteen	109

Lost in Plain Sight

Seventeen	113
Eighteen	121
Nineteen	125
Twenty	129
Twenty-One	133
Twenty-Two	137
Twenty-Three	139
Twenty-Four	143
Twenty-Five	149
Twenty-Six	157
Twenty-Seven	165
Twenty-Eight	173
Twenty-Nine	179
Thirty	187
Thirty-One	193
Thirty-Two	201
Thirty-Three	207
Thirty-Four	213
Thirty-Five	219
Thirty-Six	225
Thirty-Seven	231
Thirty-Eight	241
Thirty-Nine	245
One Year Later	247
Twenty-Eight Years Later	249

ONE

Anthony sat frozen, disbelief etched across his face. Why did his wife call to say goodbye? It didn't make any sense. The way Diane had spoken, as if in a dream, touched a knowing sense deep inside of him. Something had gone horribly wrong. He could feel the bile rising in his throat. He tried to refocus and frantically dialed her cell number, but it went straight to voice mail.

Oh God, what happened? "Think!" He pressed the heels of his hands into his temples. "Where did she go today?"

He racked his brains. "Debra!" The two women had planned to meet for lunch at the Octagon Restaurant in Fairfield.

He jumped up and ran to the driveway, finger on the redial key ... but she didn't answer. As he started the car, he dialed the State Police. Had there been a report of an accident on The Merritt Parkway?

His heart pounded, and his hand shook so hard he almost couldn't hold on to the phone. He sped down Route 106 to the entrance ramp at Exit 36, heading north, tires squealing as he took the 180-degree turn at sixty miles per hour. Just as he merged onto the highway, the phone cut out.

"Shit, Shit! No cell towers on this damn road." He slammed his fist into the dash, ignoring the pain, and raced in and out of traffic as startled drivers hit their brakes and pulled over to let him

Lost in Plain Sight

pass. He felt numb. Nothing registered. No sound, no thoughts, only fear in slow motion.

The traffic began to slow ahead, brake light after brake light blinking on, then off, then on again. Finally he was moving at a crawl. When he saw the blue and red emergency lights around the next bend he somehow knew it was her.

Anthony didn't want to believe it, but he felt it in his bones. A heavy feeling from the pit of his stomach grew and grew until it engulfed his entire chest. He didn't want to look, yet he couldn't take his eyes off the side of the road. He couldn't breathe.

Underneath it all, a faint, imperceptible hope flickered inside of him like a candle ready to be snuffed out at any moment by a random breeze.

At first, all that he could see was an emergency truck from the Turn of River Fire Station, located only a few miles south, and three cop cars, but no debris. He let out a deep breath as he frantically scanned the accident scene. Then he recognized Diane's green BMW flipped over on its roof, resting on the embankment. It had destroyed the guardrail and plowed into a tree, ending up at least twenty yards from the road. Anthony let out an involuntary wail as he pulled over to the shoulder.

"No … Noooo. Oh God, no!!"

He threw open the door and stepped out, but his knees buckled under his weight and he fell to the ground. He tried to get up and run over to the car, grasping at the air as a police officer grabbed him around the waist so he wouldn't fall again.

The emergency lights became a kaleidoscope of color and movement. Firemen, police, emergency workers and vehicles of all kinds seemed to be randomly moving around him. But, for Anthony, time stood still as he spotted a white sheet stained with blood, covering the body.

At that moment, he heard a buzzing sound from somewhere inside his head growing louder, culminating in a gentle *snap*. He collapsed and, to his amazement, realized he was no longer in his body.

As if a bird, he rose up over the mayhem. The din of sirens, lights, shouting and chaos quickly receded into the background as everything grew silent. Disoriented, he thought that maybe he had died too. The sensation of floating above the accident scene made him feel as though he was in a dream. He was alert but in a kind of half-conscious state; aware, yet blown like a leaf in the wind, as if some outside force was in control.

He looked calmly down at the scene that, moments before, had put him into a state of shock. Then he looked over to where he had been standing and saw a man lying face-up on a grassy area just off the shoulder of the road.

For a moment he wondered who it was, but soon realized it was him! The officer who had been trying to hold him up was now motioning frantically to an EMT to perform CPR on his lifeless body, while emergency workers continued to move chaotically around the accident scene.

Oddly, he felt no emotion as he studied his body's ashen face. The eyes were closed as if he were asleep, impervious to the ghoulish convulsions of his body rising and falling in step with the rhythmic ventilation the EMT applied to his mouth and the compressions to his chest.

Anthony viewed the scene with a combination of curiosity and compassion, mildly surprised by his lack of emotion. He had almost forgotten about Diane, so lost was he in this waking dream.

"Anthony." A whisper broke him out of his thoughts.

"Diane?" He turned his gaze toward a bluish white light positioned just over the tree line above him.

"Diane!" A sense of pure joy filled him, and he somehow felt her presence as the light began to grow in size. Gently, through what seemed to be his thoughts or intention, he rose toward the light, which was continuing to grow in intensity.

Diane's features were suffused with an incredibly bright light. She looked the same, yet younger, as she did when they'd first met in college. She appeared happier than he had seen her in years, all stress and worry erased from her face. Her body, transparent and illuminated in a bluish gray hue from within, was returned to the slim athletic build he had admired when she ran every morning prior to her pregnancy with Daniel. She had always been the love of his life ... and now she was gone. He suddenly realized the magnitude of his loss.

"I love you, Anthony," she spoke, gently embracing him with her eyes.

Lost in Plain Sight

"I love you more than you will ever know," Anthony whispered. He felt a rush of gentle but intense energy pulse through him.

"I didn't realize it was time to go. I'm so sorry I didn't say goodbye to you and Daniel." Her gaze was resigned, as if she had accepted her fate.

"If only I had known, I would have held you and never let you go, Diane. I want to come with you," he pleaded.

"It's not your time, Anthony." Diane's spirit moved closer. She cupped her hands around his face, gazing deeply into his eyes. "You have so much more to do in this world ... wisdom to gain for yourself and pass on to others who are here to learn from you. We will see each other again, sooner than you know. Although the years may seem long, time is but an instant on the other side."

At that moment, Anthony could not comprehend a life without her. Suddenly, he felt a tug at the back of his head and he plunged back into his physical body as if diving into a pool of ice water. Disoriented, he opened his eyes.

"No, Diane! I want to go with you," he screamed as he tried to sit up and reach for a spot above the trees.

"Sir, try and calm down. Relax, please," a voice shouted from behind him as paramedics attempted to lay him on a stretcher.

"Let go of me! I'm fine! I want to go with my wife," Anthony screamed. He tried to push the paramedics away and get up off the stretcher, but they forced him back down.

Powerless, he stared into a deep blue sky as EMTs secured leather straps across his body. A bird darted overhead into his line of vision. He blacked out.

#

Anthony finished recounting the events of that day, his head buried in his hands. His shrink, Dr. Richardson, scribbled notes on a pad while he sobbed quietly on the couch.

After what seemed like an eternity, Richardson abruptly ripped an unreadable prescription from the pad and held it out. Anthony looked up at the doctor with resignation and then begrudgingly took the paper.

"Look Doc, it wasn't a hallucination." He stared Richardson straight in the eye in challenge. "I'm not crazy." Deep down, he wasn't so sure.

Richardson shifted uneasily in his chair. "Everyone mourns differently. You've done a tremendous job facing the loss of your wife. In my opinion, you've expressed your grief in healthy ways, which is admirable. However, this experience seems to have triggered a psychosis. There's something we're not getting to—"

"Doc!" Anthony pleaded. "The visions aren't just real to me. They're real period."

The two men sat staring at each other in silence. It was a battle of wills and Anthony knew he was losing.

"So, you're telling me I'm insane?" Anthony asked in an exhausted whisper.

"I suspect you're suffering from trauma-induced psychosis, similar to the post traumatic stress a soldier experiences when confronted by violent combat. It's almost impossible to function normally after returning home from the battlefield *or* experiencing a terrible tragedy."

Anthony sat back and thought for a moment, considering the answer. It was the most sensible explanation he had heard yet, but disturbing. "Psychosis? I'm sorry, what I saw was real—"

Richardson interrupted. "The script I gave you is for depression medication that will address your mood swings and help to make you feel better on a more consistent basis. We'll start with that and see how it works."

Anthony recoiled. "Depression medication?" He'd never needed to be treated for depression before. Those medications could cause all sorts of side effects. "Doc—" he started but Richardson interrupted again.

"Millions of people take these meds, and they should help you too. We'll monitor your progress. If that's all, I only have a few minutes to prepare for my next appointment."

Anthony felt numb. "Okay." In a fog, he said goodbye to the busy doctor, who was already checking his schedule for the rest of the day.

Richardson glanced-up from his computer. "Make sure and fill that prescription today and I'll see you next week, same time."

Anthony sighed and gently closed the door.

"What the hell am I going to do?" he grumbled as he walked to the elevator. "I'm not taking those meds ... no way."

By now, it was getting dark and the street lights had come on, illuminating the parking lot with splotches of bright light reflecting off the pavement. Offsetting the well-lit spaces were areas of darkness where the lamp posts weren't functioning.

As Anthony walked to his car, he noticed the lights had illuminated the black leather seats in a glistening, silvery grey light. Something seemed different about how they looked tonight, almost as though they were the surface of a pool of water.

"I'm thinking too much," he chastised himself as he unlocked the driver's door. He leaned back in the seat and noticed something out of the corner of his eye in the rear view mirror. The hairs on his head stood to attention as a cold mist filled the car.

Anthony felt glued to his seat as a face slowly appeared in the mirror out of the mist. It was so white, it seemed illuminated from within. His heart jumped. He wanted to run but was paralyzed by absolute terror and a feeling he was being pinned in place.

Beady black eyes, deep-set and unblinking, like those of a spider ready to attack, stared back at him through the mirror. A foul, pungent stench wafted to where he sat, as if something had died and lay rotting in the back seat. He wanted to scream but no sound came out. Echoes of screams rang inside his head as if from inside a cave.

He couldn't look away from the specter that seemed to have stunned his mind and forced him to look into its eyes. Hatred emanated from the thing.

As the mist began to clear, he could make out even more features. Black hair was pulled back into a severe, unkempt ball that glistened with an oily sheen.

Anthony looked back at it in horror, frozen in time.

"*Yooooou,*" it whispered in disgust as its features slowly transformed into a scowl. "Remember me?" it hissed. "I haven't forgotten you." A sinister smile cracked the steely facade that seemed to be a female entity's face.

Anthony stared into the mirror with sheer terror and disbelief. Still, no scream was possible, only the screech of his soul permeated his awareness. He could not answer, only look into those awful black eyes that bore into him like a knife.

"We had a date, you and I." She laughed an ugly laugh. "You can't escape me through these pitiful moments you call a lifetime. I'm always there when you return." She smiled knowingly.

"Who are you?" Anthony barely managed to get the words out.

Ignoring him, the apparition continued. "You think you can run but you cannot hide. Enter my house and your time will be nigh," she spat and disappeared down through a liquefied back seat, as if pulled under water by invisible hands.

Frantically, Anthony fumbled to open the door. He jumped out onto the concrete parking lot, tripped over a broken tree branch and fell onto a grassy embankment. He kept his eyes on the car, afraid to turn his back on the apparition that had just disappeared into thin air.

The hair on his neck and head stood on end as adrenaline continued to rush through his veins. Hyperventilating, he slowly got up and carefully walked back to the car to see if the thing was still gone from the back seat. As he approached the rear door, he thought he caught wind of the rancid smell again. Was it his imagination?

He slowly reached for the door handle. A crow screeched, its wings flapping loudly as it took flight from a maple tree overhead. Anthony covered his head and ducked as it flew low over his car and out of the parking lot.

"Stupid bird," he muttered nervously. He refocused his attention on the rear door.

He reached out for the handle again, leaning away from the car for a quick getaway. Wincing, he carefully pulled the door handle, expecting the apparition to jump out at him. He finally threw open the door to expose the back seat, a chill running up his spine.

Nothing ... the seat was solid and empty. Breathing heavily, Anthony considered whether he dared even get back in, but it was getting late and he had to get home.

With great hesitation, he sat in the driver's seat eyes' glancing over his shoulder. He checked the rear view mirror to make sure the horrible reflection didn't suddenly reappear. Finally convinced it wasn't returning, he made the very uncomfortable trip home, worried the thing would return while he was driving and grab him from behind.

Lost in Plain Sight

After a minute or two, anger began to surface along with a million questions.

"Why me?" He slammed is hands on the steering wheel. What was that thing and how did it know him? And what did it mean by saying he could run but couldn't hide? It didn't make sense. Nothing made sense anymore!

Anthony broke down and cried. Nothing had been the same since Diane's death. He was alone all the time now, banging around a house full of memories and old photos. Her clothes still hung in their closet, and her shoes still littered the closet floor.

He remembered the day he could no longer smell her scent on her pillow or nightgown. He'd hugged the garment tight and cried all night.

Sometimes, he heard her voice while reading in the study. He would stop and listen, hoping Diane would appear and console him, saying that it was all just a nightmare, but nothing was ever there. Only echoes of conversations long past rang in his ears. Afterward, sadness always overwhelmed him. It seemed so pointless, so lonely.

Thank God for my dog Max, he thought. I don't know what I would do without him. With Daniel away at college, the house was a shell.

He grabbed the steering wheel so hard his knuckles turned white as he held back more tears. Had he taken a wrong turn into an alternate reality, a kind of Twilight Zone?

Finally, he shook himself out of these self-destructive thoughts. Last time this had happened, he'd spent the entire weekend curled into a fetal position in his bed. He knew if he didn't move beyond this numbing grief, the stress would eventually kill him.

He opened a window to breathe in some fresh air, took three deep breaths and headed for JoAnne's place. He needed to be with someone.

TWO

"There you go again. I can't discuss matters related to my patients, JoAnne. It's not ethical." George Richardson scowled in frustration and held the phone away from his face.

"But I need to know how to help him," JoAnne pleaded. "He's seeing things, for God's sake, and I'm in the middle of it."

"Look, I understand your concern, but you asked me if I would take on this case as a favor to you and the family. I gladly accepted, even though my practice was full." Richardson spoke in measured tones, annoyed by the intrusion. Still, he tried to be patient with her. "Divulging the details of adult private therapy sessions, even for a family member, without the patient's permission, is against the law." Maybe he could appeal to her sense of propriety if common sense didn't work.

"How can I help if I don't know what's causing all this?" she stammered.

Oh God, Richardson thought, rolling his eyes, *she's crying now*. "Come on, JoAnne. Give me a break here," he pleaded. "I know it's a tough situation. But with my sessions and your caring support, he's got the foundation he needs to begin the healing process," he stated reassuringly. "We had a very productive session today, a real breakthrough. As he faces the vision of his wife head-on and works through his grief, the intensity of the hallucinations should begin to diminish."

"He *saw* Diane?" JoAnne gasped.

Damn! Richardson massaged his brow, trying to figure a way out of his gaffe.

"George, what happened today? Did he really think he saw her? Please tell me he isn't that far gone."

"All right. You can't tell anyone I told you this. I'll only say it once … and I won't discuss another thing with you."

"Promise." JoAnne sounded satisfied. "George, hold on a second. Someone just pulled into my driveway." Before Richardson could respond, she banged the phone down on the kitchen counter, causing him to wince.

She's more insane than he is, Richardson thought as he let out an impatient sigh. Not five seconds later, he heard footsteps running back toward the phone.

"George, it's Anthony. I gotta go. We'll talk tomorrow. Thanks." With a click and a dial tone, she was gone.

"Good timing, my friend," he muttered, hanging up. "Let's hope she doesn't bring that subject up again." Could he possibly be that lucky?

#

Anthony pulled over as far as he could to avoid blocking JoAnne's car, slammed the shifter into park; turned off the lights, cut the engine; yanked up the emergency brake and leaned back in the driver's seat to let out an exhausted breath.

"What on Earth am I going to say to her?" He fumbled in the center console for his Blackberry, stalling while he tried to come up with a reason for showing up unannounced.

He already felt bad enough that she had to deal with his long list of crises, but he didn't have many people close to him to talk to. His mother and father were divorced and living on opposite coasts of Florida. His other sister, Alison, lived halfway across the country in freezing-cold Minnesota. His favorite uncle, Sam, lived nearby in Darien but was on vacation in Puerto Rico. He would only impose on his close friends Debra and John Clark sparingly for fear of pushing them away.

That left his neighbor, Elizabeth Shrimpton, who he knew through her daughter, Abby. The twelve-year-old girl loved babysitting his dog, Max, while he was out or traveling on business. There was no way he was going to speak to Liz about this stuff and risk losing the services of Abby.

Liz will think I'm nuts if I open up about what's going on. He shook his head at the thought. Realizing he had nowhere else to turn, he reluctantly shuffled up the driveway to pay his sister a visit.

#

JoAnne peered through the front windows, wondering why it was taking so long for Anthony to come to the door. Not wanting to let on that she knew anything about what had happened, she stopped herself from bursting out the front door and running down the front walkway to greet him. Instead, she made herself a martini with the extra olives she loved so much and stood by a window in her office that overlooked the driveway.

She gently pulled back the sheer curtains to get a better look at him as he walked up the front pathway, warmly illuminated by the nautical-style lamp-post and solar-powered path lights that lead to the front porch.

She took a moment to examine her brother's body language. His lean, muscular frame was stooped, and his strong but gentle hands clutched his Blackberry. He seemed nervous, his sandy blond hair more tussled than usual, as if he had been sleeping on it. She missed the wonderful sense of humor he shared with all who knew him before he spiraled downward into his current depressive state. His piercing brown eyes, always the topic of conversation among her female friends, had become as grey as an overcast sky.

Anthony's footsteps snapped her out of her reverie. She suddenly realized she was grasping the feather-light curtain so tightly she was nearly pulling it off the rod, and let go.

She took a deep breath as the front porch creaked with each of Anthony's steps, culminating in the metallic clank of the door knocker. It always seemed to startle her no matter the time, day or night, or the knowledge that a visit was imminent.

"Anthony, what a surprise." JoAnne faked a smile as she opened the door.

Lost in Plain Sight

"I'm sorry for bothering you on a work night." Anthony looked positively defeated.

"Not a problem, come in." She waved him inside, forgetting to turn on the light.

He stepped into the dark room, hanging his head as tears streamed from his eyes.

"Hey, why the tears?" she asked him. He buried his head in his hands, shuddering with emotion. "I'm so sorry," JoAnne whispered in support. She was nearly in tears herself. They had always been close, and the loss of Diane had made her very protective.

"Come and sit down." She gently took him by the arm through the darkness of the office into her kitchen, which was drenched with light from newly installed fixtures recessed into the ceiling and gleaming stainless steel appliances. The delicious smell of simmering tomato sauce filled the room.

Squinting from the brightness, Anthony followed her into the adjoining family room. It was open to the kitchen and showcased an impressive vaulted ceiling, twelve feet high, topped with four large sky lights. A freshly stoked fire burned cheerfully inside the oversized stone fireplace, creating inviting warmth that she knew would make him comfortable.

JoAnne sat on the edge of her favorite high-back chair opposite him and studied his face to get a feel for where to take the conversation. He looked terrible. The circles under his eyes had actually darkened since she last saw him.

"You can't go on like this," she began. "It's eating you alive."

"I know." Anthony sighed. He stared into space, hands locked together on his lap.

Feeling the time was right to confront the issue head-on, she decided to throw out a suggestion she had harbored for weeks. "I think you should move out of that house," she stated bluntly, holding her breath.

He slowly turned his head to look at her and cleared his throat. "I can't do that."

JoAnne shook her head. "I don't understand. You're miserable there, all alone with no one to take care of you. Why?"

"The best years of my life were spent in that house. Diane and I raised Daniel there ... took him to pre-school, elementary school, middle school, high school." He stopped, catching his breath. "And now he's in college. Every good memory I have left is there. I can't leave it." Anthony's voice rose as his emotions seemed to get the better of him. "I don't want to leave it. It's my only connection with—"

"Okay, okay." JoAnne realized she had made a mistake. "It was just a suggestion. I thought—" On the verge of tears, she stared back resolutely. "Can't you see I'm just trying to help you?!"

He took a deep breath. "I'm sorry, JoAnne. I'm just not ready to make such a life-altering decision yet. Please understand."

She held his gaze for a moment, hurt by their exchange and upset at herself for bringing it up at the wrong time. With a sigh, she rose from her seat and walked over to the bar to make herself another martini, knocking around the shaker, glasses and everything on top of the bar in frustration. She sipped her drink in silence.

"You could offer me something," Anthony said with a smile.

JoAnne accepted the truce. "I'll assume you'll want a double."

Anthony leaned back and stretched. "Nah, that's alright. Just a rum and coke with a twist of lime ... shaken not stirred," he added with a fake English accent.

"But of course," she added with her own elitist accent and a hint of a smile. It was the first attempt at a joke she'd heard from him in a long time. "Lame joke but at least you tried," she encouraged, and handed him his drink.

"Thanks, Sis." Anthony took a sip of his cocktail and placed it gently on a nearby coaster. "Can we start this conversation over again?"

"I'm all ears." The tension relieved, she hoped he'd reveal what was on his mind.

"It was a tough session today," he began carefully. "Richardson poked and prodded my psyche like a proctologist searching for a polyp."

"Anthony, really, must we have crude descriptions?"

"I've been told by someone in this room that humor can diffuse stress, so I'm trying it out." He shrugged.

"Fair enough ... go on," she responded patiently.

"I know Richardson is trying to help but he forces me to recall the same memories over and over again. It's torture. Frankly, I don't see the value. It's not making me feel any better. In fact, it's making me feel worse," he complained.

JoAnne forced herself to stay quiet and listen.

"Anyway, he made me recall the day Diane died—again. You know what that does to me, but that's not the half of it." Anthony feigned a laugh.

"Okay, I'll play. What happened?" JoAnne crossed her arms over her chest.

"You won't believe what I'm about to tell you. I wouldn't believe it either if I hadn't seen it with my own eyes."

"Try me."

"Well ... it was getting dark as I walked back to the car. My mind was racing and I sensed that something was out of place, but I couldn't put my finger on it." He looked at JoAnne hesitantly.

"Go on," she encouraged.

"After I sat in the front seat I noticed a weird mist filling the car. It wasn't fog," he added. "I felt something watching me from behind and looked into the rear view mirror and saw—" Anthony's voice trailed away as he shook his head in embarrassment.

"I know how hard this is for you. Just tell me everything and we'll talk about it, okay? No judgment from me, all right?" JoAnne wanted to be supportive, even as her heart was sinking.

"I ... I saw this awful thing appear out of nowhere."

"What kind of awful thing?"

"It looked like an old hag and, God, she smelled like—"

"You mean a witch or something appeared in your back seat?" she repeated to make sure she had heard him properly. She hoped he wasn't describing his deceased wife.

"I told you, you wouldn't believe me." He looked hurt and embarrassed.

"Sorry." JoAnne took a deep breath. "Keep going."

"She knew who I was," he added.

"She ... it spoke to you?" Joanne added with horrified surprise.

"Yes."

She carefully considered her next words. "Alright. I believe you."

Anthony let out a breath.

"But you know this is physically impossible," she implored with the best combination of concern and support she could muster.

"I don't think we're dealing with something physical. Either these are hallucinations and I'm crazy, or I've tapped into something we don't understand. Even Richardson told me trauma can affect people in strange ways. Who's to say it's all in the mind? Maybe the trauma has opened a door?"

"Opened a door to what ... another dimension or something?" she said laughing in disbelief. "You can't be serious."

"Why not? It's just as plausible an explanation as anything I've heard from Richardson in a year."

"But Anthony—"

"No, I'm serious," he continued. "I've spent the last few months listening to everyone but myself, and nothing has worked. It's gotten worse. There are thousands of accounts from millions of people all over the world about trauma-induced out-of-body and near-death experiences. People have seen family, friends ... even religious figures and have spoken with them. Why not me?"

"I've heard those stories too, but they can't be proven. The dead can't come back to life and explain what's it's like to be dead," she said emphatically.

"Countless books, scientific research and people who have treated the dying would disagree with you," Anthony retorted.

"Maybe, but until there's physical proof, it's all just hearsay." JoAnne was beginning to feel uncomfortable.

"I haven't told you, but I've started reading books about this subject," he added quickly. "There's a ton of research—"

"I can understand that these books would make you feel better and give you a sense that there is more to life than just our physical existence. I'll give you that. But, unfortunately, when someone is gone, they are gone. The living can't speak with the dead. The sooner you accept that and deal with it, the quicker you will heal."

JoAnne realized right away that her bluntness wasn't going over well, judging by Anthony's expression. But she couldn't help herself. They had been brought up in a non-practicing Catholic household, by a father who was basically an agnostic. Nothing in her life had supported either a religious or a paranormal view of the world.

"I'm sorry, I didn't mean to—"

Anthony looked stone-faced. "There's no need to apologize, JoAnne. Not everyone believes in the paranormal. Look, I really appreciate that you took the time to talk to me, but I should be going." He started to rise from the couch. The room was getting quite warm from the fire, which now had subsided but was glowing red with heat.

"Are you sure you're okay?" JoAnne felt a rising sense of panic that she might have overstepped her bounds. She had not expected this suddenly calm demeanor from Anthony, especially after such a tense conversation.

"I'm fine," he said with a smile. He gave her a warm hug, which she returned.

She stepped back to arm's length, attempting to read his facial expression.

"I'm okay JoAnne, really ... thank you," he said genuinely; a role reversal that wasn't lost on either of them.

"Alright," she responded tentatively.

#

Abby loved taking care of Max when Mr. Stoddard was out, but she hated going into the house alone to feed and walk him, especially when it was dark. She fumbled for the house key, buried in her jacket pocket, and looked around nervously at the tall oak trees looming over the front entrance of the large colonial style house.

The place seems much friendlier in the daytime, she thought, trying to keep her mind busy. I like it better in the summer when it stays light until 9:30. She finally grabbed hold of the tiny pen light attached to the key and shoved the key into the lock. As usual, the dead bolt stuck until she pulled on the door handle and it gave way with a "clunk". The sound reverberated off the black-and-white marble tile that covered the front foyer and hallway leading to the rooms in the back of the house. Abby didn't understand why Max never barked when she opened the front door, as noisy as it was. The house seemed too quiet with Daniel off at college and no one home to make dinners or keep the house in order.

Kinda creepy, she thought as she looked down the front hallway to the entrance to the kitchen. And he always forgets to turn the lights on for me. She sighed.

Finally, she heard the familiar sound of Max's collar as he got up from a nap in one of the bedrooms upstairs, shook himself, stretched with a yawn and ran downstairs, sounding like a herd of elephants. Such was Max's excitement to greet Abby.

"Okay, Max, down boy ... sit ... sit," she commanded gently. She gave him a hug and attempted to attach the leash to the animal, now in constant motion. Finally, she heard the familiar click as the leash hook found the ring on Max's collar.

"It's the same every day, Max. It's like you haven't been walked in a month the way you carry on, you big lug." She smiled and scratched him behind the ears.

"I guess you've gotta go, huh? Good boy." She held his head in her hands and gave him a kiss as his big, cold, black nose swiped her neck. "Keep that wet thing to yourself," she scolded, playfully scrunching up her own nose in mock disgust as she turned to take him outside.

Invariably, he pulled her toward his favorite tree stump so he could do his business. At eighty-five pounds, Max was a solid five-year-old black Labrador with a heart of gold. Circling the stump the way he had a thousand times before, he sniffed the ground seeking out the perfect spot.

When he was finished, Abby was always able to get him back inside with his favorite words, "Ready for dinner, Max?"

She quickly turned on every light switch as she made her way down the front hall to the kitchen. She always glanced nervously into the study located to the left because of a nagging sense that someone was watching her. It was one of many *feelings* that surfaced when she was alone in the house, and it made her shudder. If she hadn't loved Max so much, she would have told Mr. Stoddard she couldn't do the job anymore. She continued down the long hallway, her steps echoing off the hard marble tile.

Lost in Plain Sight

Her mom always told her to honor her commitments, so she would follow through until the end of the school year. Besides, the money was good and Max was always with her, which made her feel somewhat safe in this creepy house.

With Max by her side, she paused just outside the dark kitchen entrance and flicked on the switch before peering around the corner to make sure all was in order. The light over the kitchen table drenched the middle of the room in yellow light but left the far ends of the kitchen in shadow. She could see her own reflection in the bay window, her pale face staring back at her with alarm.

A large oak trestle table and four shaker-style, high-back chairs stood neatly in front of the large window, creating a comfortable eating area with a view of the side yard, now invisible in the darkness. A round clock mounted on the wall over the window stared back at her like the giant eye of a Cyclops, its steady ticking competing with her heart, now beating heavily against her chest.

Everything was clean and organized. Four placemats, one for each chair and two brass candle holders held brand new white tapered candles. A large white porcelain bowl was placed neatly in the middle of the table, filled with fresh bananas, apples and pears.

Abby turned to her right toward the newly installed maple cabinetry. Winnie the Pooh themed canisters containing sugar, tea, flour and cookies were lined up neatly on the granite counter tops to the right of the kitchen sink. Pooh, Eeyore, Piglet, Tigger and Rabbit smiled back at her from across the room, which creeped her out in a weird kind of way. She remembered when Mr. Stoddard had bought them for his wife, a life-long fan of The Hundred Acre Wood gang. They seemed out of place now in this lonely house. Abby felt a tingle on the back of her neck.

Turning to her left, she walked over to the pantry on the opposite side of the kitchen and noticed the door to the cellar was open slightly.

"That's odd," she thought aloud. The small bolt lock was always in place.

A chill ran up her spine as she quickly ran over and bolted the door shut. Without another thought, she rushed into the pantry and grabbed Max's huge bag of dog food, which she promptly

David Gerard

poured into his metal bowl with a loud swoosh. After briefly peering down the empty hallway, she turned off the kitchen light and sprinted toward the front door, still glancing nervously over her shoulder. She ran directly into Anthony coming in the front entrance.

THREE

"Whoa there, little girl! What's the rush?" Anthony gently grabbed Abby's arms, stopping her from bouncing off him and falling to the hard floor.

"Oh, it's you, Mr. Stoddard!" Abby was shaking like a leaf. Max bounded in from the kitchen, adding to the frantic scene.

"What's wrong? Why are you running?" Anthony peered down the hallway expecting to see an intruder. Adrenalin rushed into his veins for the second time that night.

"I'm sorry, Mr. Stoddard." Abby caught her breath. "The cellar door was open. It was so dark and quiet … I, I just got scared. I'm so sorry."

"Not now, Max. Sit down!" Anthony commanded, as the dog paced and sniffed Abby nervously, sensing her fear. He took a deep breath. "I'm sorry, Abby. I haven't been thinking lately. You've been an angel coming here to help me take care of Max, and I've rewarded you by making you come alone into a big, dark empty house." Anthony was disappointed with himself.

"It's okay," Abby responded through a deep breath, beginning to calm down a bit. "It's my fault for letting my imagination go wild tonight. I'm really sorry."

Anthony crouched down to be eye-to-eye with frightened girl. "I promise to leave some lights on for you from now on."

Lost in Plain Sight

Abby smiled as Anthony affectionately tousled her hair.

"Let's get you back home. I need to walk Max anyway."

Hearing the word *walk*, Max jumped up on Anthony in anticipation.

"Alright, Max. Sit … sit. He attached the leash to his collar. "Oh, by the way, please call me Anthony," he said with a warm smile. "My father was Mr. Stoddard." He looked at the girl with a big grin. "Deal?" He held out his hand, which Abby gently grasped and shook, looking shy but reassured.

As the three of them walked down the gravel driveway to the sidewalk that led to Abby's house, Anthony took a moment to enjoy the beautiful fall evening. The golden leaves were half gone and had now lost their color in the darkness. A beautiful harvest moon cast its silver glow across the peaceful landscape. Pretty clouds were scattered throughout the night sky.

I love New England at this time of year, he thought, taking a deep breath of the crisp night air. Max walked obediently by his side, the sound of leaves gently crunching under foot as they strolled down the hill, giving Anthony a moment to reflect.

Strangely, he felt a calming sense of purpose rise inside of him. He wasn't angry with JoAnne at all. In fact, he was grateful because their conversation had crystallized a new point of view he hadn't considered until tonight.

He now felt compelled to seriously explore the bizarre encounters that had plagued him lately. He wondered where all these experiences might be leading him as Abby's house came into view.

Anthony knocked on the front door, adorned with a welcoming fall wreath made of twigs, apples, pears and other seasonal decorations. He admired the cozy home, warmly lit from within, smoke gently rising from the stone chimney. The smell of burning wood permeated his senses. The house and property looked like a scene from a Thomas Kincaid painting, he thought wistfully.

The figure of a woman swept past one of the windows. A moment later, the front door swung open revealing a stunningly beautiful Elizabeth Shrimpton, wearing a classic black cocktail dress with sheer black stockings and patent leather pumps. Anthony was caught a bit off guard and quickly tried to conceal his attraction.

Elizabeth smiled. "Oh, hi, Anthony. Hi, Max." The dog wagged his tail furiously but kept to his master's side. "How kind of you to escort my daughter home this evening. Is everything alright?"

"Yeah." Anthony shrugged, still trying to pull himself together, but her emerald green eyes were making it hard to concentrate.

"Did you feed Max and remember to fill his water bowl, Abby?" Elizabeth asked with a mother's uncanny ability to identify the only thing Abby didn't take care of.

"Arhhh!" Abby grimaced. "I can't believe I forgot to check his water bowl." She looked up at Anthony. "Sorry," she added sheepishly.

"Honey—" Elizabeth started, but Anthony interrupted.

"No worries, Liz. It was my fault. I've been so preoccupied lately, I haven't remembered to leave any of the lights on for her," he apologized. "I'll fill the water bowl when I get home, no biggie."

Elizabeth's demeanor softened immediately. "In that case, thank you for bringing my little dear safely home. I'm just about to head out to a party and need to pull together some dinner for Abby, so we'll see you again soon, okay?"

"Sure ... I'll be going, then. Bye ..."

"Goodbye, Anthony." Abby smiled at him over her shoulder as she walked past her mother into the house.

"Come on, Max." Anthony gently pulled the leash and began to head up the hill, looking back one last time for a final wave. He noticed Elizabeth lingering in the doorway. She responded with a wave and a smile and then slowly closed the door.

"Oh—My—God. I acted like a complete ass." He had never reacted to Elizabeth that way before, but then again he'd never seen her dressed quite like that.

She had supported him through his grief after Diane died, listened to his work-related problems, stopped by on a whim to make sure he was okay, and not once had he been at a loss for words around her. Why now? She must think I'm an idiot.

"At least you love me, right Max?" The dog looked up lovingly at his master and wagged his tail. "I'll take that as a yes," he laughed out loud.

When he reached his driveway, he turned his attention toward the house again. He hadn't mentioned it to Abby, but he also wondered why the cellar door had been open. Without a doubt, the latch had been locked since the previous weekend when he had brought the outdoor furniture into the basement.

As he strolled up the pathway to the front entrance he realized that the only lights he had turned on before leaving with Abby were the outside lanterns, so the inside of the house was still dark. A sudden breeze whipped up a pile of dry leaves and spun them around like a miniature tornado as he approached the front door.

"I can see why she was so apprehensive about going inside," he muttered aloud. "It's making me nervous too," he whispered to Max.

He opened the front door and flicked on the foyer light. Silence met them as they stepped inside. Almost immediately, Max let out a low growl. He stared down the hallway, crouching like a coiled spring. The hair on the dog's neck stood to attention as the muscles on his chest and legs began to quiver.

"What is it, boy?" Anthony whispered, looking back and forth between the dog and the end of the hallway.

Max looked up at him, alternately whining and growling as he began pacing and attempting to break away from Anthony's grasp on the leash.

I don't like this, Anthony thought, his heart racing. Max never becomes aggressive unless something is really wrong. Somebody was in here with them. He pulled the dog outside the front entrance and dialed 911 on his cell phone.

The dispatcher picked up immediately. "911."

"Hello. I think there's someone—" Distracted, Anthony's grip loosened on the leash and Max broke free. "Max!"

It was too late. The dog ran at full speed through the front entrance and down the hall, his paws desperately scraping the tile to get traction as he turned left through the opening to the study and disappeared from view.

"Oh damn. My dog just got loose and ran inside," Anthony shouted into his cell.

"Who am I speaking to? Sir, please explain to me what's going on?" The dispatcher sounded confused.

"My name is Anthony Stoddard. I live on 713 Woodland Drive—"

"What's happening at that location?"

"I think someone is inside my house. My dog got away from me and ran back inside. I'm worried—"

"Don't go into the house after him, sir. I'll alert the police."

"Okay, I'll stay outside. Please tell them to hurry!"

"Would you like me to stay on the line with you? Sir, are you there?"

Anthony had stopped paying attention to the dispatcher. He stood frozen, listening for any sounds to indicate Max had found the intruder.

He braced for a human scream or a yelp of pain from Max, but soon realized that neither scenario was materializing. An eerie silence fell over the house.

"What's taking them so long?" Not even a distant siren penetrated the night air. He could wait no longer. He carefully pushed open the front door and crept silently over the cold tiles that lead down the front hallway.

"Max … here, Max. Here, boy." Anthony's voice was shaking as the opening to the study gradually came into view with each step. The grandfather clock, still out of sight, ticked steadily, mocking his mounting fear.

He peered into the room, every molecule of his being in a state of high alert. The light from the hallway partially lit the darkened study, illuminating his mahogany desk and a bookcase just to its right. He pressed the light switch on the wall to his left. All the recessed lights came on immediately, but they were dimmed, keeping him from seeing any details.

He pulled up on the dimmer switch and suppressed a gasp. There in the far right corner of the room stood a short man, no more than three feet tall, glaring back at him. Max sat calmly and obediently beside the intruder. The dog appeared to be in an odd, trance-like state.

For what seemed like an eternity, he and the stranger stared at each other. Unable to move or speak, Anthony was overcome with a powerful feeling of déjà vu. Long-forgotten images and memories of childhood began to flood his mind. Gradually, he realized he had seen this odd character before. He was suddenly transported back in time to one of the scariest moments of his young life, a scene that had lain buried in his subconscious for forty years …

Lost in Plain Sight

As Anthony hovered over the end of a bed, he noticed a small boy sleeping under a plaid woolen blanket. Next to the bed was a small, black folding table holding a glass of milk and two cookies. This was his first bedroom. The little boy was him!

He continued to scan the room in awe, beads of sweat forming on his brow. Light streamed in through the dormer window overlooking the front lawn, illuminating the child-size wicker chair filled with his stuffed animals. His bulldog, elephant and teddy bear looked back at him as if not a day had passed since he'd last seen them.

Anthony suppressed tears of confusion as long forgotten feelings overtook him. His breathing became shallow. His heart pounded so loudly, he felt sure he could hear the sound bouncing off the bedroom walls.

"Impossible!" he blurted out. There was his white bureau with the small lamp and gum drop lamp shade! To the right of the bureau was a hallway, at the end of which was an open closet door revealing neatly hung shirts and pants. More stuffed animals sat on the shelf above, looking back at him happily. He glanced quickly to his left and saw two framed prints of nineteenth century sailing ships hanging side-by-side, long ago forgotten.

He focused his attention down the hallway leading to the closet. It faced the bed like the dark mouth of a demon, ready to devour the child on the bed as he lay trembling under the covers. He remembered staring into that pitch-black space as it became filled with scary images created in his boyhood imagination.

Monsters had appeared from the void and attacked him while his parents slept, unable to respond to his calls for help. His breath now came in short bursts and he began to hyperventilate.

A muted scream interrupted his thoughts. He turned back toward the bed. The boy was sitting up with the covers pulled to his face, clearly frightened, watching him.

Startled, Anthony looked back at the boy, and felt the color drain from his face. How had he become the very monster he feared as a child?

Like a leaf in the wind, he suddenly found himself back in the room hovering over the bed. The little boy was not looking up at him, nor peering into the darkness at the foot of his bed where Anthony had just been. Instead, the full force of the boy's attention was directed to the right of the wicker chair where the three-foot man stood.

Anthony remembered everything now. He had seen this dwarf-man as a child, in this very room, and he was witnessing that moment all over again!

Even as a grown man, reliving the scene, he could feel the terror of the child. From his new perspective, he paid more attention to the details of the intruder as the boy slinked down between the bed and the wall. He had a sense that he needed to protect the child. He focused on the scene from a more objective viewpoint, which calmed him.

He directed his attention and rising anger at the apparition, something he couldn't have done as the little boy hiding behind the bed.

"Why are you here?!"

The specter stood silent.

His curiosity took over. "Who are you?" He waited for a response.

Let's provoke it, he thought, gaining confidence.

"It was easy to scare me as a five-year-old, but I'll be damned if you'll scare me now," Anthony taunted, the hairs rising on the back of his neck.

"He is ready." The diminutive man spoke in a high-pitched voice without moving his lips.

"Ready? Ready for what?" Anthony demanded.

"Ready for what you always knew would come." The answering voice was not the voice of the dwarf. "Let us move to a more familiar and comfortable location."

Before Anthony could answer, the bedroom began to fade. A new scene took its place. It was as if he were watching the scenes of a movie fading out, then in again, except *he* was inside this living movie.

Disoriented, he found himself standing on the grass in one of his favorite places on the shore of Long Island Sound. Reservation cards with names and the handwritten date, July 18th, 1970 were taped to tables positioned nearest to stone grills located at the water's edge. Somehow he had been transported back in time to a beautiful, clear summer day of his youth! Soon, families would be arriving with coolers full of burgers, soda, beer and chips to enjoy a picnic dinner while the kids played on the cool grass, he marveled.

The breeze was light. The calming smell of the salt water and the lapping of the waves seemed in stark contrast to the insanity of the situation.

Looking east, Anthony saw the details of Long Island, and to the southwest was the familiar skyline of New York City. Sailing yachts of all types and sizes dotted the Sound. In the distance, colorful spinnakers were suspended above the ocean while seagulls glided through the sky overhead.

He looked toward a stony outcropping at the end of the picnic point, and saw the figure of a man standing on the rocks. He was wearing what seemed to be a white shirt with billowy sleeves, and his wavy, salt-and-pepper hair was disheveled in the wind. Sitting next to him was a boy, looking out over the water. They seemed to be talking.

As Anthony took in the scene, the figure turned and began to come down off the rocks toward the place where he stood, and the boy disappeared. He was not afraid. Quite to the contrary, he felt a sense of peace he had not experienced in a long time.

As the stranger approached, Anthony studied his features. They appeared wise beyond his years. The symbol of a fish was emblazoned into a gold medallion suspended from a golden necklace. As the man drew closer, he smiled as if greeting a long lost friend.

"Anthony, welcome to your own special place. A place and time you created through your beliefs, thoughts and experiences. I am but a visitor."

"I know you, but I don't know from where," Anthony responded. "Am I dreaming?"

"This is as much a dream as the life you create every day," the man answered.

Anthony was confused. "Maybe it's a waking dream?"

The man gave a gentle laugh. "I think we have much work to do, Anthony."

"Work? What do you mean?"

"My name is Maxim. We have been friends for centuries ... in Earth time, of course."

Anthony eyed the stranger warily.

"On the other side, we know you as "Tabor". Calm your restless mind and listen to the waves lapping the shore, and it will come to you."

With each passing moment, a growing familiarity with this stranger began to take hold of Anthony's awareness. Fleeting images and long lost memories buried deep in his subconscious rose to the surface as if suddenly released by an invisible hand.

Maxim waited patiently for the knowledge to come to Anthony, his eyes gleaming in anticipation.

Anthony drew in a deep breath as he saw in his mind's eye a series of lives he had lived in other times ... families he had loved, people he had been—male and female. The sudden realization was overwhelming. He wept with joy at the recognition of those he had loved and sadness for what was no more.

"Nothing is ever lost," Maxim interjected, as if reading his thoughts.

Anthony looked back sadly. "But they're all gone. My families ... my friends." Long forgotten emotions bubbled to the surface. His face was etched with pain.

He felt Maxim's energy pull him back to the present moment. Then it dawned on him. Through all of his lives on Earth, Maxim had been there to guide him, yet he could not possibly be of this world, could he?

He felt immersed in a sea of knowledge as pieces of a puzzle began to come together in a single truth: Death was not the end. It was merely the portal back to his source, his real home.

"A gift of truth from one loyal friend to another." Maxim gave him a knowing smile.

But Anthony wasn't totally convinced.

Sensing his resistance, Maxim added, "Your lives on Earth are your dreams on the other side. You have chosen each life carefully after death, building the progression of your soul toward All That Is over countless centuries."

"This life I am in now. I chose to be here? Are all of the things I'm experiencing pre-ordained ... meant to be?" Anthony's voice rose in anticipation.

"Nothing is pre-ordained, Anthony. You have free will to think and act as you see fit." Maxim smiled patiently as Anthony thought about this.

"But if I've chosen this life to learn and grow, wouldn't I know what was going to happen so I could meet the challenges I set down for myself?"

Maxim shook his head. "With the assistance of your Oversoul, you created a map; a blueprint for this life that included specific experiences and goals you wanted to achieve. It was not set in stone but rather serves as a guide for you to follow. Subconsciously, you recognize the signposts and walk the path. Listen to your heart and your body. They will tell you if your path is true or if you have deviated from your intention."

Still stuck on the concept of an Oversoul, Anthony inquired, "Maxim, what or who is my Oversoul? Is it a part of me?"

"Good, good. Yes, your Oversoul is a part of you and so much more, Anthony."

Maxim seemed pleased.

The sound of cackling laughter interrupted their conversation as they both turned and looked toward a pathway leading to the picnic point from a beautiful horseshoe beach just beyond a sea wall. Anthony noticed a strange looking wooden cart filled to overflowing with what seemed to be ordinary boxes, suitcases and containers of all sizes. So tall was the pile of items that it completely obscured the person pushing it. There was no doubt, however, that the laughter was emanating from whomever was wheeling the rickety cart toward them.

"How strange," muttered Anthony.

"Oh, he likes to make a grand entrance, that Jaster," Maxim replied, rolling his eyes.

"What's a Jaster?" Anthony asked.

Maxim suppressed a laugh. "Not what, but who," he stated with a hint of exasperation and obvious fondness for the still invisible character, pushing the cart toward them.

"He sure does seem to be in a good mood, whoever he is," Anthony observed. He held his gaze on the cart, now squeaking its way closer.

"Oh, he's one of the happiest souls I know," Maxim added. "A bit of a practical joker. Sometimes rubs others the wrong way."

"Really?" Anthony tried to peer around the cart, but the elusive Jaster still hadn't come into view.

"Oh yes. You've got to set down boundaries with him. He is, however, one of the most loyal friends I know. I can count on him to keep an eye on my charges ... like you for instance." Maxim took in Anthony's confused expression and clarified himself. "He helps me watch over those I guide and protect."

"You mean there are others—"

Anthony was interrupted by a loud *thump* as the cart finally arrived at its destination in front of him. Containers and boxes' clattered to the ground from the tall pile of debris. A loose storage container top rolled near his feet as Maxim welcomed his friend.

"Jaster, I would like you to meet my dear friend, Anthony." Maxim gestured formally in Anthony's direction with a slight bow.

With a shuffling of feet, a little man came into view from around the cart. It was the apparition Anthony had seen in his study and as a little boy forty years earlier.

FOUR

Anthony stared incredulously at the dwarf-man. Jaster, obviously reveling in Anthony's shock and surprise, looked up at him smugly. He finally cracked a smile that revealed a rack of abnormally large gold teeth to match the gold hoop earrings poking out from underneath his white turban.

"So surprised is he, Maxim. You would never know he insisted on this meeting prior to his current incarnation. Quite amusing." Jaster crossed his arms and tapped his gold sandals with mock impatience.

Speechless, Anthony turned to Maxim for an explanation.

"He's right, you know. You did insist quite vociferously. Your Oversoul thought the meeting time premature, based on the blueprint for your current life, but relented because of your willingness to address an extraordinary number of karmic issues," stated Maxim matter-of-factly.

After a moment of confused silence, Anthony continued. "I really don't understand any of this."

Jaster burst out laughing, doubling over with uncontrollable spasms as he grabbed his belly. He fell into the cart, knocking every box, storage bin, lid and container into the air around the three of them.

Lost in Plain Sight

At first, Anthony felt hurt and embarrassed by his obvious lack of *cosmic knowledge* but the sight of Jaster rolling around on the ground was ridiculous and he began to laugh despite himself and the insanity of the situation.

"He's one of a kind, that Jaster. Keeps me on my toes, he does," said Maxim as though he had seen the scene a thousand times before. "Now that he has kindly dispersed the packages from the cart, let us discuss why he brought them here in the first place." Maxim had turned suddenly serious again.

Jaster seemed to sense the change in mood and hastily rose to his feet, wiping the grass from his tunic and standing attentively with his little hands behind his back.

"Why bother pushing around a cart full of empty containers? It seems silly." Anthony shrugged his shoulders.

"It would be except for the fact that they are not empty containers. They are symbols representing the manifestations of your negative energy, including the attitudes, beliefs and thoughts that limit your life every day. They follow you wherever you go until you become aware of their existence, recognize them for what they are and let them go. This changes your reality in the truest sense. Negative energy creates resistance between your soul and the source of your energy and vitality. That source is your Oversoul."

"My Oversoul is my life force?" Anthony was awestruck.

"Yes. Some call him your Higher Power or Spirit, but don't make the mistake of thinking he is a being outside of you. There is no separation. Your Oversoul is the most subtle part of you, just as you are the part of him that is experiencing physical life on Earth."

"And these containers represent my personal baggage?"

"Yes, excellent." Maxim was clearly pleased. "So you can see how much work we have ahead of us to clear the way, so to speak, before we begin our real training," Maxim exclaimed.

"Training?" Anthony was caught off-guard.

"I think we've covered enough for now. You have much to think about, my friend." Maxim waved his hand in a circular motion.

Before Anthony had a chance to respond, his head began to spin as the landscape underneath and around him collapsed into a million shapes and colors, re-forming into the familiar surroundings of his study.

For a moment, he thought he had woken from a vivid dream. The room was exactly as he had left it. Max was resting comfortably on his fleece bed next to the old leather couch, and Jaster was no longer in the corner of the study ...

The sound of sirens broke through his confused state of mind as patrol cars skidded into his driveway, blue and red lights flashing. Max jumped up and ran into the hallway, barking madly as the sound of men's voices outside reached Anthony in the study.

It took him a moment to remember he'd called 911. That must have been hours ago, he thought, looking at his watch. However, to his shock and surprise, only five minutes had passed since he'd begun his search for Max.

"That's impossible!" he gasped. "I've just spent hours ... " He stopped for a moment, thinking out loud. "Spent hours where? My boyhood home? On a beach at least a half-hour drive from here with invisible friends?" It had seemed so real.

A knock on the front door shook him out of his ensuing panic.

"Mr. Stoddard? Police! Are you inside?"

"Yes, uh ... come in. I'm coming." Anthony noticed that Max's leash was still attached to his collar. He jumped out from behind the desk and grabbed the loop off the floor, pulling the dog close as the officers approached, guns drawn.

"Are you okay, sir? We received a call from 911 that you reported an intruder in the house." The officers looked at Max warily.

"Yes ... I, I'm fine." Anthony tried to pull himself together. "My dog went after something in the house, but nobody seems to be here. Max won't hurt you," he added.

"Just keep hold of your dog, sir, and go outside with Officer O'Connell. We'll take a look around."

"Alright. Come on, Max." Anthony kept the dog on a short leash as he scooted past the two officers, who had now split off in different directions. One headed for the kitchen while the other carefully entered the study.

Anthony stood outside the house with Max at his side, overwhelmed by the escalating chain of events. He felt as though he was going insane. Try as he might, he couldn't make sense of the apparitions, visitations and journeys thrust upon him like an

Lost in Plain Sight

unwilling pawn in a chess game from hell. Yet, at the same time, he felt as if he was thinking more clearly than he had in months. He was just thankful he hadn't been taken away to a padded room.

His thoughts were interrupted by the two officers emerging from the entrance after completing a sweep of the house.

After exchanging a few words with the female officer assigned to keep an eye on him, Anthony noticed the lead officer motioning to him. He gave a quick jerk to Max's leash and nervously joined them on front stoop.

"Mr. Stoddard, we searched the entire house and found nothing. We're not sure what your dog reacted to. It could have been anything." The officer sounded slightly annoyed. "However, we heard a strange sound coming from somewhere inside your study. Do you have some type of fan in the wall behind your couch? Maybe a radon fan?" Both cops seemed genuinely perplexed.

"The wall you are referring to backs up to the living room. There's no place to put a vent fan or something like that. I've never heard the sound. Can you show me?"

"Follow us." One of the officers led Anthony back to the study while the other followed behind him.

Anthony thought the cops must be mistaken but was curious to see what they were talking about. As they entered the study and walked over to the far corner of the room where the old couch stood, Anthony thought he heard a low tone, almost like a musical note coming from somewhere inside the walls. It was barely audible. He checked behind the couch but nothing was there, and the sound didn't increase in volume, even with his ear pressed to the wall.

"That's odd." Anthony frowned at the two officers. "I've never heard that sound before. I can't pinpoint its location."

"We came to the same conclusion, sir. It doesn't seem to be anything dangerous. It could be the sound of an appliance somewhere else in the house, vibrating against the wall. Anyway, there isn't anything else we can do at this point."

Anthony got the feeling that the police thought the call was a waste of their time and didn't want to cause any more problems.

"I appreciate you guys coming to check it out. I'm sorry it was a false alarm." He let out a long sigh. Nothing seems to going right these days, he thought wearily.

"That's what we're here for." The officer smiled unconvincingly. "If you have any other problems, give us a call."

"Thanks." Anthony watched them walk back to their patrol cars, relieved the incident was over. All he could think of was getting to bed. He was exhausted.

FIVE

Morning arrived in what seemed like an instant. The clock radio alarm went off at its usual time, 6:30AM. Anthony stared at the large red digits in disbelief.

"Oh, man, it can't be!" He sat up, and then fell back on his pillow.

Max looked over at Anthony, laid his head back down and let out a groan.

"You can't believe it either, eh Max?"

The dog groaned again.

"I thought so."

Suddenly, Anthony remembered he had a sales presentation to finish by lunch. He had a meeting with a client at 1:30.

Oh shit! Contessa will be all over my ass if we don't bring in that piece of business, he thought. A rush of adrenaline overtook his exhaustion as he stumbled into the bathroom while Max went back to sleep. He cleaned-up and was out the door in record time.

Anthony looked at his watch. He was ten minutes late to work and the damn elevator still hadn't arrived in the lobby.

It never fails. When I'm in a rush to get to the station, I get stuck behind a school bus, dump truck or some ninety-year-old driver going fifteen miles per hour, he thought, holding back his desire to smack the elevator door. Then I get on a train with no available seats and a bathroom that smells like it hasn't been cleaned since 1974. Now, Contessa would be all over him as soon as he walked into the office.

"A great way to start the day," he mumbled as the elevator finally opened for a weary group of commuters, coffee cups firmly in hand.

He thought he had made it to the sanctuary of his office undetected, when Contessa's head appeared in the open doorway.

"Anthony, can I see you in my office in five minutes? Thanks." Then she disappeared.

"Damn!" Anthony let out an exasperated sigh and rubbed his eyes with the palms of his hands as his computer booted up. Despite the courteous request, it had been delivered in that too familiar tone, which meant he was in for an unpleasant conversation ... at the very least.

He took a deep breath and braced for the inevitable as he walked over creaking wood floors to the corner office, resplendent in leather furniture and a beautiful view of New York City skyscrapers. He stopped at the open office door, revealing an animated Contessa, busily commanding the unlucky recipient of her tirade on the other end of the line. She silently motioned for him to take a seat across from her on a hard wooden chair and mercifully ended the phone conversation.

"What is it this time?" Contessa's unblinking eyes held him in a head lock.

"I apologize. I'm going through ..."

"You have a job to do. I can't have you coming in late three out of five days a week. It's disruptive to the team. Bob was looking for you so he could finalize the research slides that *you* requested yesterday, one day before our meeting this afternoon. That's not a whole lotta time, is it?" Her eyes bored into him like a screw driver. "And then you walk in at 9:15 like everything's okay. Is it okay?"

"Well—"

"I don't think so," she barked. Her face was beginning to redden, a sure sign more was to come, he thought with dread.

"One more time and you're on probation, understand?" She glared at him.

There was nothing he could say to make the situation better. "Understood," he responded, embarrassed and upset at her lack of compassion.

"Good. Will the research be ready in time to integrate with the presentation deck?" Her expectant stare reflected a total willingness to rake him over the coals if he had the wrong answer.

"Absolutely." Anthony was far from confident he could pull it off. But he felt backed into a corner with no other choice but to tell her what she wanted to hear.

"Terrific." She looked through him for any sign of weakness. "I'll meet you in the lobby at 1PM."

"Okay, thanks." Anthony nodded and quickly left the room, mapping out the three plus hours remaining to make sense of the research and integrate it into a cohesive and understandable presentation deck. This sucks, he thought as he headed for the coffee machine.

Annoyed and stressed out, he made an extra strong mug of coffee and trudged back across a sea of cubicles. The relative quiet of the office was broken only by the incessant tapping of computer keyboards. The cacophony belied the quiet desperation of those unhappy with their careers, marriages, or the routines in which they had found themselves enslaved.

Enslaved by what? Anthony mused. He found himself surveying the scene outside his comfortable office. He had never paused long enough to consider such a thought before. What's holding them here? The thought puzzle seemed to appear from nowhere, adding an unwelcome but intriguing delay to the hectic day unfolding before him. They aren't behind bars. No physical bars anyway, he thought, sipping his bitter concoction.

At that moment, Bob came around the corner. Anthony acted quickly. With no time to waste, he did what he seemed to do best lately, apologize, explain the situation and plead for help. It worked. With a smug grin, Bob was off to his office to finalize the research slides.

"Nothing like a little shameless groveling to move things along," Anthony mumbled as he took his last sip of coffee. "I'll never hear the end of it, but I don't give a shit," he hissed through his breath, plunging back into his chair to review the agenda for the meeting.

Lost in Plain Sight

After checking a back-log of e-mails, he noticed he had a few minutes to dial his friend, John Clark, before Bob e-mailed him the completed deck for a final go-over. He realized, with a tinge of guilt, how much he had relied on John and his wife Debra over the last year to keep himself grounded. He could always count on them, no matter what.

They are true friends, he thought gratefully. No conditions, no judgments, only acceptance of a friend in pain.

Anthony thought about how JoAnne's take-hold-of-the-reins approach differed from the gentle consistency of John and Debra. He half-joked to John that he relied on their friendship as much for recovery from JoAnne's support, as for the mourning of his late wife. John always said, "No extra charge for that, my friend."

He smiled inwardly as the phone rang.

"Clark, here." John's abrupt phone greeting always caught Anthony off-guard. To his friends, John was a big teddy bear. In business he was a no-nonsense CEO.

"Hey, John. Anthony here."

"Anthony. Come' sta?" The gruff voice perked-up immediately.

"I'm alright. I was wondering if you had time for a drink after work."

"What, no lunch? You must be okay," John laughed. "Otherwise, you'd be dragging my ass out within the hour," he joked.

"I'm not that bad, am I?" Anthony laughed out loud.

"Oh, yes you are!"

"Oh well. I guess you get a break today," he retorted.

"From lunch, maybe ... but I'll pay later," John added quickly with his usual dry humor.

"Yeah ... well anyway, how about 5:30PM at The Well?" He ignored John's comments at his expense. He certainly deserved some ribbing after all he had put upon John and Debra over the last few months.

"5:30, it is," answered John. "An apt name, The Well. I'm surprised it hasn't run dry with all the time we've spent there lately."

Anthony could practically see his Cheshire Cat grin through the phone line. "Thanks, John. I really appreciate it." He didn't know what he would do without him.

SIX

A grey mist swirled and danced around Daniel Stoddard. The atmosphere was heavy with darkness, broken only by a terrible sadness permeating every molecule of his being.

He had been moving quickly through the blackness, until this moment. Without warning, the thick smoke-like clouds seemed to notice his presence and began to encircle him menacingly. Noxious fumes gagged him, and he became aware that the strange place in which he'd found himself seemed to have a mind of its own. He sensed evil; an unseen, lurking maliciousness.

"Crush him!" a voice shrieked from the blackness.

Daniel grabbed his throat, choking, feeling as if a force was pushing his entire body inward like a rubber ball being squeezed from every direction. His head felt as if it would explode with unrelenting pain. Then, the image of a woman appeared holding something shiny over her head, and a blue-white light filled his field of vision.

He sat bolt upright in his bed as if a coiled spring had suddenly released him. His sheets, wet from the sweat cascading from his pores, stuck to him like glue as he swung his feet over the side of the bed.

Gasping for breath and disoriented, he glanced nervously around the room, attempting to get his bearings. The window was in the wrong place, he thought. His heart was beating so hard he grabbed his chest with a cold, clammy hand, and his breathing became labored. Then, he realized he wasn't at home. He was in his dorm room at school. His eyes focused in the darkness, and he stumbled into the bathroom for a drink of water. He flipped the light switch and grabbed the sides of the sink trying to catch his breath.

His exhausted reflection and blood shot eyes stared back at him through the mirror. His hair was matted from sweat. He grabbed a cup off the sink and gulped down water, the overflow dripping from the side of his mouth.

Finally, beginning to calm, he noticed red marks on his neck. Moving closer to the mirror, he saw to his horror, the outline of a large hand with long fingers. It had bruised a large area on the left side. What looked like a long thumb print or claw, had wrapped around his Adam's apple, ending in a puncture wound on the right side of his neck. It was discolored; obviously a recent wound.

He quickly turned to see if anyone was behind him, searching the darkness of his dorm room through the bright florescent light of the bathroom, eyes darting left and right. He pushed the door to the wall and peered into the empty room, illuminated only by the ghostly glow of his digital clock. The sound of an old radiator hissed in the background.

He looked into the mirror again and slowly placed his hands over the impression. Not even close. The mark was easily a third larger than his right hand, which was how he would have had to grab himself to make the wound. There was no way he could have punctured his neck with his thumb, he thought shuddering. That was made by something long and sharp.

Looking closer, it dawned on him. The impression was made by one hand, not two. The strength would have had to be incredible. His hair stood on end as he bolted into his room, quickly got dressed and ran out the door.

#

As he pulled into the end of his long driveway, Anthony was feeling better than he had in months. It wasn't until he turned the curve that he saw the other car pulled up next to his back door. It was Daniel's black SUV.

He's not due home for another few weeks, Anthony thought. He closed the door and pressed the key fob. The familiar chirp of the alarm system sounded as he walked across the gravel driveway crunching beneath his feet.

Was he stopping by to say hello? Anthony decided to enter through the back door since it opened into the kitchen. It was Daniel's favorite room in the house. He smiled at the thought of his refrigerator being raided.

The screen door banged behind him as he entered the kitchen, startling Max, who looked up suddenly from his water bowl.

"Dad, where have you been?" Daniel seemed upset.

"Where have I been? How about, Hi, Dad. Sorry to show up out of the blue. I know you weren't expecting me." Anthony walked over to give his son a hug. "It's great to see you, but why the unexpected visit?" Anthony noticed something off about Daniel. He seemed as tight as a drum.

"Sorry ... you're right." Daniel pulled a chair out from the kitchen table, sat down, buried his head in his hands and took a deep breath.

"What's wrong, son?" Anthony sat down next to him.

"Something happened to me that I can't explain. It scared the shit out of me." Daniel pulled back the collar on his shirt to expose the marks on his neck.

Anthony bristled. "Who hurt you?"

"I don't know."

"What do you mean, you don't know?' Somebody choked you, for God's sake!" He inspected the wound and gave Daniel a questioning look. "Are you okay?"

"Yeah, I'm alright. I took a nap earlier today and had a really bad nightmare. In my dream, it was really dark. I heard a voice scream out and then something attacked me. Suddenly I couldn't breathe. I ran to the bathroom and saw these marks."

"Nobody was in your room?"

"When I woke up, nothing was there." Daniel stared blankly at the floor.

The implications of what he was saying hit Anthony like a punch to the face.

Lost in Plain Sight

"Dad, something tried to kill me but I couldn't see in the darkness. I don't know. It's so confusing. I panicked, ran out of the dorm and came home." He started to shake with emotion. "I miss Mom." He covered his face with his hands and cried uncontrollably.

Anthony was numb. He reached over to hug Daniel as tears began to flow for the pain his son was feeling.

"I miss her too." They hugged each other, holding on for dear life.

A part of Anthony was glad his son was letting go. Daniel had tried to be so brave for him after Diane's death that he hadn't fully grieved for himself. Anthony had tried to get him to open-up, but it usually ended in an argument. This was good, he told himself. Max walked over and rested his head on Daniel's thigh.

After a few minutes, both of them calmed down. Anthony pulled the chair closer to sit face to face with his son. He had tried to protect Daniel from the insanity that had pervaded his life but had the uneasy feeling his visions were somehow connected to what had happened in his son's dorm room. He owed him an explanation.

"This past year has been very difficult for both of us. With you away at school, it's been pretty lonely at the house. I've tried my best to give you your space so you could concentrate on your studies but—" Anthony hesitated, choosing his next words carefully as Daniel looked on inquisitively. "Strange things have been happening to me."

"What kind of strange things?"

"Scary visitations, and I've got this feeling they may be related to your attack."

"What are you saying?" Daniel looked alarmed.

"I've tried to deal with them myself and not drag you into it. You've got enough on your plate."

"Dad, how long did you think you could keep it a secret?"

"I haven't kept it a secret. I've told Dr. Richardson. I thought it best to deal with it on my own and they might go away. But never in a million years did I think what I was experiencing would affect you."

"Wait ... go back. What do you mean by *they* might go away? Who are you talking about?" Daniel looked confused and upset.

Anthony massaged his brow trying to come up with a plausible explanation. "The doctor seems to think I have a condition similar to post-traumatic stress disorder." He didn't want to use the word, *psychosis*.

"Okay, I know what that is. What else?"

Anthony knew sugarcoating the situation was not an option. "I've been seeing apparitions for about a year, and they're starting to get more frequent." He waited for Daniel's response, not sure how he'd take this news.

"What are you seeing?" Daniel looked extremely apprehensive.

Anthony could only imagine what he was thinking. "I see different things ... and I go to other places." He let out a breath of resignation.

"Where do you go, Dad?" Daniel spoke softly.

Anthony wasn't sure if it was pity or empathy his son felt for him now. "My past ... I don't understand why, but I know there has to be a reason for it."

"Are you sure?"

"I'm not sure about anything, anymore. Look, I saw a very scary apparition the other day that claimed to know who I was, and it threatened me. It was as real as this table. I'm thinking that *maybe* it knows about you and tried to scare or hurt me by getting to you."

"I don't understand. A non-existent person of some kind is threatening us? That doesn't make sense!"

"I know, I know. It sounds insane but it's true. You've got to believe me, Daniel."

"What the hell have you ever done to make someone or something so angry that it threatens you ... and me for that matter?"

"Good question. The specter told me that I can't escape her through lifetimes, whatever that means."

Daniel got up off the chair and started to pace around the kitchen, running his hands through his hair as if that would help him make sense of it all. "It does sound insane. What did Dr. Richardson say to you this week?"

"He told me the visions I'm experiencing are a result of trauma and prescribed anti-depressive medication. On the positive side, he thinks I've made progress." Anthony shrugged. "I'm telling you that these things are absolutely real on some level. I've still got all my marbles, believe me. I'm convinced some kind of door has opened up, maybe due to my grief. I had a long conversation with John about it."

"You told John? Ugh."

"Well yeah, what's the problem? He's been very supportive."

"What's the problem? This could start getting around and hurt your reputation. It's private."

Anthony shook his head. "John is a great friend. He's holding everything I've told him in confidence. Without his support, I'd be in a lot worse shape."

Daniel sighed. "It's just … this whole thing is so frustrating. I want our lives to be normal again!"

"We'll work through this together, okay?" Anthony laid both hands gently on Daniel's shoulders and looked directly into his son's eyes. "You just have to trust me on this one. I'm going to learn more about—"

"What? Apparitions?" Daniel interrupted.

"Yes. I have to get to the bottom of this."

Daniel rolled his eyes. "I don't believe this is happening. What choice do we have?"

"Look … by learning about these things calmly and deliberately, I'll be better able to address them directly instead of reacting with fear. Will you back me on this?"

"Sure. We've always made a great team, right?" Daniel cracked a smile.

"Right. We'll get to the bottom of it, but there's one more thing you should know."

Daniel rolled his eyes again. "What now?"

"I have a friend from the other side who claims to be my guide. His name is Maxim. I saw him yesterday, for the first time."

"I've got no choice but to go along with you, right?"

"Just bear with me. If he's really who he says he is, he can protect me and you from this entity that seems to be pursuing us."

"I'm getting a beer from the fridge." Daniel made a bee-line for the refrigerator.

Anthony had nothing to say about it now that Daniel was twenty-one years old.

"Anyway, John recommended that I open up to these experiences, which I plan to do. I'm going to scour the Internet for anything remotely related to OBEs and NDEs."

Daniel gagged on some beer. "What the hell are OBEs and NDEs?"

"They're acronyms for Outer Body Experiences and Near Death Experiences. Sorry, I shouldn't have assumed—"

"You mean like the experience you had with Mom after the accident?"

"Exactly."

"Alright. How can I help?" Daniel suddenly seemed less skeptical and more interested.

"You can speak with that professor at your college. I think his name is Dr. Matthew Ross. He conducted a study on NDEs and wrote an excellent book outlining the results. The name of the book escapes me."

"Oh yeah. I know the guy. He's somewhat of a celebrity on campus. Personally, I think he's full of himself. Anyway, I'll check on that book. Maybe I can enroll in his class next semester, as an elective."

"That would be great! Are you sure you don't mind? It does sort of fit your major in psychology." Anthony shrugged.

"No problem. It sounds pretty interesting." Daniel downed the last of his beer.

"Excellent. Let's get some sleep. Since tomorrow is Saturday I'll drive up to school with you, okay? I can take the train back home."

"That would be great, thanks." Daniel gave Anthony a pat on the shoulder. "I'll do whatever I can to help you through this, Dad."

"Thanks." Anthony felt as if things were finally coming together as he turned out the lights and followed Daniel and Max upstairs for the night. At least he had a basic plan and some semblance of control.

He noticed Max's empty bed and smiled at the thought of the dog keeping Daniel company for the night. He was glad for a break in the loneliness.

SEVEN

As soon as his head hit the pillow, Anthony closed his eyes. An overwhelming fatigue melted into a welcome sense of drowsiness. His body trembled involuntarily from exhaustion as he drifted slowly into a deep slumber.

He embraced the welcome feeling of impending sleep, and heard the now familiar snap in his head as a sense of floating overwhelmed his senses. Through the veil of drowsiness, the sound of the air blowing through the heat ducts caught his attention, momentarily interrupting his peace. His eyes opened for a second and closed again.

At first, the view of his ceiling-fan just inches from his face, didn't register. He opened his eyes again. This time he was looking directly at the ceiling.

For a moment, he thought he had fallen from his bed and was staring at the floor.

However, when he looked to his right, he saw the faint outline of the hallway night-light through the top of his bedroom door. Now, totally awake, he looked down and saw his body lying peacefully on his bed while he floated like a speck of dust near the bedroom ceiling. By now, he knew to relax and let the experience happen.

Lost in Plain Sight

He heard the faint sound of a distant wind become louder. An unseen force seemed to pull him up through the ceiling into a dark tunnel. As the speed increased, he heard voices but couldn't understand what was being said. The sound of chimes intermingled with the wind as a pin-hole of distant light penetrated the darkness.

Gradually, the hole became larger and the light brighter, as he burst into a vast open space filled with the most beautiful, welcoming light he had ever seen. It was brighter than the sun but didn't hurt his eyes in the least. The light seemed to exude a unique love for him that he had never felt before. Yet ... it all seemed familiar, as though he had been here a thousand times.

A voice broke the silence. "You have visited this realm for eons."

Anthony couldn't tell where the voice was coming from. He tried to speak but was unable to talk.

"Anthony, you are in your spirit body. Remember, in this world we know you by your soul name, Tabor. Communicate with your mind," the voice gently commanded.

Anthony concentrated. *"My mind?"* He heard his voice as clear as a bell. "It works!"

"Of course it works, Tabor. It's always worked," the voice continued.

The light moved away, and Anthony was transported by the unseen force to a location high above the Earth. He looked around in wonder. The huge blue orb was suspended in blackness below him. The brown, grey and green continents spread out to the horizon, broken only by the wispy white clouds swirling over them.

Above him, the stars felt close enough to touch. He reached out to the Big Dipper. Meteors streaked across the vastness of space, disappearing behind the curve of the Earth. It was incredibly vast and beautiful.

He turned away from the massive planet and saw what looked like a Greek temple. He marveled at the classic Doric columns that graced the entrance as it sat suspended in darkness above the giant blue sphere behind him.

"What is this place?"

"It is the Temple Portal," the familiar voice responded. "It is a way-station for an endless variety of travelers visiting the Earth and Astral Planes from other dimensions. It is also the location where we will begin your training, and the point from where we will travel to other dimensions and learn of the higher realms." Maxim came into view and motioned to Anthony who was now moving effortlessly toward the entrance, growing ever larger as he approached.

Maxim greeted him on the steps of the enormous structure, now towering over both of them. Two fifty-foot-tall, intricately carved golden doors, opened of their own accord as they entered the great temple. Endless rows of massive columns filled the chamber for as far as Anthony could see. The interior was backlit by beautiful, purple lights, highlighting every corner of the temple. Fantastic murals, depicting scenes of unknown origin, covered the walls in colors so vivid and wondrous that Anthony was moved to tears. He stopped for a moment, stunned by the beauty and haunting familiarity of the space.

"Welcome to one of the last places you stood before you were born into your current physical life," spoke Maxim as they continued down the center aisle of the temple.

"What is that wonderful music?" asked Anthony. "I've never heard anything so beautiful."

"All the great composers living on the Earth-plane are inspired from this dimension," answered Maxim. "The most beautiful melodies and artful harmonies are born here from their intent and manifested in the physical world as musical compositions. It is one of the great gifts and pleasures of All That Is."

Everything Maxim said seemed to make perfect sense. It was as if he was reminding Anthony of what he already knew to be true.

"You passed through these halls for eons between lives and in your dreams. It is a place where you truly belong and one of the most powerful portals nearest the Earth.

Anthony studied the interior of the temple in awe. From a distance, he noticed what appeared to be a colossal golden statue of a man at the far end of the temple, straddling an immense white-marble altar. As he moved closer, it was apparent that it stood at least one hundred feet tall. The right arm was outstretched high above his head, holding a brightly lit, golden torch.

Anthony gazed upward and saw light-rays emanating in all directions from the massive head. All he could do was gaze in amazement at the Herculean masterpiece.

"This ancient statue is a symbol representing the miracle of light and consciousness inherent in every living being in all universes," stated Maxim. "It was the model for the great Colossus of Rhodes, one of the seven wonders of the ancient world. It is the first symbol I wanted you to see and the most important of them all, for it represents a truth that has the power to change humankind."

"I don't understand." Anthony was overwhelmed by the energy of the statue.

"In time you will know and do great things with the knowledge given to you. For now, these revelations are enough. Pure truth can only be absorbed gradually. It is time for you to return."

"Maxim, I need to understand," Anthony pleaded.

"In time, my friend ... in time." Maxim raised his hand over Anthony's spirit eyes and moved it in a circular, sweeping motion.

In an instant, the surroundings of the statue and temple collapsed into a million colorful fragments, forming a beautiful mandala in Anthony's mind. He woke up in his bed staring into the darkness of his bedroom. The remnants of the mandala were suspended above him like an exploding fireworks display. Slowly, it faded away as he closed his eyes in exhaustion and fell asleep for the second time that night.

EIGHT

Anthony woke-up invigorated after his first eight-hour sleep in months. This time, he remembered everything about his so-called *dream*. He smiled, realizing that his experience was indeed real and seemed to be part of something bigger than himself. *Tabor*, he thought. I like that name.

As he lathered-up for a shave, he could feel a sense of purpose rising inside him. He had always questioned the meaning of his existence ... of life in general, but the unusual experiences since Diane's death had made it obvious there was meaning and organization in the world that he and billions of others inhabited.

He stared blankly through the bathroom window as he dried his face, wondering what kind of discoveries he and Daniel would uncover. Hopefully, they would be able to convince Dr. Ross to help them.

Daniel poked his head through the bedroom door. "Dad, are you ready to go?"

"I'm almost done. I'll be down in a minute."

"I took a trip down to Dunkin' Donuts and got two large coffees and a couple of toasted bagels with cream cheese ... sound good?"

"Soul food," Anthony joked.

Lost in Plain Sight

"This way, we can get on the road early. I thought we could stop by the library, maybe pick up one of Ross's books. I'll also introduce you to my new girlfriend, Emily."

Anthony peeked around the bathroom door. Daniel was grinning in expectation of his response. "Girlfriend!? How come you didn't tell me sooner?"

"After what happened yesterday it wasn't top of mind."

"Fair enough. That's great. I'm happy for you." Anthony shot Daniel a happy smile and disappeared back into the bedroom to grab his things.

As they pulled out of the driveway munching on bagels and coffee, Anthony tried his best to describe his latest out-of-body travels to the Temple Portal. As the time passed, the hills in the surrounding countryside were becoming higher as they headed north on Route 91 into Massachusetts. Anthony reclined his seat to relax and enjoy the view. He had made a conscious decision to embrace the strange events happening to him, but a thread of apprehension hung in the air, never far from his wandering mind.

The campus finally came into view, classic in its New England beauty. Large maple trees lined the streets, while their brethren dotted the expansive campus green.

Pathways lead over gentle rises, under shady branches and past benches filled with all manner of students. They conversed, listened to i-Pods, studied and generally enjoyed the gorgeous autumn day, sure to soon fade into the cold, dreary winter season that lay ahead.

Daniel pulled the SUV into the dorm parking lot. A beautiful granite archway lead directly into an open square.

"Dad, let's head over to the library."

"You don't want to stop by your room first? I can wait outside." Anthony was very relaxed, enjoying the lazy day.

"I'm in no rush to go back up there just yet. Let's see what kind of information we can uncover. I've heard that Professor Ross is a prolific writer, so there may be a number of books to check-out." Daniel motioned for Anthony to move along.

"Okay, then. I'll hit the computer while you check on his books."

"Sure, you get to surf the net while I have to slog through the library computer system and dig-up his books ... thanks." Daniel winked as they walked the winding asphalt pathways through the beautiful campus. They passed manicured lawns, rows of trees bursting with autumn colors and handsome stone architecture, all the while breathing in the crisp autumn air.

As they approached the new library building, Anthony noticed a middle-aged man wearing a traditional brown tweed jacket and maroon bow tie. He was surrounded by five or six students. They seemed transfixed by whatever the man was telling them.

"Daniel, who's that gentleman over there?" Anthony pointed to the scrum that had formed around the rather pompous-looking man.

"That's him ... Professor Ross."

Anthony thought for a moment. "Let's go introduce ourselves."

"What ... right now?" protested Daniel.

"Isn't that why we came up here today?"

"Well, yes ... but he's in the middle—"

"We may not get another opportunity this weekend," interrupted Anthony. "Let's stand aside so he sees us and wait until he's finished with the group.

"Alright," Daniel sighed.

They moved toward the group of students and began to pick up on pieces of the conversation.

"... but Professor, maybe people who have these near-death experiences aren't completely dead," blurted out an intense looking female student clutching one of Professor Ross's books.

Ross calmly responded. "There are many instances of NDEs where the person has no heartbeat, is not breathing and has flattened brain waves, Carla. Have any of you heard of the Pam Reynolds case?" The professor raised his eyebrows, obviously enjoying the attention. He searched the eyes of his rapt audience knowing the answer would be no. The students all shook their heads and shrugged.

"Well, the woman had to go through a rare procedure to remove an extremely large basilar artery aneurysm in her brain that would have killed her. In order to be successful, doctors had to induce what is called hypothermic cardiac arrest, also known as *standstill*. It basically requires that the patient die through the lowering of body temperature, flattening of brain waves, stopping the heart, and so forth. Of course, she wasn't breathing either," he added with a knowing grin. "Oh yes, and the blood had to be drained from her head."

Anthony and Daniel gasped along with the students.

"Does that sound dead enough for you?" The professor confidently surveyed the group again, as everyone nodded yes. "Good ... well, the operation was a success and she was brought back to life. But something unusual occurred during the time she was *dead*." The professor paused for effect while everyone, including Anthony and Daniel, leaned in closer to hear what happened.

"She recounted later, which was verified to be accurate by the way, that she heard a pop and subsequently floated out of her body and saw the operation being performed from above. She described the surgical tools that were used in detail as well as what was said by the nurses in the room. She also described floating out of the operating room and moving through a tunnel where she met with dead relatives, including her grandmother.

"Apparently, it wasn't her time because a deceased uncle led her back to her body so she could reenter it, which she described as *plunging into a pool of ice*. As I mentioned earlier, all of the information she recounted was confirmed by the doctors and nurses that were present." The professor looked quite satisfied with himself as the students turned to speak to each other in hushed, reverent tones.

"He's kind of a dick," Anthony whispered to Daniel, who sniggered in response.

"True, but he's the most preeminent authority on out-of-body and near-death experiences on the East Coast, so we'll have to overlook his character flaws," Daniel retorted with what Anthony sensed as mock impatience.

They approached Professor Ross hoping to get his attention. He finished speaking to the last two students, shook hands, and turned to the two men with an ingenuous smile.

"How may I help you gentlemen?"

"Nice to meet you, Dr. Ross. My name is Anthony Stoddard. This is my son, Daniel, a student here at Berkshire College."

"Good to meet you both." The professor maintained a look of cautious expectation.

Daniel took the lead. "Professor, I was wondering if you had room for one more student for the winter semester. I'm very interested—"

"I'm sorry ... it's Daniel, correct?"

"Yes."

"Daniel, there is a waiting list to get into my class. If you are so inclined, you may sign up with the registrar, even though the deadline passed last week. Let them know I agreed. They'll confirm with me." The professor held out his hand to part ways.

Anthony stepped in. "There's a reason why my son is so intent to learn more about out-of-body and near-death experiences." Anthony chose his words carefully.

"You mean beyond mere interest and curiosity Mr. Stoddard?"

"Well, yes, Professor Ross." The professor seemed to have an uncanny ability to make him feel like an idiot.

"And what would that reason be?"

Anthony could sense the man's dismissive attitude. He glanced at Daniel, who obviously had no idea what he was planning to say. However, his face spoke volumes. Apprehension and embarrassment seemed to dominate the surprised expression staring back at him.

"It's hard to explain, Professor, but I lost my wife and began having those out-of-body experiences and visions that you describe in your books."

The professor's demeanor changed immediately. "So, you've read my books?"

"Well, not exactly. Daniel had a similar experience recently. He told me about you. We decided to come to the school together to check out some of your books from the library and go online ... you know, to see if we could learn more. We were on our way when we saw you here and decided to introduce ourselves."

"I see. So you're hoping to find out why this is happening to you." The professor played with his bow-tie, deep in thought. "Firstly, I appreciate that you confided in me. I'm sorry if I seemed abrupt but you have no idea how many people come to me with all manner of questions, wild stories and claims to have experienced these phenomena."

"We understand," Anthony replied.

Lost in Plain Sight

"Secondly, I sense that you are troubled and surely confused ... which is entirely normal and understandable," he added with what seemed to be empathy.

"I don't understand why these things are happening to us," Anthony responded softly, surprised by the emotion that suddenly surfaced.

The professor studied Anthony for a moment and continued. "I can't tell you why, Mr. Stoddard, but I can help you understand the phenomenon, which may ultimately help with the answers you seek. I can tell you that a traumatic event of the sort you have endured is certainly one of many ways an out-of-body experience can be triggered. Would you be averse to an interview, so I can understand your particular case and formally enter it into my new study? I never divulge the names of my subjects and will always seek a written release if I ever decide to publish it in any form," he added.

"Of course. If there's a chance of learning something new or helping someone else, I'd be happy to speak with you about my experiences."

"Very well, then."

Anthony noticed that the professor's mood seemed to lighten dramatically. "I don't live nearby. How would you like to handle the interviews?"

"Are you here for the weekend?" the professor inquired.

"I wasn't planning on staying the night but I'd be willing to if you can schedule some time." Anthony felt the excitement rise inside from this unexpected turn of events. It almost seemed as if running into Professor Ross was meant to be.

"That's good of you, Mr. Stoddard."

"Please, call me Anthony."

"Anthony, then. Why don't we meet in my office tomorrow after breakfast, say 10AM. Daniel, do you know where it's located?"

"Actually, yes. I've walked by it on my way to psychology class."

"A psychology major, eh? Good for you. If you don't mind, would you walk your father over tomorrow?"

"I'd be happy to." Daniel forced a smile.

"It was a pleasure meeting you both." Professor Ross extended his small, clammy hand. With a nod, he bid them both goodbye and strolled away.

Anthony waited until the professor was out of hearing range and turned to Daniel with a surprised but satisfied look.

"Well, you got what you wanted," laughed Daniel.

They walked to the library building and a world unexplored.

NINE

Daniel headed for a computer terminal to see if the library carried any of Professor Ross's books. Anthony located the computers with Internet access to do some detective work on anything he could dig-up on the paranormal as it pertained to out-of-body and near-death experiences. Within a matter of seconds he had Googled NDEs and was presented with an extensive list of sources.

It's amazing how easy it is to find information on this stuff, he thought. There were dozens of links to scientific studies. He scanned the search results for a credible source and clicked on it. He was overwhelmed with countless topics. They ranged from scientific evidence to notable NDEs, skeptical arguments, how the experiences related to the various world religions, and even Edgar Cayce's NDEs. As he scrolled back up the page, he noticed the topic *Triggers of NDEs*.

"Interesting," he mumbled under his breath. "We've got NDE theories from all the recognized authorities and here we've got the triggers; death, surgery, dreams and stress." He made a note on a pad. "Death-bed, seizures, relaxation, coma ... here ... out-of-body." He scribbled more notes. "Anything else ... um, mental illness." Let's hope I don't fall into that category, he thought with a sigh.

"Let's look at stress." He clicked on the word and read a recounting of someone named Melanie. It didn't seem to have any bearing on his experiences except for a comment about a bright light that didn't hurt her eyes. He made a note and moved on to another topic about NDEs and the Earth.

As he scrolled down the page, he noticed a section describing the Earth being viewed from the spirit realms. He sat straight up and began reading a brief piece about an NDE experienced by a renowned doctor decades earlier. As he read, Anthony realized that the man of science was describing exactly what he had seen while visiting with Maxim at the Temple Portal. The beautiful blue light of the Earth, the deep blue seas and the continents were all described the same way, as if he'd been living in a space station looking down from more than a thousand miles up ... and it was published more than a decade before space travel had become a reality.

"Incredible." Reading on, the doctor described a massive stone temple floating in space. One quote, in particular, caught Anthony's eye. "An unusual man, small in stature, sat quietly on the steps leading to ornate golden doors and bowed, as if in greeting."

"Jaster!"

Anthony's outburst sliced through the silence of the room like a knife through a curtain. Startled students looked in his direction, yanked unceremoniously away from their computer screens and text books. He sheepishly returned their attentions, waved his hands in a gesture of apology, and then turned back to the computer screen to pick-up where he had left-off.

"As I moved toward the entrance, the doors swung open of their own accord—"

Just like the Temple Portal! He tried to suppress his emotions for fear of retaliation from nearby students immersed in their own projects. He glanced over his computer terminal and saw Daniel returning with a stack of at least five books under his arm. Anthony waved him over.

"Looks like you were successful." He was anxious to see what Daniel had found.

"Yeah, I've got most of his works. I might be missing one or two. I don't know."

"You'll never believe what I found." Anthony's excitement was obvious.

"What?" Daniel chuckled.

"I found this site on near-death experiences. Check it out." He hit the enter button. The web page appeared and he scanned the paragraphs for the section on visions.

"What does it say?" Daniel leaned in closer for a better look.

"There's a quote from a well-known medical doctor back in the late 1940s. He described a vision that matched the one I had last night, down to the last detail." Anthony glanced-up to see the surprised look on his son's face.

"You're kidding me. Show me where."

"Right here." Anthony pointed with his pen, tapping the screen. He waited as Daniel read silently. His heart was racing.

"That's exactly how you described it ... weird."

"We better get out of here before the librarian kicks us out," Anthony sniggered.

They quickly gathered the books and walked through the maze of chairs and tables to the lobby.

Daniel turned to Anthony. "That's unbelievable," he whispered to his still grinning father as they walked out the front door, down the steps and back down the pathway to Daniel's dorm.

"I know," laughed Anthony, practically giddy over the fact a respected doctor had experienced an identical vision more than sixty years earlier. Had they been to the same place? Was it real? he wondered. Who could blame him for being happy about this development. It was the first clue that his experiences might be credible, not the delusions of a madman as he had feared.

The time had flown by in their excitement to gather information. The short afternoon had given way to evening. Anthony gazed-up at the beautiful midnight blue sky, teeming with stars, and took a deep breath. This was just the validation he needed to renew his spirits and move forward. He was glad he was doing it with his son but realized they'd forgotten one detail.

"Where am I sleeping tonight?"

"I have a sleeping bag. Camp out in my room," Daniel cheerfully offered. "I could use the company after what happened the other day."

Lost in Plain Sight

"Sounds like a plan. Let's grab a bite to eat first. I'm starving. We can take a look at those books after dinner."

The two men walked to the cafeteria for a quick meal and then headed back to Daniel's room to do some information gathering.

Back for the first time since he ran from the dorm in a panic, Daniel cautiously pushed open the door to his room and hit the light switch. Everything was as he'd left it. The bed was still unmade, his clothes were strewn over the chair next to his desk, and papers littered the floor near the wastepaper basket.

"Sorry, Dad. I know it's kind of a mess." He glanced back sheepishly and shrugged.

"Some things never change," Anthony sighed.

Daniel turned to his right and noticed the door to the bathroom was half-open. The light was still on and he could see the corner of the mirror of his medicine chest. He massaged his Adam's apple as he recalled the moment and the terrible dream that had made him flee just days ago.

Anthony could see that Daniel was upset. "Hey, I know it's rough coming back here after what happened ... believe me. Every night, I come home to an empty house filled with nothing but memories." He placed his hand on his son's shoulder. "You need to be strong while we get to the bottom of this."

Daniel nodded, took a deep breath and turned off the bathroom light. "Let's take a look at these books." He dropped them all on the floor.

"What's the print date on that one?" Anthony pointed to a thick hard-cover book with what looked like clouds on the cover. "Let's see when they were published and put them in order to see how his findings progressed."

"Good idea." Daniel laid them out in a row, six books in all.

"So, we're not sure if these represent all his works, correct?" questioned Anthony.

"That's what the librarian told me." Daniel searched for a print date.

"That's okay. These look like a good cross-section." Anthony looked for a publishing date inside a particularly thick, hard-cover book, while Daniel did the same with two others.

"Excellent! It's mostly recent stuff," Daniel shot back.

"Great. We'll never get through all of this tonight. If we both skim the table of contents and some of the chapters, we should get a decent understanding of the type of studies, questions and experiences of his subjects ... so I'm not totally in the dark tomorrow." Anthony felt good about their finds.

They each grabbed a note pad and began the arduous task of reviewing the lengthy material until they both crashed at 1:00AM, too tired to dream.

TEN

Half-asleep in the early morning hours, Anthony thought he heard a light tapping on the door to Daniel's dorm room. He poked his head out from under the sleeping bag and listened for the sound again ... nothing. He shrugged it off and fell back on his pillow, enjoying his drowsy state, wrapped in warmth.

He suddenly remembered his meeting with the professor at 10:00AM. He opened his eyes again and glanced over at the digital clock-radio perched on Daniel's dresser. It displayed 7:33AM in big green, glowing digits. Still early, he thought, closing his eyes to fall back asleep.

The tapping started again ... this time, noticeably louder. Anthony groaned and peered-up from his comfy spot on the floor next to Daniel's bed to see if his son had heard the knocking. Would he get up to answer the door?

No such luck, he thought, dragging his legs out from the soft warmth into the chilly room. He slid on his jeans, stumbled to the door and opened it to find an attractive young woman standing in front of him. Her jaw dropped at the site of a middle-aged man staring back at her with puffy eyes and a serious case of bedhead. Her hand, extended in a fist to knock, yet again, pulled back quickly, and her eyes narrowed inquisitively.

Anthony chuckled. "You must be Emily," he said with a knowing smile. "I'm Daniel's Dad."

"Mr. Stoddard!" Her face softened immediately. "I'm sooo sorry to wake you up this early. I came by on Friday, and Daniel wasn't here. I was just checking—"

Anthony held up his hand to reassure her. "Not a problem. How would you have known? He came back home, spent the night and we returned together yesterday. I decided to stay over last night. As you can see, the accommodations are so luxurious." He gestured toward the dorm room.

Emily laughed, looking suddenly shy.

Anthony positioned himself next to Daniel's bed. "Wake-up! Emily is here."

A groan emanated from under the comforter.

"Come on. It's time to get moving. My appointment with Professor Ross is at ten o'clock and I'd like to have some breakfast." Anthony pulled-off the covers, which caused howl of protest. Daniel grabbed the sheets back and re-buried himself under the warm comforter.

Emily walked over and sat on the edge of his bed. "Come on, sleepy-head," she coaxed, gently shaking him. He opened one eye and smiled.

"Up ... come on. Your Dad needs some breakfast," she prodded kindly.

"Alright." He sat-up on the edge of the bed rubbing his eyes and yawned. "I see you've met," he said through a stretch.

"Sure, you'll get up for her but not your old man," Anthony joked.

"She's prettier than you." Daniel shot his father a sleepy smile as he slipped on his pants.

It was early on a Sunday morning, and the cafeteria was still relatively empty. Anthony checked out the impressive space with approval. Floor to ceiling windows dominated the walls with a beautiful view of the campus. The large room was quiet with much of the floor carpeted where the students sat to eat, away from the food service areas. Gleaming counters and countless choices of food greeted them as them as they grabbed trays.

At least I'm getting my money's worth, he thought. It was remarkable how much better this cafeteria was compared to what he had to endure in his college days. Sour-faced, hair-net wearing fraus seemed to have been replaced by smiling young men and women in pressed white linen suits. They appeared to like their jobs.

There was a cornucopia of fresh fruits, bagels still warm from the on-site ovens; delicious looking scrambled eggs, recently prepared batter for waffles or pancakes; fresh-baked ham, countless cereals, juices and on and on.

He grabbed a bagel and studied the student's faces as they filled trays with an assortment of food and beverages, seemingly unaware of their good fortune.

After a huge breakfast, Daniel and Emily escorted Anthony to Professor Ross's office located in one of the older buildings on campus. They walked through a narrow passageway with brick walls covered in dark green ivy. It lead directly to a courtyard surrounded by a cluster of three-story brick buildings. A side-door in building number four was left slightly open, as if expecting them.

Once inside, they climbed a set of stairs to the second floor, their uneven footsteps echoing loudly off the brick walls. They passed through a steel door at the top of the stairs and continued down a drab hallway. Their sneakers squeaked on the shiny, flecked linoleum floors, recently mopped and buffed but in obvious need of replacement for many years.

The door to the professor's office was wide open, exposing a large, rectangular room. The space was illuminated with a combination of natural outdoor light from a picture window at the far end of the office and bright fluorescent lighting in the high ceiling directly above Professor Ross's desk. The leather-topped desk was well-worn and piled high with books and papers.

"Dad, we're gonna head over to the campus green and hangout for a while. We'll meet you at the cafeteria for lunch."

Anthony noticed that Daniel had his arm around Emily. "No problem. Have a good time. I'll see you later." He waved goodbye as the two kids headed back down the hallway. The steel door slammed shut.

From the looks of it, the office hadn't been organized in a very long time. Anthony ran his hands over an old cherry bookcase filled with text books, manuals, papers and various odds and ends. The office was a mess but somehow comfortable; a refuge from the hustle and bustle of campus life and the outside world that lay just beyond the gates.

Lost in Plain Sight

His attention was drawn to the professor's chair, a comfortable looking brown leather high-back on casters. The arm rests were worn from constant use. He pictured the professor reaching across his desk for papers seemingly lost in a forgotten pile, only to be plucked neatly from beneath some old books and scraps of paper filled with notes and doodles.

He tried to get a sense of the professor's personality from what seemed to be massive disorganization. He knew better than to make snap-judgments. Usually, people fall into three camps, he thought, analyzing the room. Some are organized neat-freaks who know the location of every last paper clip. Others are a disorganized mess, keeping their tax receipts in a shoe-box and unable find their latest paycheck. The final category, he surmised, are the folks that give the appearance of disorganization but know exactly where everything is located. Anthony had a strong feeling that Professor Ross fell into the last category.

You can't interview hundreds of people, keep track of all these notes, organize them into best-selling books and not be organized, he decided ... "despite this disaster of an office," he muttered under his breath.

"Trying to get a sense of who I am, Mr. Stoddard?" Professor Ross smiled as if it wasn't the first time he'd caught someone inspecting his office.

ELEVEN

Anthony was startled by the professor's stealthy entrance and hoped he hadn't heard his last comment. He turned to greet the diminutive man, heart skipping underneath his courteous smile and outstretched hand. "I was just admiring your office, Dr. Ross. You're obviously a very busy man." He composed himself.

"Likely story," Ross responded. "You're not the first to wonder," he continued as he walked to his desk. "Funny business, this line of work. It generates many conflicting emotions ... and paperwork." He smiled, sat in his chair and waved Anthony over to a rather comfortable looking leather arm chair next to his desk.

"People are fascinated by the prospect of life after death, yet they have a difficult time believing there is consciousness without a physical body. Oh, they want desperately to believe that life continues beyond this three-dimensional reality we find ourselves in, but most can't grasp the concept ... with the exception of those who have experienced a near-death experience first-hand."

"Well Professor, I can't say I've had an NDE, but I've certainly experienced more than one out-of-body experience. I believe you refer to them as OBEs."

"You know the lingo, do you? That's more than most who sit in that chair for the first time." The professor's demeanor softened. "The first thing I want to tell you is this. What you are experiencing has no bearing on your sanity." He looked at Anthony solemnly but with assurance, as if he had said this a thousand times before. "Everyone I've interviewed has questioned their sanity on multiple occasions. I'm here to tell you, you're fine. I'm a licensed psychologist. Believe me, if you showed signs of instability during our conversation yesterday, we wouldn't be having this conversation today."

Anthony began to relax. Having a leading authority like Professor Ross confirm that he was okay made an immediate, positive impact on his stress level.

The professor continued. "The experience of an NDE or OBE is not as uncommon as you may think. Well over ten million people in the U.S. alone have experienced them. The true number of cases is probably much greater. Many haven't been reported due to fear of ridicule, embarrassment and denial to name a few. Most people believe death to be the end of existence itself, despite massive evidence to the contrary ... not necessarily the empirical evidence they desire but scientific evidence nonetheless. The tradition of science is based on investigation, so we do ourselves a disservice by not seriously analyzing the phenomenon to the best of our ability. Don't you agree?"

"Absolutely." Anthony was fascinated.

"One very common experience is coming to some kind of barrier that can't be crossed or the sense that if the barrier is crossed, that person will never be able to come back to tell the tale. Common themes would be a river, a wall, a door or a white veil of light."

"Tell me more about the light, professor. I think I've seen it."

"It is described as brighter than the sun, yet it doesn't hurt the eyes. It is always described as beautiful, full of love, even a manifestation of the God-head. The light draws the visitor to it like a moth, yet most say they cannot penetrate the light because it is not their time or that their soul is not advanced enough. There are different spectrums of light and different levels of reality but we won't get into that now." The professor sipped from his water bottle, eyes fixed on Anthony.

"What I need to do is jot down some basic demographic data, age; gender, and so forth; get a brief family background, religious beliefs, and then some detail regarding how your experiences began and changed over time. Fair enough?"

"Sounds good." Anthony could feel his heart beating in anticipation.

After sharing the prerequisite information on his age and religious beliefs, he delved into as much relevant family background as he could remember from early childhood on, including any significant events that had an impact on his life and self-image. He described the tragic death of his wife, but somehow it didn't seem as jolting as when he relived it with Dr. Richardson. He concluded with his most recent experiences.

"Good. We're done with preliminaries. Are you ready for some questions?"

"As ready as I'll ever be." Anthony smiled in anticipation.

"Based on your profile, I don't see much religious influence from either of your parents or from any organized religion. Would that be an accurate statement?" The professor looked-up from his notes, peering over the wire-rimmed glasses slipping precariously to the tip of his nose.

"That would be accurate," Anthony responded.

The professor slid a small digital recorder closer to where Anthony sat. "You mentioned that as a child you witnessed an apparition that seems to have returned and personified itself as a mischievous dwarf-man of Indian decent? Is that accurate?"

Anthony thought the professor was trying to hide a smile. "Yes." He shifted uncomfortably in his chair.

"If I heard you correctly, this diminutive prankster assists another personality called Maxim who has claimed to be your guide."

"That's correct."

The professor sifted through some additional notes and resumed his questions.

"Let's change gears a bit. You mentioned that your first OBE occurred at the time of your wife's death at the accident scene and that you had verbal contact with her."

"Yes." Anthony drew a deep breath and found himself clutching his knees.

"Describe where you were and what happened before, during and after the experience. I'm more interested in the mechanisms that triggered the OBE, what you experienced during the event and the trigger that pulled you back into your physical body. I'm *not* as interested in the details of the conversation. The fact that you had a conversation is noteworthy." The professor sat back in his chair, hands behind his head and waited for Anthony to respond.

He explained in detail how he heard the now-familiar snapping sound and found himself suddenly out of his body. He described how he floated toward the tree-line where he saw Diane, almost as if moving by intent and how he was *pulled* back into his body with the subsequent physical sensation of cold. He hadn't realized that he had closed his eyes while recounting the experience. He opened them to find the professor busily typing into his computer.

After a minute, the professor rolled his chair away from the desk. "Fascinating ... and not as unusual as you might think. So, did you experience an increase in the number and frequency of OBEs after this initial experience?"

"Yes, that is accurate."

"This Maxim you describe ... beyond claiming to be your guide, has he imparted any knowledge to you?"

"Oh, yes."

"Really? Can you explain?"

"Well, he describes physical existence on Earth as a school. He has emphasized love and compassion when interacting with others and even with myself, which can be a challenge for me." Anthony let out a self-deprecating laugh.

"He sounds like a wise man, or should I say, *being*," Professor Ross corrected himself.

"He is ... wise, that is."

"Are there any other things that stand out about Maxim or his teachings that you want to share?"

"Well, he told me that in order to move forward in our lives, we need to face our past so that we can let go of negative emotions and beliefs that hold us back. There are two universal truths that he seems to emphasize over and over again."

"And what might those be?" the professor interrupted.

"That time is simultaneous and that we create our own reality through our attitudes, beliefs, thoughts and ideas."

The professor thought for a moment. "That's a profound statement. Can you explain what that means to you?" He nudged the recorder ever closer and sat at the keyboard to transpose Anthony's response.

Anthony was caught off-guard by the question and gathered his thoughts. "He teaches that *time*, as we understand it, is a construct of human-kind; created from the observation of nature and the daily, monthly and yearly cycles of the sun, moon, tides, seasons, and so on. He says that all time is simultaneous, meaning that there really is no past or future, only the present moment; that in the power of that moment, we all have the ability to create any reality we desire through our focus and intent ... no matter what our circumstances."

"That's a fascinating theory," added the professor.

"I don't believe it's a theory," Anthony responded with a sincerity that surprised even him.

"You seem to feel strongly about the validity of what Maxim is teaching you."

"Deep down, the knowledge seems to touch a knowing part of me that I didn't realize existed."

"You mention *this* life. That seems to infer you have experienced other lives. Can you explain?"

"Well, Maxim has taught me that consciousness is not dependent on the physical body. Basically, it's timeless."

"Interesting ... and how do you come back in multiple lifetimes if there is no linear past or future?"

Anthony had the feeling the professor was trying to uncover an inconsistency in his statements. However, he had an easy response for the eager interviewer, eyebrows now raised in anticipation of an answer.

"If all time is simultaneous, it makes perfect sense to me," he continued. "Each personality experiences his or her own lifetime in their own time-continuum, simultaneous with other members of their soul family. They are all a part of a larger gestalt of consciousness that he refers to as an oversoul."

"Whoa, hold on there. You lost me. I *think* you're saying that each personality is part of one oversoul, as you call it, and that we all live in our own historical times, yet this is all happening simultaneously?" The professor seemed dumbfounded.

"Yes."

"That's a fantastic assumption. Do you believe it?"

Lost in Plain Sight

"At first, no. I had a hard time grasping the concept. However, he has shown me glimpses of my past, as if I'm experiencing them right now, and it makes perfect sense."

"I admire your dedication and courage, Anthony, even as I find what you say hard to believe." The professor finished typing his notes and studied Anthony thoughtfully. "This session is winding down. I would like to continue our discussions and follow your experiences. Would you be open to that?"

"Sure, but I can't come up here on a regular basis. How do you propose we continue?"

"I interview people by phone, e-mail, letter … any way I can. It was important to meet you in person. Subsequent interviews can be conducted remotely with an occasional in-person visit, at your convenience, of course," the professor added with a wry smile.

"I suppose I'd be open to that. It feels good to get my thoughts and experiences out in the open. I have a couple of close friends with whom I trust to do the same."

"I encourage you to continue that. As you've discovered, you can't keep these things to yourself for the sake of your own peace-of-mind."

"Agreed."

"One more thing. Most of what you describe is positive or neutral in terms of your encounters. Have you experienced anything negative or malevolent?"

The question surprised Anthony. After a moment of hesitation, he explained how the demonic apparition had appeared to him and likely attacked Daniel as he slept.

The professor turned serious. "If you believe Maxim and Jaster to be real, then this malevolent entity has to be considered dangerous to both you and your son."

"What do you suppose I do?" Anthony could feel his heart jump.

"I don't mean to alarm you, but be very careful. You are exploring areas and dimensions you know little about. Maxim seems to know these realms well. He is watching over you. Ask him to do the same for Daniel. Listen carefully to what he tells you and follow instructions completely." The professor leaned-in closer to Anthony. "It can be extremely dangerous for those not accustomed to out-of-body travel. Medicine Men, Shamans and Tibetan

Monks have all trained for years to leave their bodies and explore the realms you describe. You have an amazing opportunity but a dangerous one at that."

The calm that Anthony had experienced earlier disappeared. He sat in silence.

"Here's my card. Call me anytime if you need to talk or have a question. I'll do my best to help and guide you." The professor extended his hand.

Anthony took the card and slipped it into his wallet. "I appreciate that."

"Not at all." Professor Ross pushed his chair away from the desk and stood up to escort Anthony to the door.

After a brief farewell, the office door closed with a reverberating echo in the empty hallway.

TWELVE

Anthony walked the tree-lined pathways back to the cafeteria to meet Daniel and Emily for lunch. He glanced at his watch, surprised at how quickly the two-hour interview had passed. He had no idea what the professor planned to do with the information he provided or if it would be included in any of his peer-review journals or books. If he had learned anything from the session, it was to be very cautious and to arm himself with as much information as possible.

He nodded hello to a couple of students chatting on a park bench as he strolled through the campus. He entered the cafeteria, already filling-up with hungry students, despite the fact that it was barely noon.

A clock-tower chimed as he spotted the couple sitting at a table at the far-end of the room overlooking the campus green.

"Hey guys."

They both stood-up to greet him. "So how'd it go?" asked Daniel.

"Sit, please." He motioned for them to sit down and grabbed a nearby chair. "It went by quickly, but I think I gave him a lot to think about." He wondered how much Daniel had told Emily about what was going-on. "So Emily, has my son filled you in on our adventures?" He didn't want to make more out of it than necessary.

"Yeah, a little." Emily glanced at Daniel and smiled.

"Actually, more than a little," Daniel added. "I figured it was best to be upfront."

"And?" Anthony gazed inquisitively at the two love birds seeking an answer. Emily's face reddened, and she turned to Daniel with an imploring look on her face.

"Dad, she's cool with it."

"Okay, then." Anthony pulled his chair closer and filled them in on what was discussed during the interview. When he was finished, all three had a bite to eat and agreed to continue to read anything they could find regarding similar paranormal activities.

Emily walked back to her dorm, and Daniel dropped Anthony off at the train station for the trip home. It didn't seem nearly as long as the drive up.

As the taxi pulled into his driveway, he spotted Abby and Elizabeth playing in the front yard with Max. I lucked-out when I hired Abby to watch him, he thought appreciatively.

Max heard the taxi pull-in and turned to see who it was, a red ball clamped firmly in his mouth. Upon recognizing Anthony, he bounded over to greet him, tail wagging like a propeller blade.

"Hey buddy, how ya doin'?" He dropped to one knee and gave Max a big hug, while Abby and Elizabeth looked-on, smiling.

"Hey, girls, thanks for being such great babysitters." He gave Abby a hug and Elizabeth a friendly peck on the cheek.

"So, how's Daniel?" Elizabeth asked.

"He's doing well. We had a nice visit."

"Oh, I'm so glad. When Abby told me you were heading back up to the college unexpectedly and needed her to watch Max, I was a little worried."

"Sorry about that, Liz. I hope I didn't alarm you too much. Thanks for letting Abby watch him last minute. I *really* appreciate it."

"No problem. We were home this weekend anyway." Elizabeth bent over to pick-up the red ball that had rolled back to her feet as a result of a renewed game of fetch between Abby and Max. As she threw the ball back her daughter, Anthony noticed her pretty tanned legs. She was in fabulous shape and looked ten years younger than her thirty-eight years. Her hair was pulled-back in a half-pony tail, revealing prominent cheekbones, glittering silver earrings and piercing green eyes that almost took his breath away.

She glanced back at him, and he cleared his throat, trying to cover-up his obvious attraction. For a moment, she seemed to acknowledge his attentions as their eyes met briefly, followed by a warm smile. At that unexpected moment, Anthony thought that he would melt, she was so beautiful. He awkwardly steered the conversation toward the wonderful weather they had been having lately, and the moment passed.

After some small talk, Abby and Elizabeth walked home while Anthony took Max for a quick walk around the block before heading back to the house. The door knob felt like ice as he opened the front door. "God, it's cold in here," he commented to no one in particular.

They had taken two steps into the house when Max stopped in his tracks, staring to the end of the front hallway. Anthony thought that Jaster might have reappeared in the study, but the dog's attention seemed fixed on something nearby. He began to growl.

"What is it Max?"

A piercing scream shot through the hallway. Max erupted in vicious barking and then retreated to the corner behind the front door, whimpering. Before Anthony had a chance to register what was going-on, he turned his attention back down the hallway and gasped. The apparition that had appeared in his car was now directly in front of him, suspended in mid-air, barely two feet from his face.

The stench of death hung in the air from its putrid breath. Icy-black eyes cut through him with hatred so intense and repulsive, he nearly passed-out. Frozen in place, he waited for what seemed like an eternity for it to make its intentions known.

Out of nowhere, Max shot through the air to attack the specter, only to pass directly through it, landing on all fours and sliding ten feet down the slippery hallway tile. He turned to face the intruder again, teeth bared but keeping his distance. The apparition paid no attention to the dog. It hadn't moved an inch.

The entity's mouth curved into a menacing smile and uttered two words, "You're mine," before dissolving in a jumble of watery black and grey spheres that tumbled into nothingness.

Anthony ran into the small bathroom off the study and threw-up. Max followed behind and sat down next to his master, now hugging the toilet-bowl. The phone rang in the study. He pushed himself up, flushed the toilet, grabbed some tissues and stumbled to his desk.

"Hello," his voice cracked.

"Anthony, it's JoAnne."

He was glad to hear from her and attempted to sound as normal as possible.

"Hi, JoAnne, what's up?"

"I wanted to apologize for the other day. I was being a meddling sister ... sorry."

Anthony appreciated her apology but realized he had treated her unfairly. "Not necessary, JoAnne. I'm sorry I was short with you. You've been so good to me."

"Anthony, I've got an idea. If you don't like it, that's okay, but I thought I would run it by you anyway."

"Shoot." He was open to anything at this point.

"These last few months have been rough on you. Between your work, the sessions with George and everything else you've had to deal with, you must be exhausted."

He couldn't argue with that.

"I was thinking it might be a refreshing change of pace for you to get out of this town for a long weekend and fly down to Palm Beach for some R&R. What do you think?"

Anthony hesitated for just a brief moment. "You know, JoAnne, that's not a bad idea." He needed a change of scenery.

"I have a friend who will be happy to let you stay at his place. He's hardly ever there. Sound good?"

"Sounds amazing." Anthony wanted to escape. Free lodging in Palm Beach worked for him.

"Great. I'll make the arrangements for next weekend. You can fly out Thursday night and return on Sunday. You won't have any problems taking Friday off on such short notice, will you ... with that awful, Condoleezza or whatever her name is?"

Anthony managed a laugh. "Contessa ... Condoleezza was Secretary of State."

"Whatever." JoAnne chuckled.

David Gerard

"I've got a bunch of days-off coming to me. I'll deal with Contessa first thing on Monday."

"Good. I'll have a car pick you up at your place, okay?"

"Perfect. Thanks, JoAnne." He was grateful for her thoughtfulness.

"Happy to help a nice guy," she responded. "I'll see you off on Thursday."

"I look forward to it. Bye." Anthony hung-up the phone and looked around the room warily. *I do need a break from this place.*

After washing-up, he locked his bedroom door. *Not that it will help much against that thing,* he worried. However, it made him feel better. He invited Max up on the king-size bed and clicked-on the TV to keep himself company. He channel-surfed to the evening news, feeling somewhat removed from worldly events these last few weeks. Exhausted, he fell back onto his pillow and stared up at the ceiling fan.

At first he thought it was dizziness. An overwhelming sense of movement began to overtake his awareness. Suddenly, he became hyper-focused on the room, as if looking through an electron microscope. He saw every molecule and atom that made up the walls, curtains and furniture. Then, his mind relaxed as every aspect of the bedroom dissolved into a blur of swirling geometric shapes and colors. A tiny remnant of his conscious mind recognized that there was order behind this transformation and he continued to relax and let the experience come to him.

Brilliant mandalas burst before his eyes. Somehow in the deepest recesses of his mind he knew that each unique design was a symbol representing its own purpose, truth and consciousness.

Emerging from an indefinable, universal void, they paraded before him; each an artistic masterpiece worthy of exhibition at any of the finest galleries in the world. He didn't have time to wonder at the creation of such beauty, only to observe in awe. Each color exuded layers and depths of shade, so subtle as to be non-existent in physical reality. Anthony felt drawn into each, as if diving into a pool of color and sound.

The consciousness that formed the structure of each geometric shape bathed him in an awareness and understanding of himself and his place in the universe. The thought *ecstasy and orgasm* came to the surface of his consciousness and disappeared just as quickly, as if coming-up for air in a sea of churning foam.

Each creation vibrated at its own frequency, resulting in a beautiful musical tone that resonated clearly into the farthest reaches of the universe. Limitless individual notes became part of an overall symphony of sound. Melodies and chords combined in an effortless and seamless whole that sung the chorus of each individual mandala. Each one, endless in depth ... minute, yet gigantic; a fractal representing limitless reality ... the closest representation of infinity that Anthony had ever experienced.

Maxim's voice broke through the vision. "The mandalas are universal symbols of life, consciousness and light. Each one is unique in shape, color and the melody it contributes to the universe. A creation of All That Is, yet with its own consciousness and free will to create its own reality ... individual yes, but also part of a greater whole." He paused.

"Welcome to your first glance at a universal truth *and* your first training session."

Maxim waved his hand in the now familiar half-circle and the symbols disappeared, revealing the massive Temple Portal looming in front of them. He sat on the steps leading to the entrance and invited Anthony to do the same.

Despite the beauty of the setting, the demon visitations and attack on Daniel were praying on Anthony's mind. Why weren't they protected? He needed to tell Maxim.

"Maxim, before we begin, I have something I need to ask you." He didn't want to make accusations but he needed to be direct.

"Of course. What is it?"

"I'm being stalked. I'm convinced that it's the same entity that attacked Daniel. Why haven't you been there to protect us?"

Maxim thought for a moment. "Just because you can't see me doesn't mean I'm not there. There is—"

"But we could have been killed!" Anthony interrupted. Daniel was wounded and the demon was inches from my face." He was more upset than he realized.

Maxim seemed unfazed. "But protected you were."

Anthony was confused.

Maxim sighed. "Daniel *was* saved by *his* guardian angel. She knew that he was resistant to the truth about the other side. She allowed him to experience a physical mark, so he wouldn't think it was just a dream. He had to know so he could understand what you've been going through."

"Okay. Then what about me? I've had two close calls. It's only a matter of time before it decides to hurt me."

"Remember, the negative forces have no power to hurt you on the physical plane. I am watching over you in your dreams and training you for safe travel in the after-death realms. That is why we are meeting on these steps."

Anthony thought for a moment. It seemed like a reasonable explanation but he still felt vulnerable and unconvinced.

Maxim continued. "You must trust in what I say. Mastering the environments of the Astral Plane and the multiple dimensions of the after-death realms need to be your highest priority. Are you ready?"

Anthony knew there was no use in arguing further. "Of course I trust you, Maxim."

The guide smiled broadly. "A wise choice. Now, do you know why I immersed you in a sea of symbols?"

"To show me truth?" Anthony was uncertain.

"Good answer but vague." The guide held his hands together as if in prayer. "What truth or rather whose truth?"

Anthony had no answer and felt as if he had let Maxim down. "I'm sorry. I don't know." He bowed his head.

Maxim continued patiently. "Those symbols are a faithful representation of your life and your place in the universe. In fact, they are a representation of all life."

"But how?" Anthony was confused. "They are geometric patterns and I am a human being. How can they represent me or anyone else?"

"Like each one of those living symbols, you also are a unique individual, with a personality and talents that can never be duplicated. As with each geometric shape, you have your own unique makeup that is timeless and forms the human being that you became in this life ... and yet you are one *very important* part of a greater whole, made-up of your oversoul, soul family, human family and ultimately all life and all reality."

Lost in Plain Sight

Anthony attempted to grasp the enormity of what Maxim was teaching him.

"All life ... all reality works this way. The planets and your sun are individual bodies with their own consciousness. They form a single solar system in a sea of stars and other solar systems, in a single galaxy, which is one of billions of galaxies and trillions of stars and solar systems in your physical universe. You see, we all count, however small. We all have meaning and purpose, even if we can't comprehend what it is. We all contribute individually *and* as a whole." A blue aura pulsed around Maxim.

"Humans are born into the physical plane from the womb of the universe. They grow, learn and ultimately return to whence they came. You are not at the mercy of one physical lifetime. You have *and will* experience, learn and grow from many lifetimes; many births, many deaths.

"What you think, what you believe and the actions you take all have an effect on the reality that surrounds you, both positively and negatively. You choose and are ultimately responsible for the effect you have on yourself, others and the world you inhabit as individuals.

"Today's demonstration, and a good one at that," Maxim congratulated himself, "was meant to imbue you with knowledge and confidence in who and what you are so that you can meet the great challenges that await you with courage and conviction. It is your destiny." Maxim nodded slightly, indicating the training session had come to an end.

Even as Anthony attempted to absorb what Maxim had imparted to him, something mentioned at the very end of his instruction about *great challenges and destiny* gnawed at him. The words gave him a queasy feeling in the pit of his stomach.

THIRTEEN

The week leading-up to his trip to Palm Beach was one of the most difficult, yet rewarding periods of time Anthony had experienced since coming in contact with Maxim. He trusted his guide to protect him but still felt vulnerable every time he got into his car or walked into his house alone. He tried to keep it in perspective and treat it like a test, so he focused all his energy on his training. Each night he would sit on his couch in the study and use the techniques that he had been taught to quiet his mind. He became very adept at meditation, allowing Maxim to enter his consciousness to speak and guide him out of his body to the Temple Portal.

On the evening before his trip, they sat on the massive steps of the temple. Maxim told Anthony he would take him back to his childhood to re-experience both the mundane and painful moments in his life that impacted his development growing-up. He asked Anthony to immerse himself in these moments again with his current perspective as an adult living with the consequences of his beliefs. Once they had explored his *official history*, they would talk about the results of such beliefs and what might have happened if, as a child, he had the perspective of his present-self. The final exercise would have Anthony using his newfound knowledge to revisit those events again but with the freedom and ability to alter any moment that had caused him pain. He would then experience the alternate realities that would have been created as a result.

Tonight, Anthony was to experience one of those traumatic childhood events, one that had shaped who he had become even to this day. Maxim did not tell him which moment it would be, only that he needed to focus fully on the scene when it came into view.

They walked past the rows of immense columns to the middle of the temple and stood face-to-face on a beautiful mosaic made from various shades of white, amber, blue and purple glass tiles lit brilliantly from below. The intense colors streamed up through the glass and projected the shape of a huge mandala on a rotunda directly above them. It was at least one hundred feet in diameter.

Anthony now understood that the mandala was a sacred symbol of the universe, just as Maxim had explained. As he looked down to the farthest reaches of the temple to admire the huge golden statue, Jaster emerged out of the shadow of the pedestal pushing the now familiar cart filled with the metaphorical baggage of Anthony's past.

As the diminutive side-kick slowly pushed the contraption, Anthony noticed a particularly large piece of baggage prominently placed in front of all the others. Jaster paused at the edge of the tile mosaic, picked up that very item and approached Maxim, who beckoned Anthony to the center of the colossal artwork.

Hesitating, Anthony opened the old, dusty suitcase and a rainbow of light shot up through the mosaic and encircled him. Surrounded by a vortex of geometric shapes, lights and sounds, he became dizzy and closed his eyes. When he reopened them, he found himself standing in the clearing of a vaguely familiar wood.

It was a perfect spring day. He noticed two boys playing in a large and beautiful willow tree. The huge branches seemed to embrace them as they happily carved their initials into the pliable bark with their shiny, new pocket knives. Suddenly, the moment became clear in his mind. From the murky depths of long-forgotten memory, this distant scene had become alive again. It was the day his world changed forever, his innocence stolen in the blink of an eye.

"To—ney, To—ney!" The sound of his mother's voice was haunting and only underscored the boys' fate.

Anthony's mood darkened as he viewed the bucolic moment, knowing full well what was to come as he and his childhood friend, Jimmy, blissfully continued their play, unaware of the impending confrontation.

Anthony nervously turned to his left and right, peering through the trees in a frantic search for Maxim, but to no avail. He was nowhere in sight.

Confused and frightened, he screamed out to the boys to run, but they couldn't see or hear him. Two teenage thugs appeared, as if on cue, from the edge of the woods. They silently approached the willow tree, their gray silhouettes superimposed on the green clearing like two smudges on the sketchpad of a well drawn landscape.

The boys didn't notice them at first. They were startled when one of the teenagers ordered them to climb down from the tree and come over to the edge of the clearing. Tony and Jimmy complied.

Anthony panicked. "No. No, don't climb down," he yelled, but he was just a ghost of the distant future, powerless to change what had been etched in time. Again, he ran over to the tree as the attackers came closer. He screamed at the top of his lungs, but he might as well have been leaves rustling in the breeze as the boys jumped to the ground.

The ten-year-olds innocently approached the teenage boys, who were physically twice their size. One of them stepped forward. He wore a beat-up leather jacket and had a scar that ran from the corner of his mouth to his chin. He spoke first.

"What are you two doing here?" he demanded.

"Just playing," answered Jimmy innocently. "Up in the tree." He turned and pointed upwards.

"Just playing in the tree, huh?" the second teenager taunted. "Big mistake."

"What did we do?" Anthony saw the panic on Tony's face and could almost hear the child's heart pounding.

"You're in *our* territory, and now you have to pay, douche bag," snarled the boy with the scar. He pulled out a switchblade from his jacket pocket and pressed a silver button on the handle. A

Lost in Plain Sight

four-inch, gleaming blade burst from the end of the knife handle, as if appearing from thin-air.

Then, Jimmy recognized the boy with the scar and addressed him by name. "Manny, don't. Please don't hurt us!"

"How do you know my name? Come here!"

Jimmy tried to run but the older boys were too quick and jumped him. He frantically kicked them over and over again. Anthony saw the knife fly through the air and land in the grass. The teenagers punched the young boy as he lay on his back screaming in pain.

Anthony watched in horror as the young child he once was, stood frozen in place, unable to help his friend. It suddenly became clear what was going through Tony's mind ... terror and powerlessness.

Tony screamed and bolted back down the path that had brought him to the clearing. The teenage boys looked up as he tried to escape and pushed Jimmy to the ground, running as fast as they could after the terrified child.

Anthony followed close behind, praying that the teenagers wouldn't catch his ten-year-old self. He was frustrated that he couldn't recall the outcome of this scary event. He visualized the high stone-wall that bordered his parents' property from the woods and somehow was transported instantly ahead of the running boys.

Within a minute, he heard twigs snapping, as running feet trampled the leaf-strewn woods. The frantic breathing of his child-self running for his life echoed in his mind.

Out of breath, Tony skidded to a halt at the edge of a stream that passed through a copse of trees behind a stone wall. He frantically searched the woods behind him for any movement or sounds.

From about fifty yards away, Anthony watched as the young boy listened for the sound of footsteps coming-up from behind him. Within moments, the pounding of feet could be heard approaching. The stream was at least ten feet wide, but Tony jumped nimbly from one exposed rock to another, landing gently on the opposite side. His speed and familiarity with the woods gave him the ability to lose the teenage boys for a critical moment. Anthony knew they wouldn't follow him home.

Without looking back, Tony ran up to the spot where Anthony was watching. For a moment, he thought his younger self might see and recognize him, but he breezed by and quickly climbed down the wall, close enough for Anthony to see the absolute terror on the youngster's face.

He watched as Tony sprinted up the driveway and into the house, traumatized by the incident. The familiar slam of the screen door cut through Anthony's senses, as he tried to make sense of the horrific event that had been brought back to life in front of his eyes. The contrast of this terrible memory stood side-by-side with the emotions connected with seeing his boyhood home again, seemingly irreconcilable as he stood in place, numb from sensory overload.

Anthony knew at this moment that Tony's entire sense of security and well-being had been shattered. He pictured himself in his room and was transported there, as if by magic. He watched Tony sitting on his bed, hands over his face, crying. He felt the child's pain as feelings of shame came flooding back … shame for leaving his friend behind and an all consuming fear of the thugs who had invaded his world.

Anthony looked around the bedroom. His thoughts were interrupted for a moment by the feeling of awe and nostalgia of being back inside his boyhood room again, as if not a day had passed. The pictures, toys; his desk, clothes; carpet …everything was in front of him. The distraction didn't last long as the feelings returned. He tried to comfort Tony but remained an invisible and silent visitor.

He felt the lack of self-confidence and sadness of the child and tears came to his eyes as he realized how hard he was on himself during his early years. All he could feel now was compassion.

Maxim appeared as the room faded from view. Anthony found himself back in the Temple Portal standing under the rotunda. He bowed his head. His face felt strained from reliving such a painful event in his life.

Maxim spoke. "It is important that you understand that it was not your fault. You have carried the shame and guilt of that moment with you to this day, despite that fact that Jimmy was able to run home while the teenage boys chased you through the woods."

Anthony's eyes widened. "That's right. I had forgotten. Jimmy told me later that he got away but I still felt guilty for not trying to help him."

"You need to witness the truth and forgive yourself. Acceptance will allow you to finally let go and move on psychologically. Now that you have faced that reality and felt the raw emotions, you can begin the healing process. Do you have enough strength and courage to do that?" Maxim asked gently.

"I don't know," Anthony responded with a whisper.

"Forgiving yourself can be more difficult than forgiving others but just as rewarding." Maxim smiled.

Anthony returned the smile and nodded in agreement.

"Let go of the past and I have a gift to bestow upon you."

Anthony looked-up at Maxim, not sure what he meant. "Gift?"

"Yes. Forgiving yourself deserves a gift of equal value. I will allow you to appear before your ten-year-old self so that you may meet yourself as a boy, comfort him and pass on your new-found knowledge."

"He'll be able to see me … hear me?" Anthony was incredulous.

"Yes … and by passing on your knowledge in your past, you will change your future. In this case, for the better."

"How is that possible?"

"Remember, all time is simultaneous. The only moment is the present. Anyone can go back to *past* moments in their mind, visualize a different outcome and literally change their past. This will, in turn, change their present. If you are trained in out-of-body travel, then you can re-visit your past and do the same. It's like watching what you call a movie, except that you live inside the moving pictures and can participate and alter outcomes."

"Which is what I just did?" asked Anthony.

"You revisited and observed but did not participate or alter the outcome. If you truly forgive yourself, I will allow you to go back to the scene again and relive it knowing what you know now, so you can change the "official" reality you just experienced."

Anthony's eyes widened. "I'll try but—"

"Trying is not good enough. You must be committed to accepting yourself and the experiences that have made you the person you are today. You need to believe in yourself and your inherent goodness before you can fully let go of your past." Maxim allowed Anthony to absorb the wisdom being offered, and then continued. "The following statement is a universal truth regardless of any beliefs you hold to the contrary.

"It is never too late to change your present reality or your past. The only true time is the present moment. All time is simultaneous. In this very moment you can change the circumstances of the past and thus change all the moments that follow. You have the power to transform your personal reality through your beliefs, thoughts and ideas. They literally form the world that you know."

Maxim's words became imprinted in Anthony's mind. He now understood what he needed to do to free himself of a past that hung around his neck like an albatross. For the first time, it dawned on him that Maxim's wisdom could apply to anyone like himself who was a prisoner of their past.

"Are you prepared to let go?" Maxim asked expectantly.

Without hesitation, Anthony responded. "Yes. I'll forgive myself."

"Good. Next, you will meet yourself as a boy for the first time. It will be emotional but you have to remember to put him at ease. This opportunity is as much about healing your younger-self as it is about healing your present adult-self."

"I'll remember." Anthony took a deep breath to keep his emotions at bay.

"Excellent! When the visit is complete, the final step will be to return to the scene again and relive it knowing what you know now, so you can change that reality and the subsequent pain you feel to this day."

Anthony wasn't expecting to have to relive that scene again and protested.

"Remember, it won't be the same because the boy will have been given the gift of knowledge and foresight that wasn't available to him the first time."

Anthony understood the concept but had his doubts he could pull it off.

As if reading his mind, Maxim added, "Trust yourself and all will be well." Then he faded away.

FOURTEEN

Anthony found himself standing in a familiar grotto of pine trees in the backyard of his childhood home. The air was fresh and the familiar sounds of birds melded with the distant hum of a neighbor's lawn mower.

The feeling of being immersed in a time long past was overwhelming and exciting at the same time. He touched his arms, then his face and hair. He was young, maybe twenty-five. His eyesight was back to what it was in his youth. He spied the treetops. The leaves and pine needles were crisp and green, even from a distance. A cacophony of sound surrounded him. Bird calls, the whisper of a jet airplane high overhead, the rustling of leaves and the sound of a cool spring breeze on his ears were real. He was experiencing all of it as if this moment in time existed forever.

Simultaneous time, he thought ... all moments existing now. He suddenly understood that the perception of time, of a past, present and future was indeed a man-made concept.

He heard a child's laugh nearby. A young boy appeared from around the corner of the backyard patio, running and jumping over the grass. He had something in his hand ... a model airplane, Anthony realized.

The boy was immersed in his imaginary game and hadn't noticed Anthony yet. As he skipped toward the pine grove, pretending to fly the plane, he saw Anthony and stopped. He warily examined the stranger in his backyard.

For a moment, Anthony thought the boy would run but he stood there with the toy plane now at his side. He looks so innocent, Anthony marveled. He wore a blue, horizontal-striped tee shirt, khaki shorts and PF Flyers. Anthony smiled. He hadn't seen those sneakers in years.

"Hi, Tony." Anthony used the name he was called as a kid.

"Hi. Who are you, mister?"

Anthony was caught off-guard. It was a simple question that he should have thought about before he arrived. He quickly came up with the only answer he could think of. "I'm a friend from a place very far away."

The boy hesitated. "Where?"

"A place where you will be someday."

The boy seemed interested. "Really?" He started to play with the plane again, landing it on the patio wall and making engine noises before skidding it to a stop.

"We don't go to many places except my grandma and grandpa's."

"Oh?" Anthony sat on the wall next to his young self. A part of him couldn't believe that he was actually conversing with himself as a boy ... and he was cuter than he remembered too. He felt a bit uncomfortable and looked over his shoulder to see if his mother was watching from the living room window, but no one was there. He didn't want to scare anyone with his presence. When he turned to the boy again, Anthony noticed the kid was studying him closely.

"Have we talked before?" the boy asked curiously.

Anthony thought for a moment. "Yes, Tony, we have."

"We did? Where?"

"In your dreams. Remember the one about the baseball game? You hit a home run and I was the pitch—"

Tony's eyes lit-up. "Yeah!" he laughed. "You stunk!"

Anthony laughed with him. "Yeah, you killed me with three home runs in that dream."

"Yeah." Tony's smile faded. "But that was a dream. In real baseball, I stink. He fidgeted with his plane and looked at the ground, kicking the patio wall with the heel of his sneakers.

"Hey, guess what?"

"What?"

"I've got a secret to tell you. It will make you feel better."

Tony perked-up. "What, Mister?"

"Don't call me mister. Call me Anthony." He tousled the boy's hair.

"That's my name too!"

"I know."

"How come you know me, Anthony?" Tony's eyes reflected pure innocence. It took every ounce of discipline Anthony could muster to not hug him right then and there, but he didn't want to scare the kid.

"What I'm going to tell you may seem fantastic. You may not believe me, but I promise that it's true."

Tony's eyes widened.

"Are you ready?" Anthony wasn't even sure he was ready.

"Yep." Tony stared at him in anticipation.

"I *am* the person that you will be when you grow up." He waited for the boy's reaction.

Tony examined him from head-to-toe as if seeing him for the first time. Then, his face lit up. "You are?"

Anthony breathed a sigh of relief. "I am! And I'll tell you something else. I know how bad you feel right now because of what happened with Jimmy."

Tony's face became red. He was obviously ashamed and started to sniffle.

"It's okay." Anthony began to choke-up. He put his hand gently on the boy's shoulder.

"Jimmy got hurt and I ran away," he cried. "I'm a bad friend." Tears were flowing down his cheeks.

It was all Anthony could do to keep his composure. "Tony, I know how to make it better. In fact, we can actually change what happened."

Tony was still sniffling but had stopped crying. He gazed at Anthony hopefully.

"How?"

"Well, when you get to be my age, you learn about stuff ... and I learned how to change things that make my life sad."

"Really, mister ... I'm mean, Anthony?"

"Yes. Would you like to try?"

"Sure!" Tony jumped off the wall.

"Okay. Now, listen closely." Anthony described how he had witnessed the event as Tony's future adult self and how helpless he was to assist him. He reminded the boy that his mother had called for him before the incident but that he and Jimmy had ignored her.

"This time, climb down from the tree when she calls and the two of you will walk home safely like it never happened."

"Will it work?"

"Yes. It's like magic. When it's over it will be as though the whole thing never happened. Jimmy will be fine and will never know the difference. It will be erased from your past like a scribble on your favorite picture!"

"Wow! That's really neat!"

Anthony knew that Maxim was silent and invisible nearby but was waiting for the right time to act. "Okay. Are you ready?"

"Yes." Tony seemed excited, as if it were a game. But it's no game, thought Anthony.

"Everything will get kinda fuzzy. You may get a little dizzy but it's okay. Do you understand?"

"Yep," Tony nodded affirmatively.

"Close your eyes. When you open them you will be in the tree with Jimmy but you will remember this conversation. When your Mom calls, climb down immediately, no matter what Jimmy says and walk home together. Ready?"

"Ready." Tony closed his eyes.

Alright, Maxim, thought Anthony. Take over from here.

The beautiful spring day began to fade away and the surroundings began to spin. Anthony closed his eyes and waited, now used to the process. Within moments, he was back again to that fateful day. Despite his understanding with Tony, he felt extremely nervous. By now, it was all too familiar, like a recurring nightmare. He hoped and prayed that Tony would remember his instructions.

He waited and watched. The two boys were about halfway up the tree, happily carving their initials into a thick branch. Then, suddenly Tony peered through the leaves to the spot where Anthony was hiding. He smiled knowingly.

Anthony returned the smile and put his finger to his mouth to remind him not to say anything to Jimmy. Then, he leaned back against a tree, relieved that Tony had remembered.

A few minutes passed and Anthony began to get anxious. Would it play out the way they wanted it to? Would the teenage boys arrive earlier?

Out of habit, he lifted his wrist to look at his watch but he had no watch. When would his mother call the boys, he wondered? He was becoming more agitated.

"To—ney ... To—ney! Time to come home! Jimmy's Mom wants him home too! Right now!"

Anthony locked-in on the spot where the boys were playing just as Tony looked down at him, as if expecting more instructions. He frantically gestured for the boy to climb down immediately, mouthing the words, "Now! Come'on! Quickly!"

Tony got the message and seemed to be trying to convince Jimmy to leave. Anthony peered around a nearby tree, careful to stay out of sight in case Jimmy might see him. He kept glancing at the clearing where the teenage boys were due to appear.

"Come'on, Tony. You've got to move," he muttered nervously under his breath. He could feel his heart beating faster. "There's not a lot of time." He scanned the clearing. Still no teenagers. He glanced back up to the big tree again.

Finally, Tony and Jimmy had begun to slowly make their way down. Anthony couldn't remember how much time had elapsed between when his mother called and when the older boys had arrived, but it wasn't long.

He continued watching the scene with trepidation as the boys made their way down the massive trunk. "Faster ... let's go."

Finally, they reached the lowest branch and jumped to the ground. Tony glanced over at Anthony, now hiding behind a nearby bush.

"Go, go!" he gestured wildly.

Tony acknowledged him and turned to say something to Jimmy. Then, they ran playfully down the well-worn pathway back home. Tony glanced back to Anthony one more time with a huge smile, and the boys disappeared.

As two dark figures entered the clearing, the scene faded and Anthony was back at the Temple Portal with Maxim.

He shook his head happily in disbelief. "Wow!"

FIFTEEN

Thursday had come in the blink of an eye. The visit to his past was fading quickly in Anthony's mind. He lay in bed for a few minutes and watched the sunlight dancing through the branches of a maple tree outside his bedroom window. They bent erratically in the breeze as if trying to warn him of impending danger. He worried about Daniel and wondered if Liz or Abby might be targeted next but there was nothing he could do.

Maxim's training seemed to be revealing a compassion for himself that he had never experienced before. It was a humbling first step in accepting his life experiences and the person he had become. It was also a good time to take a break, he thought gratefully.

He had caught Contessa in a good mood early in the week, plus an impending media deal with a major advertiser had softened her resistance to a last-minute long weekend off. He had been much more focused at the office lately, doing his best not to allow all the weirdness in his personal life to affect his performance.

He glanced at his clock-radio. It was 7:00AM. JoAnne had left a voice mail that the flight would depart JFK at 11:30.

"Time to get-up, Max." Anthony rubbed the dog's stomach, a gesture Max never protested against, despite being woken from a deep sleep. He rolled on his back with his feet in the air, looking expectantly at Anthony from his upside down position on the bed.

"You're so easy, Max ... and so predictable," he laughed.

Max made a grunting sound, wagged his tail and sneezed on the freshly washed comforter.

"Max! No sneezing on the bed. Come'on now ... off." He waved Max down. The dog rolled over and jumped onto the area rug with a thud.

"I suppose you want to go out now that you're up, don't you?" Anthony asked, half-annoyed as he glanced at his watch. The time was passing quickly.

He ran downstairs to unlock the front door. Max rushed outside to do his business, while Anthony prepared to leave. Fortunately, he had packed everything the night before with the exception of his toothbrush and shaving gear. He checked his to-do list to make sure he hadn't forgotten anything.

"Let's see ... water in Max's bowl, he was fed and let-out this morning," he mumbled to himself. "Stove is off, windows locked, doors locked, out-of-office and voice-mail is changed. Abby and Liz will check on Max later today and bring in the mail. They have my cell number ... and I think that's it." He paused for a moment while he visualized Abby and Liz coming to the house. What if that *thing* comes back? He rubbed his temples, trying to think of a way to warn them but couldn't imagine anything he could say that wouldn't make them think he was crazy.

"I'll ask Maxim if he can watch over them," he told himself. "It's the best I can do."

He double-checked the items that he had packed one more time before retrieving Max and giving him a big hug. He noticed that the dog was getting nervous and fidgety. Max always sensed when Anthony was leaving for an extended period of time. Must be the suitcase, he thought.

He bent down to give Max another hug. "It's okay, boy. I'll be back on Sunday. Abby will take good care of you." Max followed him down the stairs to the front door, giving him the sad puppy-eyes look the whole way.

"Not fair, Max." He patted him on the head one more time and slowly closed and locked the front door.

As if on cue, the black limousine pulled into the driveway as he walked down the flagstone pathway.

Max walked slowly down the front hallway and sniffed the air warily, each step of his paws echoing off the marble floor. The deep tone that had been emanating from behind the wall in the study for weeks became louder, spooking him. He ran upstairs into the bedroom, whimpering.

A black figure with a luminous white face appeared from nowhere in the study of the empty house. Suspended in mid-air, it silently turned to survey the room as the stench of rotting meat wafted to the bedroom upstairs to where Max was curled up in his bed on the floor. The pungent odor slowly reached the spot where Max lay. He began to whistle through his nose in distress and attempt to crawl under the bed, unsuccessfully. With nowhere else to go, he backed himself into the space next to Anthony's bedside table, nervously sniffing the room.

The specter turned its head slowly and deliberately upward in the direction of the bedroom above the study. It paused for a moment as a knowing expression appeared on its face. Still staring coldly at the ceiling above, it floated out of the study and into the hallway, its black eyes burning with hatred as it moved effortlessly up the stairs. Max began to yowl, turning and backing into the space between the bed and table in a fruitless attempt to hide.

An evil grin formed on the demonic face as a filthy, bony hand with pointed black fingernails pulled a silver dagger from beneath its tattered cloak and moved with increasing speed toward the master bedroom. It appeared suddenly in the doorway and peered into the room.

Now backed into a corner, Max arched his back yowling, whimpering and baring his teeth in a primal display of fight or flight. The specter moved-in closer, raising the dagger in a grotesque jerking motion, its sickly face gleeful in anticipation of the cruel deed it was about to execute on the terrified animal.

A purple-white light surrounded Max, temporarily halting the forward movement of the specter. Suddenly angry, it lunged at the dog, only to be thrown back as it screamed and grabbed its hand, searing with pain. Consumed with rage, it glared at Max, then quickly glanced in all directions for the source of the light and its pain but found nothing. Still holding its mangled hand, it made one more sweeping look around the room, flew up through the ceiling and disappeared.

Then, the spectral shape burst through an immense wall of dense clouds like a bat shot from a cannon. It dove deeper into an endless black void, the final destination known only to the solitary traveler. Random flashes of electricity illuminated clouds of putrid gas that parted begrudgingly for the black spec passing through their midst. They were not mindless, billowy shapes but living, thinking extensions of their realm. They knew she was coming as she had countless times before. The rage and hatred emanating from her was more intense than usual and absorbed by the environment accordingly.

Distracted for a moment, the clouds took note then returned their attentions from whence they came. Evil, dark thoughts were all this region had known for eons. It was a timeless, infinite realm of misery; a virtual twilight of fear, hatred and tortuous suffering; endless in duration.

Finally at its destination, the demon appeared before the evil Nefar. Her pointed and decaying teeth locked together in a grimace of anger and capitulation to the Master of the Dark Realm. She stood facing Nefar, her black eyes averting her master's stare as he rose from his granite throne and glided closer to his lieutenant.

"You bring me bad news, Maloda," he stated with disdain. He stood uncomfortably close, by design, and glared down at his normally efficient soldier with disgust.

"He is protected. Even his pet is surrounded by the purple field."

"And who is behind this insolence?"

"I am not certain, Master." Maloda scowled, diverting her jet-black eyes away from Nefar's intense gaze.

"So, you fail me twice ... three times, if you count that pitiful dog creature," Nefar hissed in disgust. He paused for a moment, gazing into the depths of the cavern that loomed above, and then turned in one quick movement, striking Maloda across the face.

Her head whipped violently to the side as she brought her claw-like hand to her bony cheek to protect against another blow.

"Primitive violence, as satisfying as it is, won't help you do your job, will it?"

"No, Master Nefar." Humiliated, Maloda cowered before him.

"How many times have we spoken of this human, Anthony?!" Now in a rage, Nefar was spitting mouthfuls of foul silvery saliva in all directions.

"Many times, Master."

Feigning patience, Nefar continued mercilessly. "Why do we seek to destroy him?"

Maloda froze, afraid to speak the wrong answer.

"Why, you ignorant ..."

"Because of the prophecy!!" she screeched to assuage Nefar's boiling rage.

"*What is the prophecy?!*"

Maloda recited the tome word for word as she had done so many times before. "*From the multitudes, the sign of the fish will arise and take his place as a leader of men. Unknown to himself, he will suffer greatly and set out on a journey to uncover that which has been lost to mankind for eons. The knowledge, hidden in the depths of time, is in plain sight. If he fails, the pace of darkness will quicken. If he succeeds, the light will illuminate the throngs and change mankind forever.*"

"Correct ... and what of our world?"

"Our power will be greatly diminished." A guttural groan of anger seeped through Maloda's teeth as her decayed face returned an evil, unblinking stare.

"Then what I ask is simple. Find him, imprison him and take the knowledge he has gained from his mind. Then eliminate him in any manner you wish. If he is protected, find a weakness and eliminate the source of protection. Is that so difficult to understand?"

"No, Master."

"Is it complicated?" Nefar's voice rose with impatience.

"No, Master." Maloda cringed in fear as Nefar began to glide toward her.

"Is it?!" He raised his gnarled hand over his head as if to strike her again.

"No, Master Nefar!"

Nefar's voice suddenly became quiet but as deadly as ever. "Then be on your way. I expect good news at our next encounter." He glowered at her with a malicious smile.

With the message clear, Maloda turned and glided away into the swirling darkness.

SIXTEEN

Elizabeth had decided to accompany Abby to Anthony's house to keep her company while she took care of Max. Abby hadn't made a fuss about it, but Elizabeth's maternal instincts told her to be nearby her daughter tonight. She wouldn't admit it to Abby but she was not fond of large, quiet, empty houses either, especially places where there had been great tragedy. She shivered at the thought as she stirred a pot of steaming lentil soup. She gently replaced the cover and turned down the heat so it could simmer while they walked over to the house to feed Max.

She knew that Diane had not physically died in the house but was aware of the great pain that Anthony had been suffering over the last year. Houses had an uncanny way of absorbing negative energy, no matter what anybody said to the contrary, she thought.

It wasn't as if she didn't have any personal experience in this area. Her husband, Graham, had died not five years before of a sudden aneurism at age thirty-five. It had left her numb, with all the responsibility of a seven-year-old child and a home to take care of as a single parent. It had taken her two years to get back to a sense of normalcy in her life and those two years were hell. She shuddered at the thought. If it wasn't for Abby, she might have gone out of her mind with grief ... and Anthony, she thought with a lump in her throat. He came down almost daily with a casserole or pasta dish that Diane had cooked for them. She smiled inwardly as she recalled his kindness. He was very shy about it but always stayed for a few minutes to make sure they were okay and then went on his way. She had never told him how much that meant to her.

While Abby was taking care of Max, she decided to inspect the upstairs bedrooms first and then quickly check out the rooms downstairs to make sure everything was in order. The house was quiet with the exception of the furnace and the sound of warm air rushing through the heat registers.

As she reached the top step, the floorboards creaked loudly beneath the carpet runner, startling her. She stopped, surprised by her racing heartbeat and shallow breathing. After regaining her composure, she turned on the hall light and crept slowly down the hallway to the master bedroom. As she approached the partially open door, she thought she heard a faint, deep tone emanating from somewhere below. Like a musical note, she thought.

She stood there for a moment; head cocked to one side to pick-up the location of the sound. The harder she listened, the more difficult the sound was to hear, so she shrugged it off and attempted to push open the bedroom door fully, but it barely moved. She leaned into the door with her shoulder for more leverage and managed to open it a few more inches, enough to easily walk through. The hallway light illuminated the far wall of the bedroom.

Hesitantly, she peered around the door and gasped. One of the bedside tables had been knocked over on its side and the lamp thrown across the room. The shade was bent and shards of glass from the light bulb were scattered nearby. A chair had fallen over in front of the door which explained why it was so difficult to move. It wasn't like Max to destroy furniture, she thought. She walked over to the bedroom window to see if someone had broken into the house but it was closed and locked. The panes didn't even have a crack.

"How odd." The atmosphere in the room was electric and she felt uneasy. She quickly put the furniture back in place and bent the lampshade to its original position so it would stand on the bedside table. I'll have to come back upstairs to sweep up the glass, she thought. The front door slammed shut, startling her. Abby and Max entered the hallway downstairs.

"Mom?" called Abby.

"Upstairs honey!" Elizabeth quickly walked out of the room and down the stairs.

"Is everything alright, Mom? You look kinda pale."

"I'm fine, hon. I think Max might have knocked over a lamp upstairs. I'll clean-up while you finish with him. Underneath her calm exterior, her heart beat rapidly.

"Okay."

Elizabeth smiled reassuringly as Abby turned and skipped happily down the front hall to the kitchen. She knew her daughter was relieved to have her there.

After she cleaned up the bedroom, Elizabeth checked the other rooms upstairs but everything seemed to be in order so she focused her efforts on the study and living room on the first floor. Nothing seemed out of place in the living room so she walked down the front hall to the study for a quick look. She pressed the wall switch and quickly glanced into the room. Everything was in place, but the same strange energy that filled the bedroom had pervaded the study as well. Her hair stood on end, as much from what felt like static electricity as an impending feeling of dread. It was disconcerting because she had no reason to feel this way, she thought, confused.

A silver picture frame perched on one of the bookshelves caught her eye. Curiosity overtook fear as she crossed the room to look at the photo. Anthony and Diane smiled happily in the foreground while a beautiful view of The Golden Gate Bridge, the bay, and the city of San Francisco filled the background. Elizabeth smiled sadly as the couple stared back her, happily unaware of what the future had in store. She gently placed the picture frame back on the shelf. Another picture of Anthony proudly displaying the black belt he had earned years ago studying Tae Kwon Do, was hidden amongst a variety of knick-knacks.

More photos of Daniel, his grandparents, aunts, uncles and Max filled the walls. Many older photographs were placed prominently on tables representing a record of Anthony's life from a little boy to the present. "We never know how life will test us," she thought aloud.

A slight vibration underneath her feet caught her attention, and she stopped for a moment to listen. What she was listening for she did not know. An eerie silence overcame the house, punctuated only by the steady ticking of the grandfather clock which had an uneasy affect on her.

Without a doubt, there was a deep musical tone coming from the far right wall of the study. She walked slowly toward that end of the room. Her senses came to attention and her heart began to beat faster as she focused-in on the location of the sound.

The faint whooshing sound of dog food being poured into Max's metal bowl rushed into her awareness for a moment. The smell of the leather furniture and wood paneling pervaded her sense of smell. Slowly, she moved closer to the curious sound and put her ear to the wall.

"What an unusual sound," she commented to no one in particular. There was no doubt that a deep resonating bell-tone was coming from somewhere behind the wall or possibly underneath the house. The air around her seemed alive. It was an expansive sound, powerful, yet oddly elusive, she thought warily.

The closest phenomenon that came to her mind was the howl of a siren and how difficult it was to pinpoint in terms of location. The two sounds couldn't be more different, she thought, but the deep musical tone and the siren shared a common peculiarity in that they seemed to come from all directions at once.

She walked out of the study and into the hallway and listened again. There was no doubt about it, she concluded. No matter where she went in the house or outside, the tone was present, barely audible, just out of reach but present nonetheless.

"What the hell is it?" She peered into the room again, hands on her hips, as if expecting an answer.

"Who are you talking to, Mom?" Abby stood at the entrance to the study.

Startled, Elizabeth's heart jumped a beat. She turned to her inquisitive daughter as the grandfather clock struck 7:00PM. "Oh, Abby, you scared the heck out of me." She laughed nervously. "I was just thinking out loud." She gently, but firmly grabbed Abby's hand.

"Let's get out of here. This place creeps me out too. I'll be coming here with you from now on, honey." She prodded Abby down the hall, turned off the lights with one last look toward the study and closed the front door.

"Sounds good to me, Mom. What happened in there?"

SEVENTEEN

The small rectangular window of the jetliner framed the long, flat expanse that was Florida. The view of the coastline was a welcome reprieve from the monotonous sights of Anthony's daily commute to work each day. The water below was a pretty turquoise and green. From his vantage point the waves could be seen silently meeting the narrow beaches in white, churning foam.

Anthony took in a deep breath and smiled inwardly, knowing he had three days to relax and enjoy his surroundings without worrying about work, Max, or being alone in his empty house.

As he continued his descent toward West Palm Beach Airport, he noticed the tall apartment buildings that jutted up from Jupiter Island. New office towers dominated the West Palm Beach side of the Intercoastal Waterway to the south. Terra cotta tile roofs covering massive estates, blanketed the island of Palm Beach. Anthony chose to focus on one particularly large home being constructed across from the financial heart of West Palm Beach. He wondered who might be the owner, a celebrity, corporate CEO or maybe just a young family with old money, he chuckled to himself.

He had been here many times before but something about Palm Beach, especially the north part of the island, always calmed his restless spirit. He recognized the old Kennedy estate with its massive concrete breakwater and expansive back lawn leading to the main house. He wondered who lived there now.

Lost in Plain Sight

He remembered running into members of the family back in the late eighties and early nineties before the estate was finally sold. Surely, some were glad not to have the distraction of the high profile Kennedy clan in their midst. However, to Anthony it somehow seemed like a loss. How many on the island thought the Kennedy's would be there forever?

"Nothing is forever," he sighed.

A young woman sitting next to him looked-up from the book she was reading.

"Everything okay?"

"Oh yeah, everything's fine. I'm just enjoying the scenery." Anthony smiled warmly, before turning his attention back to the view below.

"That's the beauty of Florida this time of year," the woman responded. She smiled as the flight attendants announced that everyone should prepare for landing.

As the buildings loomed larger, the landing gear could be heard lowering with that strange but familiar whine. Anthony ran through all the fun things he could do after he dropped his luggage off at Gregg's house. According to JoAnne, Gregg enjoyed a very comfortable home on the north part of Palm Beach Island, including beach access rights.

She had described it as the perfect place to relax. The pool was hidden by rows of tall, thick green hedges and populated with every sort of tropical plant including his favorite, Hibiscus, bursting with gorgeous red, pink and yellow blossoms. The tropical plant seemed most at home when outside in the warm, tropical Florida air.

The plane taxied to the gate. Anthony pulled down his luggage from the overhead compartment, glad to avoid the baggage area. As he waded through the crowd and stood in the car rental line, all he could think about was grabbing a lounge chair at The Beach Club, courtesy of Gregg, and ordering an ice-cold Corona with a fresh lime wedge.

The warm, humid air enveloped him as he crossed the parking lot to the rental car.

The vacation always started with the first walk outside the airport, he thought. He admired a copse of palm trees swaying gently in the background, as if to greet him.

David Gerard

The house was a quick fifteen-minute ride from the airport. He crossed the Okeechobee or "middle bridge," and the beautiful palm trees lining Royal Palm Way came into view. They danced in the stiff sea breeze while large yachts swayed gently at their docks at the marina on the Intercoastal Waterway to the right of the bridge.

Handsome buildings in pretty pastel colors lined the right side of Royal Palm Way. He came to the light at South County Road and turned left toward the north part of the island. He drove by the gorgeous Breakers Hotel, golf courses, stores and restaurants, continuing on North County Road past perfectly manicured lawns, trimmed hedges, massive iron gates and stucco walls standing sentry over anonymous estates.

Anthony looked longingly out the window at the seagulls sailing over The Beach Club. He took the hard right turn around the back of the complex onto North Ocean Boulevard, and then a left as the road paralleled the Atlantic Ocean. He noticed that the waves were fairly large and active, crashing ashore with a steady whoosh followed by the hissing retreat of the water back into the ocean. He loved the sound of the waves crashing on the beach. He thought back to his days as a young boy at his great-grandmother's house on the shores of Rhode Island. It was as close to heaven as he had ever been in this life. He pulled over to the side of the road to take in the sight of the majestic Atlantic Ocean. In the blink of an eye, he found himself back in time ...

Anthony woke up to the delicious smell of toast and eggs filling the air along with mouth watering aromas of cinnamon, butter and freshly brewed coffee. As he rubbed his sleepy eyes and looked about the peach colored bedroom, small drawings of seashells framed with intricate gold patterns caught his attention. A cool morning breeze blew gently through the sheer white silk curtains as he listened to the steady rhythm of waves breaking softly on the beach below.

The morning sun poked its cheerful rays of light through the windowpane, playfully, as if beckoning him to get out of bed and meet the glorious summer day. He smiled inside as images of seagulls, sand dunes and tall grass glided gently through his mind.

He listened carefully and could hear his mother and father talking to Nana, downstairs, the din of conversation interrupted by an occasional burst of laughter and the sound of silverware clinking against a breakfast plate.

Half awake, he reveled in the moment of peace and security as he played with the small, gum-drop shaped cotton patterns dotting the entire bedspread. The pillow was soft and slightly cool to his cheek. The air was fresh and salty as he took a deep breath and pulled back the covers.

Standing up on the cool wooden floor, he stepped toward the window, causing the boards to creak sharply and echo throughout the room. Grasping the round cotton shade pull, he noticed the texture and pattern of the thread as he released the shade to get a look at the world outside.

He loved the view from his room in Nana's house because he could see the colorful garden below his window. Beds of red, white and yellow roses were surrounded by tall green hedges. A stone bird feeder stood elegantly at the end of a flagstone walkway, nestled in the corner of the garden nearest the patio at the rear of the house.

Beautiful white wrought-iron chairs with fancy leaf patterns were placed casually on the deep green lawn, which rolled down a small hill to a tiny crescent beach below. It was a combination of sand and small round rocks, worn smooth by the endless lapping of water on the shore.

A small wooden pier jutted-out into the bay like a pathway to the sea, while an old wooden row boat rocked gently on the incoming waves.

Looking out to the horizon, he could see the waves shimmering in the sunlight, like an endless blanket of diamonds. He delighted in the groups of colorful sailboats, bobbing up and down like little triangles dancing on the water.

The scene faded and Anthony came back to the present. The images seemed far away, yet alive; forever etched in his memory, as vivid and fresh as the day he experienced it as a vibrant six-year-old. He shook his head, closed his eyes and let out a deep breath.

"Sir, are you okay?" A policeman had pulled up next to his car.

"I'm alright officer," he lied. "Just enjoying the view."

"There's no parking or standing here. Please move on." The officer eyed Anthony suspiciously.

He put the car in gear and headed toward Gregg's house, attempting to shake-off this latest uninvited but pleasant reverie that had appeared out of nowhere. It left him groggy, as if someone had drugged him. The scene seemed as real as if it had happened yesterday. It's like someone or something turned on a TV and set it to channel *Summer 1971*, he thought bewildered.

In no time he had pulled into Gregg's driveway admiring the gardens, perfectly clipped hedges and tall palm trees that dotted the property. It must cost a small fortune to keep this place looking so perfect ... impressive. He got out of the car and was distracted by the smooth concrete, half circular driveway. It was inlaid with a large, detailed image of a compass pointing east.

"I am an avid adventurer," a voice spoke from behind ... "and Buddhist," the stranger continued with obvious pride.

Startled, Anthony turned to see a silver-haired man who looked to be in his mid-fifties. He extended his hand in greeting. "You must be Gregg."

"That I am," Gregg responded with a toothy grin. "A compass is an explorer's most precious item. As a Buddhist, I am always looking east toward the rising sun ... kind of obvious, but it makes a great driveway decoration, don't you think?"

Anthony laughed. He liked this guy already. "It makes a wonderful decoration."

"Can I help you with your bags?"

"No, thanks. I travel light." He closed the trunk lid.

"Unlike your sister," Gregg remarked with a hearty laugh.

"Absolutely. You'd have to break out the dolly for her wardrobe," Anthony joked at JoAnne's expense.

"True, but your sister is worth every piece of luggage I'd have to drag into the house," added Gregg sincerely.

"That she is," Anthony agreed.

"Hey, JoAnne told me you're hardly ever here. It's great to meet you, but I'm honestly surprised that I ran into you."

"Yes, I'm sorry about that. My trip was unexpectedly cancelled. The airport is barely fifteen minutes from here. I decided to come home and meet JoAnne's brother first hand." Gregg let out a booming laugh.

"Well, I'm glad it worked out." Anthony was happy to have the company.

Lost in Plain Sight

The two men walked through the meandering pathway that led to a black iron gate protecting the front door. Gregg pulled out an old-fashioned looking key from his pocket and placed it inside a large keyhole. The lock released with a well lubricated *clack*, and the gate swung open ever so slightly in welcome.

"It seems the house is expecting us," Anthony joked as Gregg feigned an evil laugh and pushed open the door.

They stepped into a large foyer adorned with lush tropical themed paintings. Anthony paused a moment to admire them.

"Early John Kirali ... a good investment," commented Gregg nonchalantly.

"Nice." Anthony followed him into the living room, eyebrows raised as he scanned the countless crystal, jade and rose quartz carvings that filled every side table, cocktail table, sideboard and curio cabinet.

Gregg took note of Anthony's reaction. "It's a weakness of mine. Everywhere I travel, I am compelled to buy a stone or crystal carving as a memento of each unique trip."

"It must be a nightmare to dust this place." Anthony looked around the room, shaking his head in disbelief.

"Do you think I clean this place myself?" Gregg joked as he walked into the kitchen.

"Ahh, of course you don't." Anthony laughed and changed the subject. "Lovely dining room." He ran his fingers lightly over the hand painted walls, admiring a mural depicting a fountain made from white marble in the shape of a mythical dolphin. Water sprayed from its mouth into a beautiful pool ringed with blooming hibiscus plants.

On closer look, he noticed what looked like a Greek temple reflected in the water, yet the structure wasn't painted on the mural to cause the reflection. That's odd, he mused. The temple was lit from within and a large book lay open on a pedestal with the letter "A" inscribed on the base.

Wispy looking figures of light surrounded the temple grounds while a small cluster of figures gathered around the pedestal gazing into the immense book. The painter was obviously gifted. Anthony stepped back from the wall and admired how the detail came to life from a distance, as when he observed his favorite impressionist paintings.

David Gerard

A moment of recognition suddenly overcame him. He thought he saw one of the figures glance up through the painting and smile. Startled, he checked the living room to see if Gregg was watching, but he was out of sight. Entranced by the figure, he continued to stare deeply into the painting until all else around him seemed blocked out. He began to feel light-headed but continued to concentrate on the bucolic scene.

"Something seems familiar about that face," he whispered.

Gregg entered the room. "Anthony, are you alright? You look …" Gregg's voice faded as Anthony was drawn deeper and deeper into the painting.

EIGHTEEN

Anthony was transported into the painting as if drawn by a magnet. The atmosphere shimmered like tin-foil as if it were trying to fully materialize around him. As the surroundings came into focus, he found himself sitting on a grassy knoll gazing down into a beautiful pond. Disoriented, he began to focus on a cluster of large trees on a hill just beyond the pond. He studied the landscape in an attempt to locate anything recognizable.

Something seems oddly familiar about this place, he thought as a column from the temple entrance caught his eye.

He turned to face the temple and gasped in delight as he saw members of his soul group coming toward him. In the background, standing on the steps of the temple was Maxim. Standing next to him was a stunning woman emanating a beautiful blue aura.

Anthony recognized her immediately. "Heather!" he exclaimed, as if he had always known of the elusive guardian angel. He stood in place, his heart filled with joy at the impending reunion with his guide and eternal friends, now smiling in welcome.

He suddenly recognized an old friend running to greet him. "Sophia! I've missed you!" His familiar energy combined with hers in a loving and ecstatic embrace. He was home … how could he have forgotten?

"It's not your time, Tabor." Sophia spoke softly to Anthony's mind.

Lost in Plain Sight

He instantly recognized his spiritual name.

Other members of his soul group stepped forward as Maxim and Heather smiled in the background. "Gram! Deva!" One by one, timeless friends appeared before him in welcome. "Mana, I saw you in a dream the other night. Wanetta ... Durriken, you sly dog! You appeared to me as a sage in a dream recently." They all nodded silently in acknowledgement.

He noticed a tall spirit at the back of the group, and his eyes lit up like a Christmas tree. "Narain! It's been forever." Anthony was beside himself with joy as a veil of amnesia continued to lift like a fog in this mystical environment.

"Forever is but a moment here, my friend," Narain responded in a familiar, deep tone as he came forward to embrace him.

"Why am I here?" Anthony looked deeply into his friends' faces for a clue.

"Because the time to act on your destiny has arrived." The familiar voice of Maxim broke through the mists of joy surrounding the group as he came forward. "By now, you must know that there is more to reality than your current physical life."

In his super-conscious state it was easy for Anthony to grasp the implications of the reunion and his surroundings. It seemed almost silly that he had forgotten.

"What you may not know, Tabor, is that you chose to incarnate as Anthony Stoddard in twentieth century Earth time, precisely to address the challenges that began with the passing of your wife and the events that have followed. With the permission of the Elders, we are being allowed to lift a portion of the amnesia that is necessary for you and all incarnated Earth souls to learn the lessons chosen before your birth."

Anthony stood transfixed by Maxim's words amid the backdrop of the dreamlike scene that surrounded him.

"You chose a very difficult life in a very challenging Earth environment. This is commendable, and in line with the growth that you seek through the lessons you have chosen. How you respond, especially in the face of adversity, will reflect the strength of your character and the evolution of your soul."

Anthony collected his thoughts while Maxim stood patiently before him. "I understand, Maxim, but where do I begin? What is this destiny you speak of? I still can't see it clearly. Why have you brought me here?"

"Your destiny is yours and yours alone. We cannot tell you what to do, despite its importance to your fellow souls on Earth. It is for you to uncover and act upon. The reason you were summoned was to inspire you to reach deep within your being for the tests that will come. We offer the gift of knowledge and truth that transcends physical existence.

"There is despair among many of your brethren that feel divorced from their source. They feel that life has no meaning and that death is the end of existence as they know it. This has caused unnecessary suffering. It has not always been this way.

"Ancient human ancestors understood at the deepest levels of their being that they were connected to nature, that there was more to life than physical existence. They lived in harmony with the land and the other creatures that shared that land. They expressed their belief uniquely based on their culture and the physical location of their tribe. Their many gods were a reflection of the most important aspects of nature that sustained them. They knew that every rock, plant, animal, tree or lake was alive, as indeed they are. They expressed their gratitude and reverence through the many gods that represented the world around them.

"As civilizations grew and settled down from their nomadic ways, these gods became more human-like. The dogma and power of early religion began its ascension into the organized religions you know today, each with a *piece* of the truth.

"But with this *progress* came abuse and ultimately a weakening of the original power, intent and connection the religions had on earlier generations. Much of the meaning and relevance has disappeared for current generations. This has led to a disconnection from the source ... an absence of meaning in the daily lives of billions.

"This has not gone unnoticed by the Council of Elders who have allowed more of the ancient wisdom about the afterlife be communicated to the populace through thought placement, mediums and guides. This assistance has begun to help the awareness and evolution of the human species on Earth, but there is more to be done. Your destiny is tied to that intent. That is all we can say."

A sense of awe and purpose rose in Anthony, buoyed by his all-knowing state.

As if reading his mind, Maxim added, "When you return, much of what you experienced here will be temporarily blocked from your conscious mind. However, deep down, you will retain what you need to move forward. We will continue our training and assist you, but be forewarned. Danger will be present and success not assured without great wisdom and effort. Be on your way, my friend, Tabor."

Before Anthony had a moment to think or respond, the scene exploded around him like a fractured stained-glass window and he found himself back in the dining room of Gregg's house examining the mural, as if not a moment had passed.

"Anthony, can you hear me? Are you okay?" He shook Anthony's shoulder as the dining room came back into focus.

"I ... I'm okay, just a little light-headed." He steadied himself and grabbed a chair to sit. "I think I need something to eat."

"I'll see what's in the pantry. Stay right where you are and relax." Gregg dashed through a swinging door to the kitchen and out of sight.

Anthony felt terrible about imposing on Gregg and the unpredictability of the episodes over which he had no control. However, the implications of this last vision overrode any immediate concerns he had about being a good guest.

He took a moment to process what had just happened. The images of Maxim and the dream-like location were quickly fading. He did remember one thing, he was about to embark on an important mission of some kind. He had a vague feeling that the events leading up to this day were just a precursor for what was to come, and a chill of apprehension ran up his spine.

NINETEEN

As it turned out, Gregg hadn't filled the pantry with food. He gave Anthony a granola bar and suggested they head over to The Beach Club for lunch, not more than three minutes away. They grabbed their things and hopped into Gregg's Aston Martin, which Anthony eyed enviously. He looked forward to some fresh ocean air and laps in the pool.

They noticed the parking lot was half-full as Gregg drove up to the covered entrance to the clubhouse and handed the keys to the valet.

"Should be quiet today," Gregg commented as he signed the guest book.

"Perfect." Anthony followed him out a back door to a large pool area dotted with chaise lounges, colorful umbrellas and palm trees swaying in the stiff breeze coming off the beach, barely two hundred feet away. The ocean was a beautiful aquamarine. The sound of the crashing waves put Anthony at ease immediately.

"Do you want to sit under the awning near the bar?" asked Gregg.

"Absolutely." Anthony was barely seated when he noticed a flamboyant attendant prancing in their direction.

"That's Arthur," commented Gregg. He's the best waiter here. A little over-the-top but harmless. You aren't homophobic are you?" he laughed.

Lost in Plain Sight

"Ah, no. Of course not," Anthony responded with a chuckle.

"Mr. Gregg Hanson. What a pleasant surprise to see you here. Who's your gorgeous friend?" Arthur hugged his drink tray and stuck his hand out to Anthony.

"Anthony Stoddard." He smiled warmly, shaking the waiter's hand.

"Pleased to meet you, Mr. Stoddard. What's your pleasure?" He glanced over at Gregg and winked as they shared an obvious joke.

"Arthur! He just got here. Give him a break." Gregg winked back coyly.

"Oh, okay." Arthur quickly turned back to Anthony with order pad at the ready.

Anthony laughed. He liked this guy. "Martini ... dry, as many olives as you can spare ... oh and straight-up," he added jokingly.

"Touché," Arthur responded with a smile and a glance at Gregg as he lipped, *I love him*. He abruptly turned away to retrieve their drinks.

The two men looked at each other and broke out laughing. "He certainly makes a visit to the club entertaining, don't you agree?" Gregg asked through bursts of laughter.

"I guess you could say that," Anthony wiped his eyes and took a deep breath.

Gregg continued. "He makes getting a drink fun. We need more of that around here." He observed the sparsely filled pool cabanas. An elderly man and a woman with a wide brimmed straw hat sat quietly reading their books. A solitary swimmer diligently traversed a lap lane, and two primly dressed ladies shared a quiet lunch. "Decidedly humorless," he added.

"What'd you expect? Everyone's a hundred years old. They're just grateful to be alive."

Gregg burst out laughing again. "Here he comes ... be nice." He sat up in his chair.

"Hey, you never ordered your drink," noted Anthony.

Arthur overheard the comment. "Not necessary, Mr. Stoddard. He has a standard drink order unless I'm told otherwise. That would be a sea breeze, Mr. Hanson?" Arthur handed Gregg the pink drink.

"That's right, Arthur. Appropriate for the day, don't you think?" Gregg nodded to Anthony as he accepted the tall glass topped with a lime.

"As always, Mr. Hanson."

"Hey, my bad," Anthony put up both hands and apologized with a laugh, as Arthur hand-poured his Martini with a flourish.

"Is five olives enough, Mr. Stoddard?" asked Arthur in obvious jest.

"Absolutely, Arthur. Well done!" Anthony emphasized with obvious pleasure sprinkled with a bit of sarcasm.

Arthur held his gaze on Anthony for a moment. Anthony waited for an equally sarcastic response, enjoying the friendly dual of words.

"Your pleasure is my command," Arthur added with a wry smile. "I'll be on my way. Just shout if you need me." He turned to Gregg. "Later, darling." He winked and strutted to a nearby table.

After a couple of martini's and a delicious lobster salad sandwich, Gregg asked if it would be okay if he headed downtown to Worth Avenue for a meeting regarding some artwork while Anthony relaxed at the pool. Anthony was more than happy to have some time to himself on one of the nearby lounge chairs.

"I'll be back in a couple of hours ... enjoy." Gregg waved and headed for the lobby while Anthony found a secluded spot under an umbrella to take a nap.

He closed his eyes and listened to the cacophony of seagulls, crashing waves, the clinking of silverware on plates and a nearby flag whipping in the wind. Within moments he was asleep and found himself standing on the beach where he had first met Maxim and Jaster. The sound of the flag flying was still fresh in his mind but now it was coming from another larger American flag atop a tall pole at the far end of the beach, adjacent to a club house. He breathed in the fresh salt-air and enjoyed the moment, knowing Maxim couldn't be far away.

He had become accustomed to the lucid dreams and out-of-body travel. He looked forward to his meetings with Maxim, although he was nervous about what lay ahead.

Lost in Plain Sight

Within moments, Maxim appeared from the rock outcropping where they had first met. Always smiling, he approached Anthony, his fish pendant reflecting brilliantly in the sunlight.

"Hello, Anthony ... or should I call you Tabor?" Maxim smiled.

"Anthony is who I am now. I'd like to keep it until the time is right."

"A wise decision. You have already grown from the scared and confused man I first met to a calmer, more thoughtful individual. It is a good time to take our training to the next level."

"I don't—"

"You are ready, Anthony," Maxim said calmly but firmly.

"What is it you wish to show me?"

"Before we can begin our exercises, you need to learn about the many realms beyond the Earth plane that you will be visiting. You need to be familiar with the unique geography of each, including important landmarks to help you on your journey. There are entities, native to each realm that you will encounter, some with benign intentions, others who are malicious in nature. You will be versed in the laws and the languages of these realities so that you may be protected in your quest for knowledge."

"Maxim, why have I been chosen for this? Certainly, there are countless other souls on Earth that have more talent, courage and knowledge than I have. What if I fail?" Anthony felt a deep-seated fear rise within him.

"We all feel afraid at many points in our lives and sometimes unworthy of the tasks that are laid before us," Maxim gently responded. "We will never grow as individuals or souls if we don't take a chance and step into the unknown."

Anthony knew it was fruitless to argue and had begun to tire of his constant resistance to change, however bizarre that change might be. He wanted to get on with it.

"Where do we start?"

Maxim smiled. "With your dreams."

TWENTY

Anthony and Maxim stood on the beach for what seemed like an eternity compressed into a moment in time, while Maxim projected classic dreams onto a transparent screen suspended above them. Long-forgotten dream sequences, locations, and characters came to life before him as his memories rose to the front of his consciousness. What had seemed like unrelated, nonsensical images became suddenly clear.

He was allowed to process the meaning of each dream as it related to various stages in his life from an infant to the present moment. The vastness of the information and the clarity of his understanding made him euphoric. What had seemed like dead-ends in his life were exposed as necessary and important trials for his growth. Each seemingly coincidental encounter and event miraculously followed a general blueprint that was laid out prior to his current life, just as it had been explained to him.

Then, Maxim faded from view. Anthony was surrounded by an endless expanse of space filled with millions of stars suspended directly overhead like spotlights on a stage. He maintained enough self-awareness to objectively take-in his surroundings, although he wasn't sure how he was doing this or if some unseen force was supporting him.

Unlike his normal dreaming state, he was lucid and able to observe and think independently of what was going on around him. He heard the familiar, deep tone but couldn't pinpoint the source. It seemed to permeate every corner of the vast environment that surrounded him, including his spirit body. In fact, on some level he knew it was sustaining him, as if it *was* the source of his very being.

He was able to control his movements based on mental desire and experimented until he became comfortable with the process.

In the distance, a faint hum could be heard over the deep tone that dominated his senses. Through desire, he began to move in the direction of the hum. He felt the sensation of incredible speed and of crossing a great distance in a matter of an instant.

Just as suddenly, he appeared in what looked like a town-square surrounded with trees, benches and a beautiful fountain of light in the shape of a large orb. It reflected vibrant colors into what seemed like infinity. The sound of wind-chimes played softly in the background, creating the most peaceful environment he had ever experienced.

He discerned some movement at the far end of the park as a spirit, not unlike himself, appeared, radiating an aura of golden-yellow light. A second spirit came into view just behind the first, emitting hues of light blue. That must be his guide, Anthony thought, recognizing the color blue as an indication of a more advanced soul.

He recalled what Maxim had taught him about the spectrum of energy colors displayed by young, mid-level and highly developed souls. Young souls started out as pure white. If they learned and evolved from each lifetime, their auras shifted subtly, adding reds, yellows, golds, greens, light blues, deep blues, light violet and finally the deep violet and purple hues of the ascended masters.

The spirit he was watching seemed to be an early mid-level soul because the energy color was radiating a yellow-gold. The soul's guide exuded a beautiful light-blue hue tinged with gold, denoting a much more advanced spirit. He had taken the shape of an American-Indian Shaman replete with hair beads, face markings and a gold medallion around his neck, similar to the one that Maxim wore. Rather than the sign of a fish, the medallion had the imprint of a torch with some sort of symbolic etching around its perimeter. It reminded Anthony of an Olympic medal.

He felt a deep sense of exhaustion combined with relief coming from the newly arrived soul. How he knew this he couldn't tell. He realized he was witnessing an after-death orientation period which was a privilege. It must have been arranged, he rationalized. There was no way he would be allowed to be here otherwise.

Anthony observed the spirits as they made their way to the center of the park. The newly arrived soul was drawn into the middle of a large, clear round sphere. An intense beam of light enveloped the soul from above as the sphere filled with what looked like red steam. The light showers permeated the very essence of the soul, healing a lifetime of damaging emotions and physical hardship. He watched in awe as the transformation process began. Dark areas of the soul's aura were brought back into alignment and made whole again.

When the process was completed, Anthony was able see the soul's spirit body more clearly. It had taken the shape of the person it had been in the life it had just left, a tall, attractive woman with silvery-blond hair and deep-blue eyes.

The spirit guide spoke. "You are whole again, Kenda." He gave her a warm and loving smile. She returned the smile, appearing euphoric and totally at peace as she left the sphere and moved on with her guide to a quiet area of the park. The guide then moved behind her and to the left as a semi-circle of spirits appeared before them.

Anthony stood transfixed as he witnessed the emotional scene. He recognized it immediately as a *homecoming*. Suddenly, a cry of joy echoed throughout the park as a spirit stepped forward from the semi-circle toward the newly arrived soul.

"Grandpa!" The souls embraced in a joyous reunion. The spirit of her grandfather had assumed the body he had in life for Kenda, although Anthony knew that they would have recognized each other's energy regardless of the spirit body chosen.

Even communication was telepathic in this timeless world, he thought, realizing that someone had blocked the conversation between Kenda and the soul of her grandfather to protect their privacy.

He watched the emotional scene continue, as beloved family members and close friends who had predeceased her stepped

Lost in Plain Sight

forward to welcome her home. Love and acceptance radiated outward from the soul group. He felt changed by the experience.

When the reunion was complete, the spirits moved away and disappeared as the shaman spirit guide escorted Kenda to a quiet chamber for her orientation. Anthony sensed that he wasn't supposed to follow. The orientation was a very personal experience between guide and the soul under care, a place to review the life just lived, the good and the bad before the soul appeared before the Council of Elders for a life review.

He felt a gentle tugging and began to move away from the park. He felt privileged to have witnessed this soul's return and thanked Maxim, wherever he happened to be.

"Anthony, wake-up!" Gregg pushed frantically on his shoulder.

Anthony's eyes opened slowly and blinked.

"What happened? You scared me to death." Gregg sounded panicked.

"Feeling ... sleepy." Anthony sat up slowly, running his hands through his hair as he got his bearings. "Wow, I must have really been out of it," he mumbled.

"No kidding. I've been trying to wake you for the last two minutes. I was on the verge of calling 911. Are you sure you're okay?" Gregg took a deep breath.

"Yeah, I'm fine, thanks." Images of this most recent out-of-body-experience were still flashing into his mind and competing with his immediate surroundings, giving him the sensation of being drunk. "I thought you were downtown for a meeting?"

"I was ... just got back."

TWENTY-ONE

Professor Ross had been feeling uneasy all week. He wasn't sure why, only that something didn't feel right. Ever since the meeting with Anthony Stoddard all sorts of questions had been crossing his mind uninvited, and he was having second thoughts about taking on the case. He stared blankly at the ceiling of his office.

He had been in the business of the paranormal for some years now and had learned to follow his instincts. He didn't believe in coincidence and knew that to ignore his intuition was a recipe for unpleasantness. However, he had the feeling he was stepping into something where extraction might be difficult, if not impossible.

He tried to focus on a pile of student essays on his desk as a nagging question regarding quantum mechanics kept interrupting his thought processes. Namely, if the act of observing subatomic particles can affect how they behave, can our mind have an effect on our reality? He didn't know where this thought puzzle had come from, only that it must be addressed in some form.

But why? he thought. He rubbed his eyes and sighed as he followed his thought process. He knew that when a single quantum particle is observed, it appears as a particle but when it is unobserved, it appears as a wave. There's no doubt that the particle is in a state of potential when we aren't observing it, he thought. This would mean all that is needed is an act of observation to manifest the particle into existence.

Lost in Plain Sight

"Okay, what of the mind?" he stated out loud to himself. Mr. Stoddard had told him that we can create our own realities through thoughts, beliefs and ideas among other things. He threw some papers down on his desk. "What does this have to do with human psychology and near death experiences?" he bemoaned to no one in particular.

Then it suddenly came to him as if whispered in his ear. *Physical reality is an extension of the non-physical.* He looked around his office suspiciously, as if someone had popped out from behind his desk to give him the answer to a quiz.

"Locality ... non-locality," he muttered to himself as he rummaged through his bookcase searching for old books on classical physics and quantum mechanics.

"Ah, here it is." He turned the yellowed pages impatiently. "Let's see, in local reality ... the physical universe," he muttered, "information cannot travel faster than light. Yes, Mr. Einstein's theory of relativity ... all signals are restricted to the speed of light. Okay. In a nonlocal reality, objects; particles, etc; can influence each other in an instant, no matter the distance." He looked up from the book. "The brain is physical, the mind, however, is not. And there are layers." He drew a diagram of the outermost portion of human consciousness, the ego, then inside that he drew a circle representing the subconscious followed by a third circle representing the area he focused on during hypnotic regression ... the super-conscious. He sat back in his chair to connect the dots in his mind.

The super-conscious, he pondered. The most subtle part of the human psyche; the timeless connection with the non-physical. It makes sense ... all those cases of NDEs where brain wave functions are completely inert and the patient is clinically dead, yet consciousness survives. Yes. It seems so simple, yet so grand, he thought.

He considered the connection between mind, body and consciousness. It had been proven many times over by subsequent interviews with the people who had experienced these life-altering events. Accurate descriptions of procedures, medical equipment and conversations in the operating room from untrained patients, observing as they floated above the ceiling out-of-body, had been documented in numerous books and case studies including his own. He knew these experiences were as close to empirical scientific evidence as was possible.

As far as he was concerned, consciousness could exist outside the body while living *and* after death. "So communication with the deceased or those traveling out-of-body while alive must also be possible." He concluded his thought problem with some surprise.

Reality creation and communication from the non-physical to the physical in a seamless connection? He wondered. "Maybe Mr. Stoddard is on to something!"

He drew a deep breath and pushed his chair back to raise his feet onto the desk. He would perform two experiments to test telepathic communication from the physical to the spiritual realms, one through meditation and the other through his dreams. He would give himself a pre-dream suggestion and keep a note pad handy near his couch and bed. Yes, that's what I'll do tonight, he thought.

When he was ready for bed, Ross placed his glasses on the bedside table along with a fresh notepad and pen. He got comfortable and took some deep breaths, closing his eyes so he could focus on the rhythmic sound of his breathing. Once he was totally relaxed, he gave himself some suggestions, primarily that he would attempt to contact Anthony with his mind and see if he received any telepathic communication in return. In the event he fell asleep, he planted suggestions in his mind to stay as alert as possible so he could make notes of his surroundings.

He would do his best to be proactive rather than passive which demanded a high level of technique and training that only a relative few possessed. His training in hypnotherapy made the experiment worthy. However, conducting hypnotherapy on his patients was very different from self-administered techniques and success was far from assured, he warned himself. Taking this into consideration, it was well worth the effort. He was a scientist and true science demanded experimentation.

He realized it might take multiple efforts to achieve successful communication and record tangible experiences that could be corroborated by Anthony at their next meeting. He ran through all the steps he needed to take one last time as he arranged his pillows.

Lost in Plain Sight

Since Anthony had no idea that he was conducting these thought experiments, careful questioning would uncover any connections. He would know at once if the communication was valid. Not a controlled experiment, he concluded, but enough proof for his purposes at the moment.

Maybe I'll get lucky, he thought with a laugh as he prepared to go into a deep, meditative state.

TWENTY-TWO

The Lower Realm of Gore was a vast world existing in a sickening and endless twilight of misery. A black specter stood like a statue amongst craggy peaks and plateaus of stone, staring into the Lake of Sorrows and pondering her next move. The waters were opaque and knew no depth. The dead who had been cursed, lost their way or had committed unspeakable deeds while in human form, wandered the desolate land screaming for those few they had loved in life, but it was too late.

Their moans of pain echoed off the cold and impenetrable mountaintops to no avail. For those inconsolable souls seeking an alternative to wandering alone for eternity, Maloda offered the limitless depths of the Lake of Sorrows where they could float just below the surface; cold and alone, neither dead nor alive amongst the damned; in a soup of decaying flesh and hopelessness. A generous alternative, she thought, laughing coldly.

She had learned that threats would not keep the human known as Anthony from his incessant quest for truth and knowledge. His destiny was strong. "But not written in stone," she spat. "All is but a probability until it becomes reality." She scowled. "And I will do what it takes to see that his destiny dies in a painful heap of anguish!"

Then an idea came to her and she curled her claw-like fingers into a fist and smiled as her eyes narrowed into black slits. Her breathing became louder the more she became excited, nostrils flaring in a sickly rhythmic wheeze.

"Yes," she whispered to herself as she stared into the foul depths of the lake. "How could I have overlooked it? So easy ... like leading a child astray with the promise of candy," she laughed out loud to the damned below her.

She would take the form of his late wife and intercept him in the Astral Plane. Entice him, she thought with venomous intent. She would play on his grief and love for her. "Tempt him!" she screeched and then her voice lowered as if trying to keep a secret from unseen eavesdroppers. "A reunion with his love ... oh how quaint. Lure him away into the dark realms where he will be sealed in the Mountain of Dark Crystal until the time we annihilate his soul!" She was hardly able to contain her delight.

"Eliminate his very consciousness from the universe! It will be a better place for the lack of it," she snorted in disgust. "Nefar will be pleased." She glided off into the mist to tell him of her plan.

TWENTY-THREE

By now, Maxim's training had made Anthony quite adept at leaving his body, whether through meditation or in his dreams. When he "woke-up" floating on the ceiling again it was such a common occurrence that he used it as his cue to move-on. However, he never missed an opportunity to take a quick look at himself sleeping in the bed.

His body was face-up, mouth open wide, snoring loudly. That's a picture worth a thousand words, he laughed to himself as he turned his attention upward.

Slowly, a black hole formed in the ceiling. This was his gateway to the Astral Plane. He would travel through the now familiar geography to meet Maxim at the Temple Portal at the edge of space, just above the Earth.

He always marveled at how such a large structure could be floating in space and not be seen by telescopes on Earth or crashed into by orbiting satellites. He had to keep reminding himself that the Astral Plane, and everything occupying it, was not physical but a dimension sitting parallel to physical reality.

As he passed through misty cloud-like formations, he relished the feeling of freedom and lightness of his spirit body. A silver cord protruded from the back of his head which was connected to his physical body back on Earth. It seemed to thin out to the size of a thread the farther away he traveled. This unnerved him a bit because he knew if it was somehow severed, he wouldn't be coming back.

So much of what surrounded him in this place was a mystery. Maxim had told him to exercise mental discipline in these realms so as not to manifest something negative. If by mistake or lack of concentration he did create a negative thought-form, he was instructed to remember that it was a creation of his own mind and not to give it power by being afraid ... just move on.

He journeyed through a familiar pathway running between a series of rocky hills lined with wild flowers and noticed some movement in a distant valley. It was a fleeting shadow, moving quickly amongst tall grass and rock cliffs. He stopped to see what it was but nothing appeared. His senses were perceptive beyond anything he had experienced in his physical body. All ailments had disappeared, to be replaced by perfect eyesight and hearing. His spirit body had the ability to fly anywhere it wanted ... at a high rate of speed. As he considered investigating the source of the shadow, he found himself instantly transported to the valley below.

He was about to explore an area partially hidden by the cliffs when a familiar bluish light appeared from above. He peered into its brilliance, transfixed. A rush of recognition overwhelmed him.

"Diane!" He immediately rose to meet her. "I've missed you so much." He lost himself in the long awaited embrace.

She returned the gesture, but something felt odd and cold about her energy. A small voice inside him nudged his consciousness to heed the warning, but the joy of the moment pushed it aside. They were together again.

"I've missed you so," she whispered softly. "Come with me. There is a beautiful meadow at the base of a mountain of crystal where I rest my spirit. We can talk and be together for a while."

The scent of Diane's perfume permeated his senses, overwhelming his ability to think clearly. Happy memories of his life with her burst into his mind, and the scent triggered feelings of nostalgia, momentarily erasing any concerns about their encounter.

She took his hand in hers. They flew through the mountains and over fantastic cities of crystal radiating colors more brilliant than any he had seen on Earth. An enormous double spire of crystal rose from the center of a city well below them. They must be two thousand feet tall, he thought, amazed at the sight. As they flew between the massive structures, he felt a burning sensation on his face from the bright crimson red energy pulsing from the tips of the spires.

Despite the exhilaration of being with Diane again, he was lucid enough to question why the color energy would burn him. Maxim had taught him about the healing properties of light. Something seemed off about this place, he thought warily. The beauty of the landscape was at odds with the heavy feeling now coursing through his spirit body.

He looked over at Diane. She glanced back with a smile before looking ahead to their destination again. A gargantuan mountain suddenly came into view, distracting him for a moment. Then he set his eyes upon her again, this time with a sense of doubt slowly creeping over him. Something about her eyes wasn't right, he thought with alarm. Diane had green eyes but the eyes that just looked back at him seemed darker, almost black.

As if reading his mind, the grip on his hand grew stronger. Anthony looked down to see a dark, claw-like appendage slowly tightening its grasp. He quickly looked-up and recoiled. The face of the apparition he had seen in his car glared back at him with an evil smile as the dark mountain loomed ever closer.

"You are in my house now, Tabor."

He tried to wrest his hand away from the foul claw, but it was impossible. A powerful force had taken over, as if invisible hand cuffs had chained him to the demon. He began to panic but a strange amnesia began to overtake his consciousness and he didn't know who to call for help.

From the depths of the mountain, tiny black figures flew up to meet them. As they came closer, Anthony could see that they resembled the hideous gargoyles that adorned ancient churches. Their grotesque faces and large orb-like eyes focused on him intently, like prey. Their grey and black wings flapped rapidly like bats in a cave as they moved in on him, claws outstretched. He screamed and lost consciousness.

#

Lost in Plain Sight

Professor Ross sat straight-up in his bed, the terrible scream still ringing in his ears. His heart pounded like a sledgehammer against his chest, and his breathing was labored. He looked apprehensively around the bedroom. The moon was almost full, and the walls were blanketed in a silver glow from the light penetrating the sheer window curtains. The lamp on his dresser projected an eerie shadow on the wall opposite the bed. It stood like a silent specter, uninvited and unmoving. Half-asleep, he stared at it for a moment with trepidation as it loomed before him in the semi-darkness.

"Oh, this is silly, Matthew," he scolded himself. "You're letting this whole situation with Stoddard make the imagination run wild. It was just a bad dream. Enough!"

Exhausted, he sat on the edge of his bed and turned on the lamp to get his thoughts in order. He grabbed his notebook and pen off the bedside table and forced himself back into analytical mode. With some effort and a few deep breaths, he managed to recall the last images in his mind prior to waking-up, including any corresponding feelings. He needed to record them as quickly as possible before they faded from his consciousness.

"There was something large ... dark. It felt like a barrier, blocking ... something stopping me from going where I wanted," he whispered. He focused on the image, trying to relax and not force the recollections to the surface of his mind. That would end in failure anyway, he reminded himself. He wanted to retain the feelings that were still fresh in his mind.

"It was very negative ... I sensed feelings of hate." He wrote down a few notes, more to do with feelings than images, but better than nothing.

He tried to tap into more detail but came up blank, laying his notepad on the bedside table with a sigh. He knew this wasn't going to be easy. He turned off the light, determined to try again.

TWENTY-FOUR

Elizabeth tossed in her bed during a fitful night of sleep. Something kept waking her for no reason. She would lay there, half awake, half asleep surrounded with feelings of unease, only to fall back asleep again and wake-up an hour later. After a few minutes, she nodded off again.

The man in the purple robe came to her again. They stood outside a beautiful marble structure that looked like a Greek temple. It stood on a small hill overlooking a clear pool lined with lush green plants and intense blooms of red and white. Entranced by the scene, she listened to the familiar, soft-spoken entity.

"Elizabeth, I am your guide, Kamalli. *We* know you as Candra, named after the ancient moon that shines upon the Earth, giving it light and the rhythm of the tides. Your gentle soul reflects the waves that break softly upon the beaches."

Elizabeth's awareness suddenly expanded, and she knew Kamalli spoke the truth. The guide nodded as recognition spread over her face. She rushed to greet him as one would embrace a long-lost friend. Kamalli's energy surrounded hers with gentle warmth.

"Kamalli, why am I here now? Have I died?"

Kamalli laughed. "No, you are quite alive, my dear. Have you forgotten Tabor's destiny with which he challenged himself so selflessly?"

Elizabeth thought for a moment, and the memories returned as if not a moment had passed since their decision. Yes, she and Tabor *had* agreed to be born near each other physically, in the same historical time period. Images flooded her mind of an immense sphere where Tabor's life selection took place. He was there as well as his guide, Maxim. There were others too, including Kamalli.

More images came to her of meetings in places that looked like school rooms. The conversations centered on how to help each other while on Earth so they could learn the lessons needed to continue their soul development. She reflected for a moment on a distant, yet familiar scene of the two of them conversing affectionately.

"Tabor is Anthony!" she realized with surprise. "We have always been connected. Kamalli, why didn't you tell me," she laughed.

"For what purpose, my dear," he smiled kindly. "You've always known."

"You are wise, as always, dear Kamalli."

He motioned to the temple structure. "Let us view the life records."

They entered the immense hall and paused for a moment to view the endless rows of scrolls tucked neatly into white walls, as far as the eye could see. Long white tables and benches sat empty, save for the occasional soul or guide reviewing the living records that would give them insight for their own development.

It was at once familiar to Elizabeth and awe inspiring at the same time. How could she have forgotten this beautiful place with all its magnificent structures like the Hall of Records?

Kamalli motioned for her to begin. One scroll in particular glowed brighter than the rest. She retrieved the document from its home and laid it on a table before him. As his hand waved over the scroll, it rose up and unfurled, suspended magically between them.

Everyone and everything is magic in the place, she thought with delight.

"You see the world with the wonder of a child," Kamalli responded, reading her thoughts. "It's one of the traits I've always loved about you."

"Oh, Kamalli. You've always made me feel special." Elizabeth gave him a kiss on the cheek and turned her attention back to the scroll. By now, it had transformed into a large, television-like screen.

Images of Anthony's life selection process began to appear before them. She noticed that he was looking very apprehensive about his life choice and could sense his doubt about whether or not he would succeed. They had both been through the process countless times before, however this life was to be particularly challenging and pivotal.

She watched as Anthony's guide, Maxim, reviewed the signposts he would encounter along the way that would trigger his subconscious mind to take action or get back on track if he made poor decisions. She recalled that the life selection process was designed to help the incarnated soul move toward alignment with the chosen blueprint and destiny for the next life.

She also remembered his concerns at the time. So much was riding on his success. Twentieth and twenty-first-century Earth was a difficult time to be alive, so many pressures, and so much hopelessness. He had chosen America, specifically New York City and surrounding areas to be his home ... because there was more stability and freedom than other parts of the world.

She re-witnessed her conversations with Anthony as if not a moment had passed. They were lively discussions about the various probabilities that would be open to him. Some would lead him astray or cause him pain; others would keep him on the path of his destiny.

It was at that time he had chosen Arella, another soul in their close-knit group of mid-level souls, as the most probable choice of his first wife, Diane. As a group, they had all advanced dramatically since their days as new souls thousands of Earth years earlier. Many soul groups had been split up by the time they had reached the middle stages of development, but their cluster group had grown together and learned their lessons very much in tandem.

Arella was close to Tabor. They had shared many lives and roles as husband, wife, brother, sister and close friend, but Candra shared the deepest bond of all. As Elizabeth, she had been completely unaware of her connection with Anthony. They were fond of each other but only as friends, she thought, puzzled.

"Kamalli, how could we be so close and yet unaware of our bond in this life?"

Lost in Plain Sight

"The pathway for Tabor's current life *and yours*, Candra, were not meant to intersect at the deepest levels until the time was right. You already know this to be true."

As Kamalli spoke, it was as if a curtain had lifted and truths, long buried within her, became apparent. "Why do we forget?" she asked.

"Amnesia is applied so that the lessons set out to be learned for the life to be lived can best be realized. If you carried the knowledge of your soul with you consciously while in human form, you would never experience the joys and sorrows of life. Only through direct experience can our souls learn, grow and develop," Kamalli explained patiently.

"It's hard, Kamalli. Few believe in life after death. They think that death is the end of their existence, of their very consciousness. It is the thing they fear the most. It seems so cruel to hold back the truth."

"But there are signs all around you on Earth," Kamalli responded. "They speak to those who would listen that all is not lost at death. It is the doorway to your true home, as you have learned ... again," he added with a knowing smile.

"What signs are these?" asked Candra.

"The seasons reflect the stages of life. Spring, birth; summer, youth; autumn, adulthood; winter, old age and death. And what occurs after winter every year, my dear?"

"Spring, of course." She felt silly for asking.

"Deep down, every soul and every human being understands these truths. As civilizations have progressed, humans have become more divorced from nature. They have forgotten the wisdom bestowed upon them many lifetimes ago."

"Yes, but there is such despair because people feel as if life has no meaning. They become addicted to power, money, relationships, drugs and sex. They don't see the justice of the universe working in their favor. They are surrounded by violence, indifference and ignorance. Then they are told to have faith in something they can't touch, see, hear, taste or smell."

"You state only one side of the equation, Candra. There is also love, forgiveness; beauty, happiness; friendship and tolerance in the world. You just have to look for it."

"But not enough of it, Kamalli."

"Remember, everyone has free will. You create your own reality. It will faithfully reflect your beliefs and intentions. We all experience what we put out into the world. Love expands, hate contracts and ultimately destroys itself. That is a universal truth whether one chooses to believe it or not."

"It is true, but not enough people understand this. We need these truths to resonate inside of every human being. If people remembered, it could change the world, give them hope and a reason to live life differently ... to the fullest," she pleaded.

"The Council of Elders understands, Candra. Earth has become conflicted ... so conflicted, that humans damage the very planet that sustains them. They have instructed countless guides to help bring humankind back into balance."

"Does this connect with Tabor's destiny as Anthony?"

"Precisely! He chose, as part of his development, to reincarnate as Anthony and learn the difficult lessons needed to resonate with his soul. Why? To impart the truths of which we speak with authenticity and credibility to those on Earth that would listen. Does this sound familiar, dear Candra?"

"He follows in the tradition of the modern-day prophet," she responded.

"Arella knew this too," Kamalli continued. That is why she chose to be his wife and then move on when she could teach him no more. She fulfilled *her* destiny. It was her time, and in the depths of his soul, Tabor knew it was time for the difficult lessons that lay ahead to begin. The door had been opened and he willingly straddled two worlds, putting his life in jeopardy to seek the truth."

"What do you mean?" Elizabeth was alarmed.

"Forces inhabiting other dimensions, denser than what you and your group know, threaten him. These forces are sustained by hatred and conflict and have poisoned men and women's souls for eons. They are tricksters and shape shifters. The marks of their influence are evident wherever there is discord. They feed off misery and become stronger. They abhor the absence of negativity. Where love, tolerance and happiness are strong, they become weak ... but always seek a way to destroy that positive energy to maintain their power."

Lost in Plain Sight

Elizabeth had so many questions that she thought she would explode. "How can one soul like Tabor ... one person like Anthony change what has taken centuries to create?"

"By touching the truths that lie within every human being, but have been forgotten."

"How will they know?"

"If they believe what he teaches, they will see it become their reality. Not with their eyes but with their heart. It will manifest in every part of their lives. Great change can begin with one positive idea and quickly grow into a formidable shift in human consciousness. Remember, love expands. Light overcomes darkness."

Elizabeth understood and had nothing more to say.

Kamalli proceeded to direct her attention back to the screen.

As they reviewed the last moments of Tabor's life selection process, one probability stood out among the rest. It was a brief but peaceful moment, a loving embrace between two soul mates.

Elizabeth awoke from one of the most vivid dreams of her life. A feeling of happiness tinged with an undercurrent of concern remained with her for a moment, suspended in time and then faded as the sun's rays filled her bedroom with morning light.

TWENTY-FIVE

"Is anyone there? Hello ... please, is anyone there?" A voice whispered in the darkness.

The sound brought Anthony back from unconsciousness. Disoriented, he peered into the dark and unfamiliar space that surrounded him. He touched something hard and cold with his foot and pulled back instinctively.

Where was he? Was he dreaming? He looked upward. He could see nothing with the exception of a faint light but couldn't pinpoint its source. The walls of this strange place were as smooth as glass and shimmered slightly in the dim light.

He placed his luminescent hand on the nearest wall, which was cold to the touch. A shiver of panic coursed through him as he realized that he was still in his spirit body.

How much time had passed?! Was he dead ... separated from his physical body forever? He glanced at the wall behind him. It reflected the image of a silver cord extending from the back of his head. The cord was illuminated and intact. He breathed a sigh of relief. If the cord was attached to the spirit body, he couldn't be dead because it was still connected to his physical body.

As he became more focused, he began to examine the room or whatever it was. His thoughts came with much effort. How had he gotten here? He ran his hand over the hard, smooth surface of the walls and felt a faint but powerful vibration. He tried to recall where he had been before appearing in this dark chamber, but his mind seemed devoid of any recollection.

"Hello, is there someone there? If you can hear me, please speak to me!" a faint, disembodied voice pleaded.

Anthony pulled his hand away from the wall and stopped to listen but was surrounded by silence. I'm hearing things, he told himself. Fear and doubt began to seep into his mind. He placed his hand on the wall again and forced himself to calm down and think clearly.

"Please ... if you're there, give me a sign."

There it was again! Every time he touched the wall, he felt the vibration. This time, he placed both his hands on the wall and with great concentration sent a message telepathically to the voice. He couldn't tell which direction the sound came from, but maybe it would hear him if he concentrated hard enough.

"I hear you." He waited for a response which came almost immediately.

"Thank God! I thought someone was there," it answered. Then silence.

"Who are you? Where are you?" Anthony responded.

"I'm Tom. I've been imprisoned here for what seems like a lifetime." The voice sounded calmer.

Anthony could barely hear the stranger and pressed his hands harder against the wall, hoping that it might help the connection. "Where are you from?"

The voice seemed to sense Anthony's frustration. "Look up to the light. A small crystal is embedded in the wall. It glows brighter than the rest. Put your hand over it and our communication will be stronger. There is a telepathic pathway between us."

Anthony reached up to the light and found a narrow ledge. In it, a small crystal did indeed glow brighter than the rest. He put his hand over it and spoke with his mind.

"Is that clearer?"

"Oh yes!" Tom's voice was now as clear as if it was in the same room. "Who are you?"

"I'm Anthony."

"You're the first person I've spoken to in a long time," Tom echoed.

It was reassuring to be in contact with another human, thought Anthony. "How did you know about the crystal?"

"There was someone in your chamber before you. He knew how to use the power of crystals to communicate and taught me to do the same. Then, he tried to escape. I never heard from him again. We need to be careful. They check these chambers often." His voice became a whisper.

"Who are they?"

"The dark forces of the lower realms."

The image of Diane morphing into the demonic apparition came flooding back. The winged demons ... the massive mountain. Anthony's memory was slowly returning. I must have blacked out, he thought.

"What is this place?"

"The Mountain of Dark Crystal," answered Tom. "We've been sealed in one of the few places our souls cannot escape. It has been under the spell of Nefar for eons."

"Who's Nefar?"

"Nefar is the darkness that suffocates men's souls; the extinguisher of light. He will stop at nothing to diminish or erase love from the world. He is the embodiment of ignorance, appearing in the form of the Devil himself."

Anthony was confused. "Then who was the female entity that took the form of my deceased wife and brought me here? It purposely deceived me!"

Tom was silent.

"Did you hear me?" Anthony repeated.

"I am afraid you are in more trouble than I thought," Tom finally replied.

"Why?"

"Some fear Maloda more than Nefar and believe that one day she will rule the Lower Realm of Gore. She is his lieutenant and far more dangerous and sadistic. He knows this and uses her for only the most wanted ... those who pose the highest risk to their world. I'm afraid for you."

Fear shot through Anthony, but he stayed calm and refocused. The only way to have a chance in this environment was to stay alert and not to panic, he told himself.

"They must have a weakness, Tom. Everyone and everything has a weakness."

"If they do, I don't know what it is."

"How long have you been imprisoned here?"

"I'm not sure ... months, a year? Time is not the same here. I just graduated from high school ... class of 1976."

That's impossible, thought Anthony. How could he think he's only been imprisoned for months if he was taken thirty-four years ago? He reminded himself that solitary confinement can do strange things to a man's mind.

"What year did you say?" Anthony asked again just in case he'd heard it incorrectly.

"1976. You know ... the bicentennial. My friends took the train down to New York City to see the tall ships. I had nothing else to do so I meditated and continued my work on out-of-body travel. My friends thought I was nuts," he laughed.

Anthony laughed out loud.

Tom continued. "I wanted to see if I could replicate some of the experiences I had read about like the tunnel and the light. I thought that maybe, if I was lucky, I might make contact with my grandmother who had recently passed away."

"So you successfully entered the Astral Plane, only to be taken to this God forsaken place?"

"I guess so," Tom answered sadly. "And now it's too late. I'll never be able to go back. This must be Hell and I must be dead." Tom became silent again.

Anthony sat in his cell for what seemed like hours. What had he done? He was in serious trouble. Maxim probably had no idea where he had been taken. Panic began to take hold as the solitude gnawed at his state of mind. Then, an idea came to him. He felt for the ledge and placed his hand over the crystal.

"Tom, do you still have a silver cord extending from the back of your head?"

"Yes, why?"

"Of course!" Anthony shouted telepathically. "You're still connected to your physical body ... and your historical time!"

"Please, don't draw attention to yourself!" warned Tom.

"Sorry." Anthony stopped for a moment to listen for danger. He heard nothing and continued.

"My guide explained to me that, as humans, we each live in our own time continuum ... that time is simultaneous. In three dimensional reality, we perceive time in linear fashion, moment to moment which is an illusion. Everyone accepts it as reality without question, but the only real moment is the present moment."

"I'm sorry. I don't understand."

"Your time ... 1976 and my time ... 2010 are happening concurrently. As long as we are connected to our physical bodies, we both have the ability to go back into those time periods. Don't you see? It's not too late."

"So does that mean you are from the future and I am from the past?" Tom sounded confused.

"What it means, is that your time and mine are happening at the same time because the only real time is the present. You could say that I am from a probable future. Call them future present moments if that helps you conceptualize it."

Tom's silence gave Anthony a moment to reflect on the conversation. He needed to escape from this prison cell before that thing came back to get him. He would try and get Tom out too.

He was confident that if they escaped, they could both go back to their bodies in their respective historical times. He had learned that a full life-review spanning decades in Earth years could happen in an instant in these realms. If someone could travel back to their physical body after such an experience with only a few hours of sleep, then it must be possible for him to do the same, he concluded.

He worried about Tom, though. He had been imprisoned for months or possibly much longer in Earth time. He would get back to his body. He was sure of that. The silver cord was still attached. But in what condition after all this time? He couldn't think about that now. Anything is better than this place, he rationalized.

"Tom, has anyone ever escaped from this mountain?"

"I heard stories from Narro; the prisoner who occupied your chamber before you. Every moment was spent working on a plan of escape. He was always hopeful that a breakthrough was just around the corner ... and he did come close one day—"

"What happened?" interrupted Anthony.

Tom recalled the fateful moment he lost his fellow prisoner. "The boredom of our imprisonment was driving us both mad. Our communication was the only thing keeping us from falling into the abyss of insanity. It was a quiet moment for Narro and for me," he recalled. "We were tired from the constant conversations outlining how we would escape. The faint vibration permeating the crystal walls blended with my thoughts. I was thinking that the relentless, never ending sound might drive others mad but for me it was soothing ... a companion reminding me there were other energies around besides myself." He paused for a moment.

"Anthony, I know you've just arrived and this place hasn't affected you to the extent it has me, but I have a question. Are the constant energy vibrations wearing on you or do they soothe your state of mind?"

"Neither," Anthony answered truthfully. "It doesn't seem like negative energy but more like a higher frequency reaching out to us from somewhere outside this place. After all, it's allowing us to communicate. I don't believe that the forces that imprisoned us would allow this secret communication pathway to exist. They must not know about it," he surmised.

"Interesting. I hadn't considered that the energy could originate from outside this dense mountain. Someone, at some point must have discovered a way to create it. Narro had heard about the ancient art of using crystals to focus energy and break through the dense layers of the lower realms. He learned that the higher frequencies could not be detected by beings that existed on a lower frequency but wasn't sure if it was really true.

"He decided to take a risk. He had nothing to lose. He spent all his time trying to locate and tap into this ancient communication pathway and finally broke through to me. He told me that legends described how old souls used it to speak with their guides as they traveled in the lesser known and dangerous lower realms. These souls didn't have the need to incarnate as often as they used to. They explored other realms outside their higher dimensions to better understand how all levels operated and interacted. They also searched for lost or imprisoned souls intercepted by the forces that brought you to this dark mountain so they could be freed."

Anthony thought for a moment about the implications of what Tom was saying. "If this is true, are those souls still wandering these realms? Where are our guides? They're supposed to be protecting us." He felt a pang of abandonment and was angry that Maxim hadn't come to rescue him.

"I don't know," answered Tom. "I thought the same and then came to the conclusion that Nefar and Maloda bring certain souls here precisely because they know we can't be found, even by our guides. There is something about this mountain that has sealed our energy inside; a place where we have become invisible to those who would search for us. Somehow Narro was able to find the small pathway that allows us to speak, but I am afraid nothing escapes this evil place."

"Then what of Narro?" asked Anthony. "How did he escape?"

"After exhaustive searching of the frequencies in your chamber, using techniques of which I know nothing, he was able to uncover a portal. He told me he had found a crystal ... a perfect fractal that replicated itself infinitely—"

"Maxim told me about fractals," interrupted Anthony.

"They are powerful expressions of the infinity of the universe," explained Tom. "Within that fractal, he found a tiny wormhole. It took him many tries and stretched his ability because it was infinitely small, but when he finally understood its coordinates, he was able to locate it consistently."

"So what happened?" Anthony was excited. Maybe, this was the key to his escape.

"After what seemed like an eternity, he spoke to me one last time." There was sadness in Tom's words. "He said he had discovered how to enter the portal and return to the chamber. Slowly, he journeyed through the strange pathway making notes of the landscape along the way. He said he had stayed clear of any alien beings.

"Gradually, a route to the other side had become apparent. He knew this because the horizon became brighter and he began to feel lighter. He described it as the frequency becoming more in alignment with his own. It felt more comfortable ... more like his home realms."

Anthony agreed. "That makes perfect sense to me. I've learned about the ten dimensions and how beings naturally gravitate toward levels of their own frequency. I need to find this portal."

Lost in Plain Sight

"That's easier said than done," Tom cautioned. "He left me no clues ... and there is one more thing you need to know. After he said goodbye, I heard the energy vibrations we hear now become much more pronounced, followed by a very brief scream. In a panic, I called out to him but he never answered." Tom's voice lowered. "I haven't heard from him since."

TWENTY-SIX

Anthony heard a booming sound in the distance. At first it sounded like a distant drum, struck once ... then silence. He thought nothing of it. But then, the sound became more pronounced, as if moving toward his chamber. There was no way to see outside the cell. He was completely closed in. He quickly called out to Tom.

"Tom, what's that noise? It's getting closer."

"What noise? "I don't hear a thing."

"How can you not hear it?" implored Anthony.

"Like the beating of a drum?" Tom was clearly alarmed.

"Yes, that's it. What is it?"

"Oh God. They only send the Ipos after the most notorious prisoners. They are cruel demons, massive in size. They take the shape of a lion-headed eagle. They're coming for you."

"What can I do?" Anthony began to panic.

"There is no escape. I'm sorry, Anth—" Tom was cut-off.

"Tom ... what?"

"I hear them now. They're coming for me too."

"Tom!" His friend didn't respond. Anthony turned toward the entrance to his chamber and waited for the inevitable. The sound of gigantic footsteps reached a terrible crescendo as they raced up the corridors outside his cell. Anthony covered his ears, but it made no difference. The chamber shook violently ... and then the noise stopped.

An eerie silence fell over the chamber. Slowly, a door cut into the crystal walls began to open upwards into the ceiling. Anthony sat frozen on the floor with his back to the far wall. A scaly, grey claw with pointed black nails came into view as the door continued its slow ascent. He tried to crawl into a corner but there was no place to hide. Three demons, the size of grizzlies, stood glaring down at him with eyes like pools of black oil. A sensation of frigid air rushed into the chamber. Anthony shivered uncontrollably.

Terrified, he could do nothing but wait to be annihilated. The demons seemed to smell his fear and stood patiently, snorting like bulls on a cold winter day. Silvery snot ran from their noses, and their cold black eyes pierced Anthony as though he wasn't even there. Huge claw-like hands grasped black, long-handled axes tipped with razor-sharp daggers. They stepped into the cell and threw Anthony out into a hallway.

Not far away, he could hear Tom screaming as he was being dragged from his cell. The demons proceeded to pull Anthony down a long passageway and pushed him into a cavernous chamber supported by hundreds of stone columns the size of redwoods. A massive claw grabbed his shoulder and pushed him into the floor, holding him motionless. Moments later, he glanced-up briefly and saw Tom being thrown to the ground next to him.

Minutes passed, followed by what seemed like hours before a dark figure glided into the room. Massive claws hastily yanked their heads up so they could see the monster that stood before them ... and what Anthony saw revolted him.

He stared, transfixed, at the demonic specter. He was scared ... and angry. This was the demon that had threatened him in his car and then pretended to be his wife so it could take him to this godforsaken mountain.

"Oh, you're angry are you?" Maloda growled. The demons joined her in a sickening cacophony of hissing laughter. "Don't be so surprised. I warned you not to leave your feeble world, but you would not listen ... and here we are, finally." She seemed beside herself with glee as her boney hands rubbed together like the scraping of sandpaper.

"Whatever shall we do with you, Tabor? You've outdone yourself this time, but we've got you now ... and your pathetic friend, Rad. It is Rad, isn't it?"

"Tom managed to eke out a response. "It's Tom, not Rad," he whispered. He looked away from the taunting personification of evil.

"He doesn't even know his true name!" She shrieked in laughter as the demons laughed in unison. "You think the name you are given in one pitiful Earth life is your real name ... you fool. Rad is your real name, you insignificant human. You young souls are all the same. You think you know everything but you know nothing!" she screamed. "It doesn't matter anyway," she added quietly. "You will both be eliminated."

Anthony saw Tom struggling to get free but the demons pushed him down hard with their huge clawed feet.

"Don't worry, we'll make sure it hurts," she glowered.

A faint light reflected on the hard crystal floor in front of Anthony. He gazed into the shiny surface and saw what looked like a golden light flicker from above. Maloda and her henchman didn't seem to notice. She continued with her verbal rampage, now fading into background noise as he focused his attention on the figure descending from above. He couldn't lift his head to see it directly but the reflection was clear enough for him to make out a woman garbed in white, carrying a long shiny object. As she slowly descended, a brilliant white light tinged with gold began to fill the enormous chamber.

Maloda became silent and looked upward. A beam of intense blue-white light shot down from above and shook the room violently. The pressure on Anthony's neck released amid guttural screams of pain from his captors.

In the commotion, he broke free and ran over to Tom as the demons stumbled backward, gazing upward in raging agony. Strange bubbles of energy encircled Anthony and Tom, protecting them from the light beams bouncing off the walls and striking nearby columns, now beginning to crack.

"Let's get out of here now!" Anthony screamed. He grabbed Tom and ran for the nearest pathway out of the mountain. There seemed to be endless tunnels leading to empty chambers. By process of elimination they peered into every doorway seeking an escape. They raced through a main passageway, now spiraling downward, ever mindful of the guards, who by now had heard the commotion.

They wound their way down the massive mountain, fearful they would run into a demon at every turn. Finally, they burst-out into an enormous cavern. Anthony could see light coming through the gaping entrance to the cave about one hundred yards away. There didn't seem to be anyone around. The faint sound of explosions could be heard through the passageways behind them.

"The guards must have left their posts," whispered Tom. "Let's run for it."

Anthony surveyed the cavern for movement. "I don't know. They could be hiding. I can't believe they left the entrance unguarded. I don't trust them."

"If we don't get out now, we'll be caught again," Tom urged.

Anthony sighed. "You're right. Let's stay close to the perimeter of the cave. Once we're within ten yards of the entrance, we'll make a run for it and hide in that thick scrub brush over there." He pointed to a small hill located a few hundred feet from the cave opening.

Silently, they crept along the cavern wall, ever mindful that danger could be lurking behind every rock outcropping. The entrance to the mountain grew larger and the light became brighter as they neared their goal. Suddenly, they heard a deep scraping sound coming from another cave off to their right. They jumped and hid behind a large boulder.

The sound became louder as a gigantic, hairy appendage came into view. They backed into each other as an enormous spider lumbered into the huge chamber. It stopped, head jerking from side to side, inspecting the cavern. As it turned to face the direction where Anthony and Tom were hiding, they could see its massive fangs. The creature was so enormous that the curved fangs had to be three feet in length. Anthony was repulsed. Behind him, Tom shook with terror, doing everything he could not to scream.

The beast stood at least thirty feet tall. Eight unblinking black eyes peered into the corners of the massive cave. It was so huge they could hear it breathing in a slow, deep rhythmic pattern. Anthony froze. He couldn't take his eyes off the monstrosity.

Two huge melon-sized eyes were positioned in the middle of its head, protruding from their sockets like polished bowling balls glued to a wall of hair. Two baseball size orbs were positioned on either side which offered the spider a better side-view, exactly where Anthony and Tom were hiding.

They ducked out of view but could still see the creature just over the top of the boulder. Long, brown hairs protruded from every inch of its gigantic body. They heard strange popping sounds as multiple hairs burst-out from its body and shot through the air like spears.

The spider moved deeper into the cavern past the frightened prisoners. With each step, the massive, hairy legs moved six inches of dirt and kicked-up small rocks and debris which ricocheted off the cavern walls. As its huge abdomen loomed over them, it dropped a disgusting pile of excrement not ten feet from where they stood. A foul stench filled the cavern.

They waited until it was well past their hiding place. Then, with a quick nod to each other they ran for the cave opening. The spider turned to see them running out of the massive entrance and pursued them. For just an instant Anthony looked back. To his horror, the spider had made up half the distance in a few seconds as razor-sharp hairs flew overhead and landed around them. Both men screamed and ran faster than they ever thought possible over rock outcroppings and hills dense with bushes and scrub-brush, until they dove exhausted into a nearby ditch.

They waited for the spider to appear above them, but there was only silence. Anthony found himself gasping for breath as if he was using his physical lungs. It was an odd sensation, almost like muscle memory. He knew he didn't need to breathe in his spirit body but was reacting out of habit as he would have on Earth. Knowing this, he immediately calmed himself and helped Tom to do the same.

After what seemed like a few minutes, they slowly rose from the ditch and peered over the edge, expecting to see the monster's deathly stare but nothing was there. They looked at each other, exhausted but grateful.

"That was way too close," Tom sighed with relief. "I've got to rest."

"We've got to keep moving," urged Anthony. "Let's go ... now."

He dragged Tom through the countryside. He wanted desperately to teleport to the nearest city; the one he had flown over before the ambush. Try as he might, the best he could do with significant concentration, was teleport fifty feet or so from his current location with little directional accuracy. Tom wasn't much better. The two of them hop-scotched a half-mile before stopping, mentally exhausted from the exercise.

"We've got to keep moving. Someone will know we've escaped—and soon." Anthony glanced nervously at Tom, hoping his new friend might have a suggestion. Tom's expression told him otherwise.

The two lost souls sat there as vulnerable as newborn chicks. Strange electrical storm-clouds gathered overhead as they nervously pondered their next move. Anthony gazed at the odd formation swirling above them. "They're coming," he blurted-out suddenly. "We can't stay here."

Exhausted and frightened, they continued the only way they knew—on foot. Anthony marveled at the landscape. Intellectually, he knew he wasn't on Earth, but the world that now surrounded him felt as real as the Rocky Mountains. They were hiking on a trail with views more spectacular than the majestic Continental Divide.

The mountains in this realm were enormous. They would dwarf Mount Everest, he thought, as he gasped at a particularly high peak to his right. By his estimation, it was triple the size of Everest, reaching a staggering 90,000 feet in height. The land emanated power.

Anthony heard Tom shout, "Hold on!" He stopped to see what was wrong. His friend sniffed the air as if there was something nearby and surveyed the landscape warily.

"What is it?" Anthony focused intently in the direction Tom was looking, eyes narrowed suspiciously.

"We're being watched." Tom's eyes were locked on a point in the distance.

Anthony continued to scour the foothills looking for movement but was unable to detect a thing. Without warning, he heard a low but powerful thud as if an enormous animal had taken a step toward them.

Tom flinched. "It's them."

"Who?"

"They call them Argons. They're controlled by Maloda and roam the countryside in packs looking for anything that wanders into their territory. They're like dogs the size of horses. They hunt by surrounding and ambushing their prey. We have to leave now."

The two men quickly moved on, keeping fear at bay with conversation. Tom's eyes darted left and right seeking a place to hide.

"Can we fight them?" Anthony looked over his shoulder into the distant forest where the sound seemed to be emanating. The two men crouched behind an outcropping on the side of a hill.

"No. They are too big and strong ... highly disciplined." Tom continued searching the landscape as he spoke. "I saw an Argon demon once as I was being taken to my cell. I was standing in one of the corridors. You could tell it wanted to attack but was instructed to stay where it was. Maloda threatened to have it extract my essence and leave nothing behind but a husk." Anthony could see the fear in Tom's face.

"Those that have lived to describe them tell of an evil so pure, that the sight of an Argon will freeze a soul where it stands so it can experience being eaten alive. They feed off that fear. For amusement, they uncover every painful memory within their victims, driving unsuspecting souls to despair, after which they offer to put them out of their misery."

"How? A soul cannot be killed."

"By consuming its life force and leaving a shell. Travelers to the Astral Plane would often refer to these 'shadow souls' as lec'ita or the lost. They live in a perpetual twilight of loss and pain."

"How cruel. Can we hide from them?" Anthony's sense of adventure had long disappeared. In its place a feeling of dread coursed through him. He didn't know how to fight in this strange world, only communicate and travel through it ... and he didn't do that well either. Then, suddenly he remembered what Maxim had told him about thought forms and turned to Tom.

"What if we calmly acknowledge their presence and move on without showing fear?" he asked hopefully.

"You will just make them curious and delay the inevitable," answered Tom.

Lost in Plain Sight

Anthony began to feel a sense of anger rise within. How could Maxim fail to prepare him for something like this?

Boom ... boom, boom. A series of deep, hard thuds sounded in the distance like a herd of animals coming to a sudden halt. Both men paused, expecting something to burst out at them. The sound repeated ... this time closer, louder; more menacing, like a herd of wildebeest honing in on their position.

Anthony motioned silently to Tom and the two men scrambled over the rocky hillside and made their way toward a small cave opening approximately fifty yards away. The terrain was treacherous and full of loose rocks. Unexpected depressions threatened to send them hurling off the cliff onto one of the massive boulders dotting the landscape below, like giant motionless dinosaurs.

A thunderous crash smashed the ground just yards from where they stood. They were no more than fifteen yards from the cave. After a moment of shock, they stumbled awkwardly toward the small opening. It was just large enough for each of them to squeeze through. They dove head-first into the darkness hoping to lose whatever was pursuing them.

They sat as still as mice, suddenly prey in a realm they didn't understand. Just as Anthony glanced at Tom, a deafening crunch shook the ground outside the cave opening, startling them both. In the faint light, Tom's face reflected pure terror. Anthony put his finger to his mouth in a desperate gesture to keep him from screaming.

Minutes passed and not a sound could be heard.

Whatever it was hadn't moved from the cave entrance, thought Anthony. He was afraid to peer around a natural stone column that blocked his view of the opening. They were cornered.

TWENTY-SEVEN

Daniel and Emily strolled through the campus green enjoying a break between classes. They were engrossed in their conversation about the partisan state of politics in the United States and didn't notice the portly, middle-aged professor waddling quickly up the pathway to intercept them. Before Daniel could finish his next thought, the professor urgently called out to him.

"Daniel! Daniel Stoddard, may I speak with you a moment," barked an out-of-breath Professor Ross. He was obviously in some distress.

"Professor, what's wrong? You look as though you've seen a ghost."

The professor stopped to catch his breath, hands on his knees. After a brief moment, he composed himself.

"I had a dream like no other I've ever had before ... too real." He shook his head as if to make whatever image was burned in his memory go away. "I believe your father is in trouble."

Daniel was jolted to attention. "How do you know? He's on vacation in Florida."

"Sorry to burst your bubble, my boy, but I've never been so sure of anything in my life." The professor took in a deep breath.

Daniel stared back incredulously at the diminutive man. The nightmare and attack in his dorm room immediately came to his mind. The prospect that Professor Ross was right about his father sent a rush of adrenaline into his veins.

Emily grasped Daniel's hand. "What do we do?"

Daniel stared blankly into space for a few seconds in an attempt to calm down and get his bearings.

The professor interjected. "There's no time to waste. Follow me."

Daniel had never seen the professor move so quickly. His short, stubby legs jerked up and down like pistons, propelling him almost absurdly down the pathway to his office.

In a daze, Daniel and Emily ran after him, unsure of what to do or where the professor planned to take them. They could barely keep-up and tried not to draw attention to themselves as they intermittently ran, stumbled and jogged to keep pace.

The professor seems possessed, thought Daniel, now out-of-breath. He glanced over at Emily, who was lost in her own thoughts.

They ran through the ivy-clad alleyways leading to the professor's building and came upon the exterior door, wide open, likely from the professor's entrance a few moments before. They sprinted up the stairs, pushed open the heavy steel door and skidded into the hallway. They hadn't reached the office when the professor emerged, signaling for them to stop.

"Not ... here," he ordered between gulps of air. "The access road leading to the reservoir ... pick-up the trail near the old pump house."

Daniel and Emily watched him scurry past, waving at them to follow. They exchanged glances, clearly confused. Daniel had no ideas of his own, and Professor Ross seemed to know where he was going so they hurried down the stairs after him, doing their best to keep up with his frantic pace.

The odd threesome burst past students on their way to class, leaving curious stares in their wake. The asphalt pathway gave way to an empty access road that lead to some sort of water treatment facility built on the edge of a large reservoir. Behind the building lay the beginning of a dense forest of pine trees that stretched for miles.

"We'll take that trail over there." The professor pointed to an opening in the trees carpeted with fallen pine needles that quickly lead into blackness.

Daniel's facial expression changed from concern to suspicion. "Why would we want to go in there?"

"There's no time to waste." Professor Ross shrugged-off the question and entered the forest first, waving them on again. "Come! You'll see what I mean in a moment."

They both let out a deep breath and followed the professor into the darkness.

As their eyes adjusted, they could see the green canopy above. A faint light broke through the uppermost boughs as the wind gusted overhead. Hundreds of tall trees surrounded them, standing at attention like columns in a vast temple. The pine needles crunched beneath their feet as they headed deeper into the forest.

They barely kept pace with the diminutive professor as he scurried between gargantuan tree trunks, pock-marked with the stubs of branches long torn away by the elements.

It seemed like a bad dream to Daniel, who was numb with exhaustion and concern for his father's well-being. A shout from about twenty-five yards ahead brought him back to attention.

"There it is!" The professor stopped dead in his tracks in front of a huge, circular boulder. It was flat on top and reminded Daniel of an altar. Strange markings, faded by time, had been etched into the smooth surface along the entire circumference, as if they had been burned into the rock by a laser.

A few uncomfortable moments passed as Professor Ross stared reverently at the symbols. Daniel couldn't stand the suspense any longer. "It's a boulder professor ... with some markings, probably Native American. Is this what you insisted we see ... an old rock in the middle of a pine forest?" Daniel glared at Ross in disgust as he impatiently paced back and forth across the clearing.

Emily interjected. "I'm sure there's an explanation," she implored. "Isn't that right, professor?"

"My dear girl, this is no ordinary boulder, I daresay. It is an ancient dimensional accelerator!" he stated with excitement.

"Dimensional accelerator!? What the hell is that?!" Daniel growled. He felt stupid for blindly following the crazy old coot and angry at himself for buying into the theory about his father's predicament. "I think I've had enough." He turned to Emily. "Let's go. There's nothing here."

As they turned to leave, the professor continued. "Ye of little faith. You have no idea of what you speak." His confident tone made Daniel stop suddenly as Emily lost hold of his hand. He turned to face the professor and challenged him.

"Then show me how it works ... now."

"By all means, the professor responded, unfazed by Daniel's abrupt command. "If it is proof you desire, I shall give you a brief demonstration."

The professor placed his hands on two depressions in the rock, worn down from eons of rain and wind. He took in a deep breath and gently laid his forehead on the sign of an eagle.

At first, Daniel saw no discernable change in the boulder or the surrounding area. The eccentric professor seemed to be muttering some kind of incantation or affirmation. He thought he saw the surface of the rock vibrate but shrugged it off as an overactive imagination fueled by an adrenalin rush.

A moment later, Emily tapped his shoulder and whispered in his ear. "Do you see that?" She pointed at the top of the boulder.

"See what?" He didn't want to admit that he *was* witnessing something odd.

"That shimmering, vibrating ring," she answered.

By now, there was no doubt something unusual was occurring. Daniel noticed that the professor was becoming opaque as he vibrated in time with the huge boulder.

"He's disappearing!" Emily shouted over the low, deep tone that was increasing in volume and intensity.

The louder the sound became, the more transparent the professor seemed to appear until the sound of the vibration began to hurt their ears. Before they could scream in pain, the sound stopped and the professor was gone. All they could hear was the wind blowing through the canopy overhead while the massive trees swayed and creaked in response.

Cautiously, Daniel walked over to the place where the professor had stood, arms outstretched as if he might run into the now invisible man.

Emily broke the stunned silence. "We didn't just see that, did we? I mean, it's not possible to just disappear, right?"

"I don't know what to believe anymore," Daniel answered distantly as he searched behind the boulder and nearby trees.

He found nothing and turned to Emily in confusion and disbelief.

"I believe you're looking for me?" a familiar voice called from behind them as they whirled around to see who it was.

Professor Ross stood in the pathway sporting a look that said, *I told you so.*

"But ..." Daniel looked quizzically at the boulder and back at the professor while Emily stood in stunned silence.

"Impossible? My dear boy, just because you can't see something, doesn't mean it's not there. The five senses do have their limitations," he added with satisfaction. "But enough philosophy, we need to help your father."

Daniel immediately refocused with a new-found respect for the eccentric teacher.

"We need to call on a guide who can take us to your father," the professor continued. "Someone familiar with the non-physical realms closest to the Earth plane."

"How do we do that?" Daniel was not convinced such an entity existed much less could be called upon to help them.

"Your dream," Emily answered. "You told me you saw a woman surrounded by light appear from nowhere as you were being attacked! She must have protected you."

"Good!" interrupted the professor. "What did she look like? Did she speak?"

Daniel attempted to gather his thoughts. "I ... I was being attacked by something. There was a flash of light, and I woke up in my dorm room." It suddenly occurred to him that Emily could be right. Maybe the woman he saw so briefly might have saved him! It was almost too much to believe.

The professor nodded his head as an almost fanatical grin crossed his face. "Yes, yes ... that's it! A warrior angel or guardian angel, if you prefer, saved you from that demon. Did he or she have a name?"

"I don't remember." Daniel tried to recall the encounter but came up blank.

Professor Ross sensed Daniel's frustration. "Take a deep breath and try to remember. These entities always give you a sign. If not a name, then some kind of signature." The professor waited patiently.

Daniel stared blankly into the woods attempting to remember the minutest details of the dream that he had pushed from his mind. Nothing stood out with the exception of the bluish-white aura that surrounded his protector. "I can't seem to remember anything specific. It could ..."

"Keep trying, Daniel." The professor was patient but adamant.

Daniel closed his eyes. Emily interjected. "Remember the strange lines you told me about ... that burst from the flash of light?" She gently stroked his hair.

"But I never could make out what it was," he replied.

"Try and focus on that moment," added the professor.

Daniel closed his eyes again and pictured the angel in his mind. From the cloud of white light, details began to emerge. She was tall and although cloaked in a bright bluish-white light, very beautiful. She wore what looked to be a long robe or gown. In her hand she grasped something that rose up ...

"A sword!" he shouted.

"Good, look closer at the sword," the professor encouraged.

Emily gently massaged Daniel's shoulders as he tried to visualize the fleeting images of his dream. In his mind, he honed in on the sword. It was very long and narrow.

He saw a sheath and what looked like a belt. He put aside all doubts and focused on the belt which intersected with two wide sashes attached on either side of some sort of ring or buckle. The sashes crossed over her chest before disappearing over her shoulders. Something glittered on the upper-part of each sash. He looked closer. Now, in an almost out-of-body state, the pictures in his mind became even clearer.

"I see a gold medallion, about four inches in diameter. There are symbols etched into the outer band, but I can't make out what they mean. Maybe they are some kind of ancient language. Four wavy lines begin at the border of that band from different points and meet within a circle in the center. The circle is indented and is a deep purple, like a smooth, beautiful amethyst."

"Do you have any idea what the symbol with the wavy lines means?" asked the professor.

"She's talking to me ... Jenny?!" Daniel became distracted and began mutter something unintelligible.

"Daniel, who is Jenny?" asked the professor. Can you tell us the meaning of this medallion?" He waited patiently as Daniel conversed with the unseen entity.

"Yes, I will tell him, Jenny." Daniel's face lit up with joy. "Jenny is my guardian angel." The professor eyes widened and Emily gasped.

"She said the wavy lines represent the different pathways we can take in life toward our ultimate goal. Because we are all imperfect beings, the pathways meander and make the medallion looked fractured. This is a reflection of the fragmented and disjointed nature of life. Ultimately, we all go down many paths but eventually arrive at the same place, represented by the center. Her spirit is tied to the universal symbol of unity."

"Can she help us find your father?" implored the professor.

"Yes, she is here to lead me to him. She said I can communicate with Emily through my dreams while I'm on the other side."

Emily looked suddenly panicky. "But what if you don't come back?"

The professor tried to comfort her as Daniel explained what he was about to do.

"Jenny will keep a watchful eye on me. It's not without danger but if my father doesn't receive help, he may be trapped in the death realms and his physical body will die. She's asking for you to stay here with me until I cross over. You'll both be given a sign when I am ready to return, at which time you can come back to this accelerator." Daniel sounded oddly calm.

"Emily, we have to listen to her," pleaded the professor.

She stood before Daniel and gazed deeply into his eyes. He looked back at her with determination. "Do what you need to do and get home alive. Don't leave me, Daniel Stoddard." A tear slowly appeared and ran down her cheek. She threw her arms around him.

Daniel smiled. "I'll make it back ... promise." He turned to face the ancient accelerator, closed his eyes and told Jenny he was ready. The boulder began to shimmer, and Daniel gradually disappeared. There was silence followed by the sound of a distant wind in the treetops.

TWENTY-EIGHT

Anthony and Tom huddled in a corner of the dark, cramped space, their eyes locked on the light streaming into cave opening. They dared not move and give whatever had come their way an excuse to enter their hiding place.

Was it gone ... or waiting for them, thought Anthony? He turned to Tom in the oppressive silence, who barely acknowledged Anthony's questioning look.

A light mist began to filter into the cave. Anthony noticed that it wasn't behaving like a typical fog bank on Earth. Rather, it slowly penetrated the cave opening then retreated in a rhythmic sequence, as if someone was breathing on them. The implication of such an idea coursed through him like an electric shock. Something was out there ... waiting, but he sensed that it wouldn't wait forever. They had to do something fast, and simply walking out of the cave entrance was not an option.

I'm thinking and moving as if I'm physically back on Earth," he told himself. How could he have forgotten so much of his training? Tom was obviously as clueless as he was, but at least he had an excuse ... total ignorance of the laws of the non-physical realms. What would Maxim do? he thought desperately. He tried to picture himself on the steps of the Temple Portal talking to his guide.

Lost in Plain Sight

Maxim's words echoed in his mind.

"In the realms beyond time, there is only the present moment. To think of a place is to be there. You are in a world where thought builds cities but also propels you to locations based on your desire. It is easy to forget that you aren't walking the Earth, so similar is the landscape. Do not walk ... picture your destination in your mind and you shall arrive but in a moment ... the present moment."

The scene faded away as the dark surroundings of the cave brought Anthony back to reality. He turned to Tom. "Do you trust me?" he whispered.

Tom seemed surprised by his question. "Do I have a choice?"

"No." Anthony glanced back to the entrance. "I know how to escape, but you have to do exactly what I say."

Tom's eyes widened. He leaned toward Anthony. "How can we possibly do that?" he whispered incredulously.

"We've both forgotten how to move in these realms telepathically. The key is focus and attention. Visualize a location, focus on it with the intent of being there and you will travel there. I'm not well versed in this area but we have to try. It's our only hope."

Something moved into the cave opening as if reading their thoughts. A plume of mist slowly began to fill the small chamber.

"The crystal city of lights I passed on the way to the mountain. Do you know of it?" Anthony whispered anxiously.

"Yes. Tambora."

"Picture Tambora in your mind. I remember flying over the huge spires ..."

"Yes," interrupted Tom. "They call it God's Finger."

"We'll meet there. No more time." The stench of rotting flesh had entered the cave and was quickly bearing down on them. Fear had them hyper-focused on their goal.

Tom muttered over and over; "God's Finger, Gods Finger, God's Finger."

"Now!" They closed their eyes and visualized the enormous spires. Almost immediately, the cave began to spin. Something made Anthony open his eyes again for a brief moment. Geometric shapes were flying off the cave walls as Tom continued his mantra, eyes closed. The last thing he saw was the face of a surprised demon, Maloda, leering at him from the cave entrance.

Before Anthony had a chance to register what had happened, he was instantly transported to the front entrance of God's Finger. It took him a moment to acclimate to his new surroundings. The enormous building stood before him like a giant monolith. As if by magic, Tom appeared next to him, unsteady and disoriented. He shook off the effects of teleporting and gawked at the massive tower looming over them.

Speechless, they walked over to the gigantic structure admiring the smooth, glittering foundation. It was like no material they had ever seen or touched.

"It's as smooth as machined aluminum," Anthony whispered, unsure what might be lurking nearby.

Tom ran his hand over the wall. "It feels like it's vibrating, pulsing ... almost like it's alive," he said, distracted by its beauty.

"Yes," Anthony agreed. But something didn't seem right. There were no spirits here, and no activity ... "a city with no soul," he thought aloud.

Tom was caught off-guard. "What do you mean?" He stared at Anthony.

"Look around," Anthony gestured. "No one occupies these streets—these buildings. There's nothing but silence."

Tom took his eyes off God's Finger long enough to register what Anthony was saying. He scanned the streets and buildings for signs of life but nothing moved. "You're right. It seems dead."

The two escaped prisoners surveyed the alleys, streets and buildings trying to come up with a plan. Surely they would be found if they didn't move on.

From a distance, they heard what seemed to be the steady clang of a bell. They rushed behind a building, afraid it might be a warning. It soon became clear that there was nothing to fear, so they emerged and moved carefully toward the sound.

Anthony followed what looked like a track carved into a deep trough in the ground. As they moved closer to the steady rhythmic clang, they noticed a strange looking man astride the top of a pole. He was very short but strong, Anthony noticed. His stubby bare feet stood on metal spikes hammered into the sides of the pole; his left hand grasping a similar spike to hold himself

Lost in Plain Sight

aloft. His left arm was skinny, almost atrophied compared to his massively strong right arm. In his right hand he gripped an enormous mallet-like hammer with which he pounded a vertically hung, golden bell. It was similar to the bells Anthony remembered from his high school days, hung invisibly on the walls until they startled students and teachers alike with their shrill commands.

At first, the peculiar carnival-like man didn't notice the pair slowly approaching. His face was pinched tightly in concentration as he bit down on his tongue. He hammered the bell frantically as if his life depended on it.

"Hello." Anthony looked around to make sure no one nearby had heard him. Tom gave him the all-clear sign as the strange man continued ringing the bell. "Excuse me!" Anthony didn't want to jump onto the track to get the man's attention, so he waved his arms.

The bell-ringer slowly moved his head in Anthony's direction and stopped swinging the hammer in mid-air. For a moment, the two strangers stared at each other warily. Anthony began to wonder if the unusual creature was a mute as he studied its blank stare. It was as if this alien being could see right through him. It was making him uncomfortable.

Just as the bell-ringer looked as if he would speak, Anthony noticed a slight glint in his eye, almost as if he recognized him.

He began to speak, slowly and deliberately. "You are in grave danger. They are watching you ..."

"Who is watching us?" Anthony interrupted, as Tom moved closer behind him.

"You must leave or you will be punished. They show no mercy. Tambora is doomed." The glint in his eyes disappeared.

"Where is this city?" asked Tom.

For the first time the bell-ringer smiled. "You know not where you stand?" he asked incredulously.

Both Anthony and Tom surveyed the surroundings blankly. "We're in the city of Tambora. That is all we know," Anthony replied.

The bell-ringer burst out laughing. "You wandered into the capitol of the Fourth Realm unknowingly?" He could barely hang on to the pole, he was laughing so hard.

"Nefar's army has infiltrated the city and captured its citizens one-by-one, imprisoning them within their own memories."

The two men stared back at the bell-ringer with obvious looks of confusion. He jumped down off the pole and looked deeply into Anthony's eyes with suspicion.

He was bigger than Anthony had originally thought. The creature lumbered over to where he stood.

"What are your names?" he asked.

"I'm Anthony and this is Tom."

"Why are you here?" He sniffed as if expecting a foul scent.

Both men took a step backward.

"Are you afraid?" The odd creature surveyed the strangers, obviously enjoying his advantage.

Anthony had had enough. "What's *your* name?" he asked with a suspicion of his own. The bell-ringer hesitated a moment before answering. His eyes narrowed. "You are the stronger one." He stared deeply into Anthony's eyes, as if searching his soul.

"Answer my question. What's your name and why do you ring that bell?" Anthony was getting impatient, but he had to be careful not to anger him. His fears were calmed when the bell-ringer's body language softened.

"I was testing your resolve, traveler. You can trust no one while the negative forces control the city. I am Medrar. I was once leader of the Kos but have been banished to Tambora and forced to ring the bell of capture."

"What's the bell of capture?" asked Tom.

Medrar quickly surveyed the surrounding streets for eavesdroppers. "You can't be too careful," he whispered. "The city is infested with spies. Nefar's soldiers are methodical. They target and capture citizens unaware, then lure them into plasma bubbles created from thoughts of the places they hold dear. The poor souls become trapped in a perpetual memory from which they cannot escape. I am notified of every successful imprisonment and expected to ring the bell. This signals to any remaining citizens that they are one step closer to their doom. It also alerts the commanders that they are one soul closer to their goal."

"Why do you agree to such a job?" Tom asked. "It's psychological terrorism."

Medrar responded angrily. "Do you think I wanted this job?" He glared at Tom, who was now looking sheepish.

"Still," Anthony interjected. "It is a fair question. There are no soldiers forcing you to ring that bell. Why not just escape?"

Medrar's expression went from anger to hysterical laughter. The sight of him caused both Anthony and Tom to crack a smile despite themselves. After a few moments, Medrar regained his composure, all suspicion erased from his face.

"I haven't had a laugh like that in a long while. Let me take you to a neutral area where we will be safe." He led them to a nearby building made from a strange metallic substance that glowed a beautiful golden hue.

"They haven't discovered that this building blocks all energy. No thoughts or words can escape the golden dome and find the wrong pair of ears." Medrar winked. Then he became serious. "Listen to me for your own safety. Nefar's legions don't need to be standing next to me to hurt me or you for that matter. The only reason they haven't attacked you is because your auras are different from anything else in this region."

"Auras?" interrupted Anthony. "What do auras have to do with being attacked?"

"Everything," answered Medrar. "I am not nearly as adept at reading auras as they are but yours are strong."

"In what way?" asked Tom.

"As your eyes are windows to your soul on the physical plane, your aura is the window to your soul in these realms. It reflects your inner strength, wisdom and level of protection, among other things. Do you not know this?"

"Auras aren't as important in our world as they are in yours, Medrar," Anthony explained. Tom nodded in agreement.

Medrar rolled his eyes. "How is it you are still alive? You know nothing of the realms you travel."

"I take exception to that," said a disembodied voice that Anthony recognized immediately.

Appearing in the doorway to their secret chamber stood Maxim, resplendent in purple and gold. His fish medallion glowed rhythmically with the dome high over their heads.

TWENTY-NINE

"Maxim!" Anthony ran to embrace his friend. Tom and Medrar watched the reunion with surprise.

"What have you gotten yourself into now?" Maxim chastised gently.

Anthony was embarrassed. He knew he had overstepped his bounds.

"And you have dragged another innocent soul along with you." Maxim looked across the room at Tom and nodded in greeting. Tom acknowledged the gesture with obvious reverence for the guide, while Medrar stood respectfully silent. It was well known that guides wearing the hues of purple and gold represented some of the highest level souls in any realm. They didn't appear often.

Medrar finally bowed in greeting as Maxim approached.

"Are you of the Kos group of souls?" asked Maxim.

"I am."

"I knew Hathrar well during a particularly tumultuous Earth incarnation at the time of the Roman occupation of Gaul. He was known then as Carausius ... a talented military commander for the Romans. I was Maximian, Roman emperor under Diocletian."

Medrar's eyes widened. "You were ultimately deified."

"That is true, but I was anything but a deity. I committed suicide which had to be addressed in subsequent lives," clarified Maxim.

Lost in Plain Sight

"You had no choice. Emperor Constantine ordered you to do it," protested Medrar.

"You always have a choice," Maxim responded.

Medrar changed the subject. "Carausius was one of our greatest leaders. He bravely fought the Bagaudae rebels in northern Gaul."

"I know," Maxim smiled. "It was my campaign. He was also the man I appointed to police the Channel shores. However, he rebelled in AD 286, causing the secession of Britain and northwestern Gaul."

"He was always a rebel," laughed Medrar. "Until he was assassinated by Allectus."

"Ahh ... his finance minister," sighed Maxim. "That is the treachery the citizens of Tambora are now enduring from Nefar and his commanders." He motioned the unlikely band of souls to the middle of the chamber and paused to gather his thoughts.

"Maxim, may I speak?" asked Medrar.

"Of course."

"Nefar is very close to controlling all of Tambora. I am afraid it is too late to fight. We have no army."

Anthony stepped forward. "It is never too late." He turned to Maxim. "There must be something we can do to help the city."

Maxim searched the faces of the rag-tag trio. Anthony thought he detected a momentary expression of doubt from his guide, but it was immediately replaced by resolve.

Maxim continued. "Are you two prepared to risk your physical lives to eradicate the scourge upon this realm?" He looked Anthony and Tom squarely in the eyes.

They both hesitated before answering the question. Deep down, Anthony knew it was the right thing to do, despite the risk. Too much was at stake. He wouldn't back down. How could he? He turned to Tom who nodded yes. "We're in."

Maxim turned to Medrar. "You know the circumstances of this conflict and the enemy better than any of us. Would you brief us on the situation?"

"With pleasure, master guide. Tambora, the greatest city of the Fourth Realm, also known as The City of Hope, has been attacked by Nefar's demons and his army of the damned. This hand-picked legion of souls was given the choice to languish in the hellish conditions of the lowest after-death realms or fight the forces of light. Nefar's army is lead by general Butu, a sadistic demon responsible for the kidnap and torture of countless souls who had wandered into the lowest realms." Medrar gave Anthony and Tom a look of warning.

"Maloda, Nefar's personal lieutenant, has had a contentious relationship with Butu since the war against the Kos when they were captains under the brutal reign of Zar. Both seek to be Nefar's chief commander. Their hatred and evil know no boundaries as they seek to please their leader and ultimately the supreme manifestation of evil and suffering that humankind knows so well ... the Devil himself." Medrar searched for his next words carefully.

"Nefar's army has entered Tambora disguised as souls traveling through the city and have positioned themselves in key areas of commerce. They catch inhabitants unaware and lure them into plasma bubble force-fields created from thoughts of the places they hold dear, trapping them in a perpetual memory.

"Since all realms are created from thought energy, the occupiers set out to infuse the City of Hope with negative energy and thoughts of hatred and destruction. When the population is finally freed from their prisons, the city will already have been poisoned. It is all but assured that the citizens will turn on each other leading to Tambora's demise. The ultimate goal of Nefar is to embrace Tambora back into the lower three realms and expand his power base." Medrar finished and lowered his eyes.

"I appreciate the information, Medrar," praised Maxim. "It was very brave of you to tell us of these secret plans."

"I will be killed if they find out," Medrar warned.

"Your secret is safe with us," assured Tom. Both Maxim and Anthony nodded in agreement. Medrar seemed satisfied.

"Now," Maxim sighed, "we plan our own strategy." He faced Anthony. "Tell me, what can kill even the largest beast on Earth?"

Anthony was caught off guard. "Maxim, I don't—"

"Humor me," Maxim interjected.

Anthony threw out the first thing he could think of. "A powerful weapon."

"Too vague. I'll give you a hint. It replicates."

Lost in Plain Sight

Anthony pondered a moment followed by a look of recognition. "A disease!"

"Better ... I'm thinking specifically of a deadly virus that spreads when animals or humans are in contact with each other."

"Are there virus's in these realms?" asked Tom. "If so, how would we infect the army?"

"Good, Tom! Now you're thinking," responded Maxim. Everyone looked puzzled. "It's as plain as day. We plant a rumor and allow it to replicate and infect the army." Maxim seemed pleased with the idea.

"How?" asked Medrar. "There's no guarantee it will spread. What could we possibly say that would destroy an army?"

"Even the strongest armies have a weakness. Find the weak link in the chain, exploit it, and they will destroy themselves."

It seemed too easy ... too simple to work, thought Anthony.

As if reading his mind Maxim continued. "The best ideas are the simplest."

"True," added Medrar, "but we'll never get a rumor, even a dangerous one, to the highest levels of the command structure."

"Not true," Maxim disagreed. "Can you get a message to a mid-level commander; someone with access to the high command who has a propensity to talk too much?"

"Possibly, through a scout," responded Medrar doubtfully.

"Good. Then we use the animosity and paranoia between Maloda and General Butu to our advantage." Maxim paused to think for a moment. "We need a scout that is close to the local commander; someone who will report not only what he hears but what he thinks he hears. How many scouts cover this section of Tambora, Medrar?"

Medrar considered the question. I know of at least three regulars ... and two others who come on occasion."

"What is the name of the local commander?"

"That would be Drakar." Medrar scowled at the mention of his name.

"Whom does Drakar trust the most with information?" Maxim gave Medrar a moment to think.

"Hector. He is constantly trying to get in Drakar's favor. He is persistent ... always seeking information. Drakar despises him but keeps him close because Hector delivers details that others miss."

"And who does Drakar report to?"

"The mid-tier commander, Mandible."

Maxim peered blankly into the distance, deep in thought. "Does Mandible report to any of the top leadership?"

"Yes," Medrar answered immediately. "To Butu himself."

"Good, that's only four levels to the top—five including Nefar. We need to plant a rumor that casts doubt on the mission and the command structure of Nefar's army; something that will cause suspicion, begin to break the chain of command and seep into the lower ranks. What do you think that could be, Anthony?" Maxim turned suddenly to his student again, catching him off-guard for the second time.

"Um, I ... let me think a moment." Gradually, his eyes widened as an idea came to him. "Medrar, I have a question."

"Go ahead."

"Is there more than one scout assigned to your sector?"

"Yes. Most of the time Drakar sends two, Hector and Recce, as much to keep an eye on each other as for protection. There are spies everywhere, and danger lurks down every alleyway. One scout usually keeps a lookout while I brief the other. If Hector had his way, he would always choose to be the information gatherer, but Drakar splits that duty between them."

"Who is due to speak with you next?"

"Recce," answered Medrar without hesitation ... and he is not as smart as Hector."

"Good. Maxim, I'm not sure what information we can pass to Recce, but we can have Medrar do it in a way that makes Recce feel important and at the same time doesn't raise the suspicions of Hector," said Anthony.

"I see," Maxim replied. "A good plan. Recce would likely want to pass that information on to Drakar to gain favor with the commander—"

"... and it needs to be something Recce would *want* to keep from Hector," interrupted Anthony.

"Good!" Maxim was clearly pleased with Anthony's plan and nodded approvingly. "Then, what idea should we plant with Drakar that would have the highest probability of being communicated to the high command?" There were blank stares all around. "It will need to strike fear and indecision into the key leadership to be able to affect their strategic plan—leader will turn on leader." Maxim turned to Medrar. "You know the inner workings of this army better than any of us."

"I know only what they want me to know, Maxim," Medrar cautioned.

"Still, you are closest to the situation. You understand the impact of the information you report to these scouts. You know how they think. What kind of information would rattle you if you were in Drakar's position? Put yourself in his place." Maxim crossed his arms as he waited for a response.

Tom glanced at Anthony. They knew Maxim meant business and expected an answer from Medrar, who by now was feeling the pressure.

Medrar began to describe the situation as best he could. "Even as they silently round-up every leader, defender and citizen of Tambora, there is an unspoken fear that someone will escape to tell the leaders of the Fifth Realm; the region most likely to be affected by a takeover of Tambora.

"Nefar has taken many precautions. He is a trickster, and his army is stealthy, well-trained and motivated. If the mission is successful, the conscripted legions that contribute to the victory but are damned to the lowest realms, will be freed. Imagine, thousands of prisoners on Earth being released into the law-abiding population. Well, you can see the implications for disaster."

Maxim stared grimly at Anthony and Tom. Anthony was suddenly overwhelmed by their task.

Medrar continued. "There has to be a credible rumor of a security breach. Tambora is fairly isolated from the higher realms. It is self-sufficient. Travel between realms is infrequent and easy to control."

"You would be referring to the dimensional accelerators?" interjected Maxim.

"Precisely," answered Medrar.

Anthony and Tom exchanged a confused glance. "What's a dimensional accelerator?" asked Tom. Anthony was about to ask the same question.

Maxim waved-off Medrar, indicating he would answer. "It is a shortcut from one dimension to another, a type of portal if you will."

Anthony and Tom tried to speak simultaneously, but Maxim raised his hand.

"Let me finish. You can't just enter one of these coordinates and expect to be transported to your heart's desire. It takes training. Many a soul has been flung to distant dimensions, lost in frightening and unfamiliar surroundings. There is real danger that a soul could be harmed, entrapped, or isolated by the inhabitants or laws of these least understood realms. Do not attempt to enter a dimensional accelerator if you come across one. Am I clear?" Maxim and Medrar fixed their eyes on the two inexperienced travelers.

Maxim continued. "That being said, I will carefully demonstrate how to approach and travel through these portals." Anthony thought he detected a slight smile on Maxim's face. "There are methods and tools to assist you if one knows where to find them ... but first things first."

Maxim turned to face Medrar again. "We need to convince Recce and ultimately Drakar there has been an escape ... and there needs to be evidence."

Suddenly, Medrar's face lit up and a wide grin appeared. "Why fake an escape when we can create a real one!"

THIRTY

Even Maxim was surprised by the announcement. "How do you plan to do that?"

"No, how do *they* ..." Medrar pointed to Anthony and Tom, "plan to do that."

"Medrar!" Anthony protested.

Maxim interjected, "You can't expect these two—"

"Hear me out, Maxim. I have a plan."

Medrar explained how he could keep his post, so as to not raise suspicions while Maxim helped Anthony and Tom conduct a reconnaissance mission to the accelerator.

"The key to our success will be enlisting the help of Retarius, leader and defender of Tambora. He knows other important leaders from the higher realms. He was recently captured and is now imprisoned in an alternate reality created from his own memories.

"Nefar tricked him, and now he parades aimlessly inside a plasma bubble near the sentries guarding the accelerator in Sector 8. He has become an amusement to the local regiment." Medrar became angry at the thought. "I will do whatever it takes to help you get access, however brief, to the accelerator and ultimately free Retarius. The key is enlisting the help of the Realm of Symbols. They will know the secret that will free him."

"That sounds extremely dangerous," protested Tom.

"It is dangerous just being here," responded Maxim. "If we do nothing, your situation is just as critical and the city is lost. If you attempt and fail at least you had the courage to try despite the danger to yourselves. If you succeed, you save a world, engender the gratitude of countless souls and learn the value of selflessness as hatred and evil retreats to the lowest realms for eons. Do you see the pathway?" Maxim waited for a response.

"You know we can't say no when you put it that way," Anthony protested.

Maxim just smiled. "Then the decision is made?"

"Yes." Anthony sighed.

"And you, Tom?"

It was obvious that Tom was frightened, but he managed a reluctant, "Yes."

"Alright, then." Maxim swept his arm counterclockwise, and a three dimensional map made of tiny pin-points of light appeared before them, floating at eye level. Maxim asked the trio to gather around the holographic map to plan an approach to the heavily-guarded accelerator.

Inside the map, Anthony thought he spotted small figures moving about. He looked to Maxim for an explanation.

"This is not a two-dimensional depiction of a location—what you call a map. This is a real-time, three-dimensional image," Maxim explained.

"Interesting." Anthony was fascinated by the technology. Like a satellite video image on Earth ... Google Earth on steroids."

Tom looked completely confused. "What's a Google?"

"Yes, what is a Google?" asked Maxim. A rare look of confusion crossed his face. Medrar seemed perplexed as well.

Anthony held their gaze for a moment and relented. "I'm sorry. It's a technology from my time. Tom, if we make it back home, put a big chunk of money into it in about twenty-eight years and you'll be rich."

Tom smiled. "Oh, okay. Thanks for the tip. I guess it pays to time-travel."

Maxim had had enough. "Can we dispense with the financial recommendation and focus?" he pleaded with mock impatience.

Anthony and Tom couldn't help themselves and broke out into laughter. Even Medrar seemed to understand and joined in.

Maxim waited patiently, allowing them to briefly release some tension. When they had recovered, he continued.

"Medrar will keep his normal lookout while we quietly head southwest toward Sector 8." Maxim moved his hands over the images as the miniature landscape moved to their current location. "Normally, we would teleport to the accelerator instantly, but you boys would most definitely get into trouble if you attempted mind travel to this dangerous region. I will accompany you the physical way—on foot." Maxim seemed amused at the thought.

"We need to stay close and follow the dark alleyways and trenches through the western part of the city. Once we reach the outskirts, you will see the foothills and the forests just beyond. From that point, the accelerator is approximately, to use three-dimensional terms, a mile away."

"You won't be able to get near it," interrupted Medrar. "Drakar has demons fanning out in concentric circles. They don't ask questions. If they see you, they will stun you and feed your spirit body to the Argons. They are the worst kind of demons. They will make sure that every part of you feels the equivalent of extreme physical pain as they slowly ingest your essence. The screams of those unfortunate enough to be taken, still echo in the mountains of the lowest realms, begging to be released from their suffering."

"We know of these beasts," responded Anthony. "They guarded the Mountain of Dark Crystal. We barely escaped." He noticed a surprised look on Medrar's face.

"The two of you escaped the most feared prison in the Fourth Realm ... guarded by Argon demons? There may be hope for you yet," he added cynically.

Tom and Anthony rolled their eyes.

"There's no time to waste," interjected Maxim. "As we near the accelerator, I'll teleport to the guard station, survey the sentries' movements and read their thoughts. I'll attempt to enter Retarius's mind, but I'll need to be very close to have any effect. I'm sure Nefar's master hypnotists have taken every precaution to wipe their short-term memory clean and place them in a persistent past memory state. It's very difficult to break through that level of unawareness."

Tom interrupted. "I don't understand, Maxim. If Retarius sees you, wouldn't he want to communicate with you and find a way to escape?"

"If I appeared in one of your dreams, would you have enough self-awareness and control to break from that hypnotic state, even for a moment so I could get through?"

Tom considered the question. "No. I would have control over nothing ... my thoughts, my actions." His voice trailed-off. He had nothing more to say.

"We have one advantage," Maxim continued. Retarius lives in these realms and has training that you do not. I may be able to exploit a weakness in their mind control. But in order to probe his mind, I have to get much closer than is safe. I will take the form of a nearby tree and hope I am not discovered by a guard paying close attention. It is the best I can do on such short notice."

"And let's say you are successful, then what?" Medrar asked doubtfully.

"I will create a distraction, so the two of you ..." Maxim pointed to Anthony and Tom, "can enter the accelerator to find help in the Realm of Symbols."

Anthony protested immediately. "How? You, yourself said to never enter an accelerator—"

"On your own. I also said I would show you methods and tools, ancient in their origin, to have you safely on your way."

By now, Anthony knew not to argue with the master guide. "So, what is this method—these tools?"

"Each of us is made up of energy, fantastically unique in its properties. We all emit a tone, a frequency if you will, that naturally attracts our essence to one of the ten after-death dimensions aligned with it. If you sit quietly in meditation, you can sometimes hear this tone. It has a musical quality and resonates from within us to the ends of the universe. It is the essence of your being. Think of it as your *being tone*."

"When I spoke earlier about your auras, they are tied to the frequency of which Maxim speaks," added Medrar.

"Both of you," Maxim nodded to Anthony and Tom, "have different being tones but match the same frequency. I don't want to get too technical, but your meeting was no accident. You both vibrate at the frequency of the Seventh Dimension and the realms that that occupy that level. It is where you will find the Realm of the Symbols. Ask for the Symbol of Consciousness when you arrive."

"Where is this place? How will we find it?" asked Tom.

"Advance guides will show you the way."

"And what do we say to this symbol when we find it?"

"Speak of the fate of Tambora and Retarius. Be truthful and of clear intention. The Symbol of Consciousness will know what to do."

"That's it?" Anthony was unconvinced the plan would work or that they could even find the realm of which Maxim spoke.

"You need to demonstrate faith and courage. Trust that what I have told you is enough. I will give you both a gift, but it will also act as a conductor between the energy of the accelerator and your spirit body and consciousness."

Maxim reached into a hidden pocket in his robe and pulled out two clear medallions, one with the sign of Pisces and the other the sign of Sagittarius.

"Our birth signs," noted Tom. "They're beautiful, but what purpose do they serve?"

Maxim handed them their medallions. "Place them over your heart but do not be alarmed. They will melt into your spirit body and act like a tuning fork. When you stand before the portal, it will begin to vibrate and spread through your spirit body. When the frequency aligns with your individual frequencies, you will be automatically transported to your home ... the Seventh Dimension. That is all you need to know."

Anthony and Tom stood resigned to their fate. There was no turning back. For the first time they saw each other as friends ... even brothers. They placed the medallions over their chests. In a matter of moments, the clear disks became one with their spirit bodies.

THIRTY-ONE

Every molecule in Daniel's body buzzed. He felt like a lightning bug hurtling through a tunnel of white cotton-candy clouds. Points of blue and pink light sparkled like diamonds while a musical symphony played in the background; a hidden orchestra performing the soundtrack of his life. He knew the music supported him. He felt as if he was riding on the notes as the music rose to a crescendo and came to a sudden stop.

It all seemed vaguely familiar. Had he been here before? He reached out to touch the billowy clouds that surrounded him but every time he moved, the cottony walls moved further away, almost playfully. Daniel laughed. The pinpoints of light seemed to wink as if they knew who he was, and he could hear the sound of giggling in the background.

"Is there someone here?" he called out, but all he heard was more giggling. Then, he heard a beautiful melody. It began as a single line and blossomed into full-blown chords and then stopped just as suddenly as it had started.

"Who's there? I know someone is here," Daniel laughed again. He wasn't afraid at all. He could feel love emanating from every crevice of this strange place, and he felt wonderful ... like a child wanting to play with his imaginary friends.

"Cometes is here!" a childlike voice cried out. Daniel heard more giggling as a single black note bounced from the folds of the cottony walls. He watched in fascination as the musical quarter-note danced playfully in front of him. With each jump, he heard the sound of middle C being played on an invisible piano. Somehow he knew that the note *was* Middle C! He cried-out in delight.

"Hello. Who are you?"

"I'm C ... and I'm D ... and I'm A Flat ... and I'm G ... and—"

All of a sudden musical notes of all shapes and sizes burst from the cottony walls. Each sounded their own note in a beautiful cacophony of melodies and chords. It wasn't so much a musical piece as a greeting, and Daniel was delighted with his new friends. And yet ... it was as if he knew them from the past.

Then, all the notes jumped to attention and arranged themselves in treble and bass clefs. They formed a living musical notation suspended before him and became silent. Daniel had the feeling something was about to happen but wasn't sure what. He wasn't scared. A feeling of excited anticipation filled him.

A moment later, the cottony clouds began to part. The notes moved to the side, and a bright blue-white light filled the chamber. It was brighter than any light Daniel had ever seen, even brighter than the sun, but it didn't hurt his eyes. The light began to form into the shape of a woman, and her features appeared before him like magic.

It was as if a veil of amnesia that had covered his awareness like a fog had been lifted. There standing before him was his guide, Jenny. He recognized her at once and wept with joy. He ran into her arms, and they embraced as if not a day had passed since they had parted ways before his current life.

"Jenny, I've missed you so. I didn't know it until now." He relished the unconditional love infusing his spirit body. He didn't want the moment to end.

"The time has come, Cometes. You remember the plan, don't you?" She smiled as recognition crossed Daniel's face. He knew his spiritual name at once. His earthly name, Daniel, seemed awkward in this environment. He was truly home.

Images of the outline for his life came into his awareness, as if Jenny had laid a book in front of him. He saw it all, including the large translucent sphere where he reviewed many opportunities for a new life. The different life choices appeared on the walls of the sphere like movies that he was able to control with his mind and process very quickly, yet time seemed to stand still. Beside him stood someone he didn't recognize but was assisting him with his choice of scenarios.

He saw images of his mother and father ... then his boyhood home, and knew this was the life he would select.

Jenny encouraged him. "Remember, Cometes, nothing was pre-ordained. It was just a pathway. But it was followed faithfully by you, your mother and your father, and has brought you to this point."

Daniel understood it all now. His mom had fulfilled her life as a loving mother and wife. With her destiny completed, she stepped aside so that Anthony and Daniel could fulfill theirs.

"You all knew it would be difficult, but you also knew it was the right choice based on your individual karmic issues and the lessons you needed to give each other as part of the same soul group. A hard life ... yes, but one of accomplishment and spiritual growth. However, the work is not completed. The most dangerous is yet to be." Jenny gazed into Daniel's eyes with love and determination for him.

"What haven't I done? I'll do whatever it takes."

"Your father, Cometes. He is in danger in the city of Tambora, located in the Fourth Realm. An army of evil has taken the entire population hostage, including their leader Retarius. You must help your father. Find him in the Realm of Symbols. Seek the help of the Symbol of Consciousness. You will know him by the universal sign of the swirl. Your lives are intertwined. He cannot succeed without immediate assistance."

"But how? I've never been there before."

"But you have, dear Cometes. Follow your heart. I cannot do it for you. Go to your friends here in the Realm of Music, and they will help you." Jenny placed her hand on Daniel's shoulder and faded away.

For the first time, Daniel felt alone. A terrible sadness welled up from within and he began to doubt whether he could help his father. He looked around the room, but the notes had disappeared and he didn't know where to go to find them.

From behind him he heard the plucking of an upright jazz bass. He turned and saw a standing double-bass, the kind played

Lost in Plain Sight

in jazz bands and orchestras. It stood there watching him, as alive as he was. Where the top two tuning keys should have been were two large blinking eyes. It floated over and spoke to him between the syncopated plucking of strings. It had a deep, lyrical voice and an obvious sense of humor which Daniel didn't necessarily appreciate considering his predicament.

"I've been, dum dum ... instructed to take you, de dumm dum to the realm of the notes ... da dooo dum ... yeah."

"Just lead the way." Daniel was in no mood for riddles or pranks.

"Happy, do dum, to oblige, da do dum," it responded as it floated ahead.

"Oh brother, I'm trying to help my father and I'm talking to singing basses." He followed the instrument through hallways of billowy white clouds as the sound of a beautiful symphony broke the silence. His parents loved classical music, and he had heard many famous movements played at home from Mozart, to Beethoven, Schubert, Brahms and others, but this was like nothing he had ever heard before.

Suddenly the bass stopped and turned to him. "It is your piece, dum dum, born from your mind, de dum. In the realm of music, thought becomes music, da da dum dum."

Daniel noticed the music had stopped as he listened to the bass, so he thought of a symphony and the music began again. "It does work!" he shouted to the bass, delighted by his newfound ability.

"Of course it works, dum dum. This is where all music is born, doo doo dum."

Daniel couldn't suppress a smile. "Thanks, Bass. I feel better."

"That's my job, dum dum."

"Hey, I know what you really mean when you pluck your strings like that."

"You catch on fast, kid, da doo doo," answered the bass with a wink of one of his saucer-like eyes.

They moved down a wide hallway, and an enormous archway came into view. As they got closer, a cluster of whole-notes, half-notes, quarter-notes, eighth-notes, sixteenth-notes, thirty-second notes and sixty-fourth notes streamed through the archway on ribbons of musical notation, as if reams of sheet music had come to life. The notes surrounded Daniel, playing the melody written before his eyes like magic. Together they entered through the arch to the center of a massive domed amphitheater. The music stopped.

From up above, a gigantic face made from various symbols of musical notation descended and appeared before him. At first, Daniel was afraid, but after a moment he saw that it was the leader of the Realm of Music. Its eyes were half-notes with accent eyebrows and a quarter-note nose. Staff-lines formed a mouth that curved up from its naturally straight position into a wide smile.

"Welcome, Cometes," a deep, velvety voice boomed throughout the dome. "We are pleased to see you again. How can we help you?" Thousands of notes began to pour into the chamber to listen.

"Sir—"

"Call me Stave. I am the latticework, the foundation upon which all these notes and symbols are placed."

"Stave, I was instructed by my guide, Jenny—" The notes began to speak among themselves in excited chatter.

"My friends, please let Cometes speak. My apologies. Your guide Jenny-Angel, as we call her affectionately, has bestowed many a kindness upon our realm. We would do anything for her."

"She asked me to come to you for help. My father is in grave danger in the city of Tambora. Residents of the city have been held hostage including their leader—"

"Retarius." A chorus of gasps from the multitude of notes filled the chamber. Stave's face was still with thought and concern. "He is a strong and gentle leader of the City of Hope. The Fourth Realm is particularly vulnerable as it is closest to Nefar's territory. He never rests. Only the Symbols know the secret to breaking the spell that imprisons Retarius and the citizens of Tambora."

"Yes, Jenny said I had to take my father to the Symbol of Consciousness."

"She is correct. They can choose to impart the ancient truth that can free the city. They may even accompany you. But be warned, the pathway to the Realm of Symbols, though well travelled, is fraught with danger. Entities that have come for *the gift* but have been denied, are angry and lie in wait for unsuspecting travelers. They journey to these dimensions to seek a truth that would give them power over others. The symbols know when your heart is pure or filled with selfish intentions. They will not share the ancient truths with those they deem self-serving. Only those that seek to help others will be given the gift. Is your heart pure, Cometes?"

"Yes, I am sure of it, Stave."

Stave turned to the musical notes and symbols that had by now crept ever closer to hear the exchange. "Shall we help Cometes find his father?"

A deafening roar filled the chamber as all manner of notes and symbols cried out, "Yes we will help!" The excitement was electric, and Daniel felt rejuvenated with energy, hope and gratitude for his friends.

"There is little time to waste," boomed Stave. "But first let me brief you on how and where you will be traveling. The symbols spend most of their time in the middle and upper-middle dimensions. Once a soul advances to the ninth and tenth dimensions there is less of a need for their presence, as the highest realms exude pure energy. The quickest and safest meeting place is fortunately in the Seventh Realm. However, like all realms, it is vast, encompassing many physical galaxies in size. We can see that you have not mastered the art of mind travel, so we must use more conventional means."

"And what would that be?" asked Daniel.

"Light beams," said Stave matter-of-factly. "Some of the younger souls returning from Earth incarnations find them, how do I say it in your terms ... *fun*?"

"In what way?" Daniel was concerned and looked about the chamber for an answer.

The notes giggled again. "What's so funny?"

"That's enough," Stave gently commanded the notes. Most of them stopped immediately, save for the occasional chortle of a half-note. Stave waited patiently and then continued.

"When the recently deceased arrive they are disoriented ... mentally and spiritually exhausted but relieved to know they have not disappeared into oblivion. They are met by their guides, a relative or perhaps a beloved religious figure ... whatever makes them most comfortable. After a period of joyous reunion with their soul group, followed by rejuvenation, a life review with their guides and a meeting with the Council of Elders, they are free to find recreation. A favorite is a ride on the light beams." A broad smile crossed Stave's face.

"What on Earth is a light beam ride?" asked Daniel, intrigued.

"It is not of the Earth," laughed Stave. "At least not of the physical Earth you know and love. It is what underlies the physical world you think you understand ... what your scientists call a quantum; in this case, a photon. We will reduce your spirit body to pure energy, and you will travel faster than the speed of light to your destination. I hear it's a fabulous way to see the universe," he added with a knowing smile. "I cannot accompany you. My most reliable and experienced chords will escort you. Sixteenth notes will lead the way and clear any obstacles that may arise. Good luck, my friend."

Stave nodded respectfully and floated away, leaving Daniel at the mercy of an army of notes.

A small eighth-note floated over to him. "Are you ready for the ride of your life?"

The other notes cheered him on. "Sure. Where do we go?"

"To the Vector Field Port."

"What's that?"

"An electromagnetic field. This is where your energy will be transformed into a low-energy electron, brought together with a low-energy positron and converted to gamma ray photons. Your scientists refer to this as quantum electrodynamics, but descriptions matter not. Your energy will be infused with the photons and shot through space-time to the Realm of the Symbols."

"Sorry I asked," Daniel half-joked. He was concerned. "Is it safe? It sounds quite dangerous."

The eighth-note laughed. "It's as natural a way to travel as when you fly in an airplane over the Earth ... but safer."

"Okay. I haven't been hurt yet." Daniel shrugged.

"Just stay where you are and let us take care of you," spoke a quarter-note.

Hundreds of musical notes began to encircle Daniel, increasing their speed until he began to feel dizzy. Before he knew it, he was floating over a sea of electrically charged particles as an overwhelming sense of speed engulfed him.

A bright sphere appeared in the distance as a pinpoint of light. Before he could register what it was, the object was upon him. He collided with it, creating a massive explosion that seemed to reach to the ends of the universe.

Then his awareness condensed and he became an elementary particle blasting through the universe at unimaginable speed. He let the forces take him where they wished and observed the stars, galaxies, planets and gas clouds of the Milky Way with awe. Then he circled the Earth, as if something was purposely leading him on a guided tour. The blue oceans and swirling white clouds spread out below him. The familiar shapes of the continents peeked through in hues of green, brown, grey and white.

Suddenly, he was abruptly lifted into space and hurtled through the solar system. He passed Mars and then the giant, Jupiter, like he was driving past a building on the highway. The smooth rings of Saturn appeared in the distance. In a matter of seconds, he was upon them, now filled with rocks, gases and other debris as he zoomed past. The planet soon became a pinpoint of light as the blue giants of Uranus and Neptune rose into prominence and vanished just as quickly. Pluto seemed barely a blip when he blew by the dark sphere and into deep space.

Instantly, his speed increased again, and stars began to fly by looking like they were no more than a few feet away. Impossibly massive gas clouds in hues of red, gold and purple, rose up to infinity as he burst through them like a bullet. Galaxies flew by like pinwheels at a carnival as he headed straight for a white star in the distance.

A voice whispered in his mind. "Sirius." Before he registered the name, the enormous white star was upon him, and he gasped at its dimensions now filling his entire field of vision. In moments, it too had been reduced to a pinpoint of light. Each successive star became indescribably larger than the last. The voice continued to speak to him.

"Pollux, Arcturus."

The orange giants were beyond anything he could comprehend. Then massive red stars appeared at least one hundred times larger.

"Betelgeuse and Antares."

… and then Daniel stopped. There was only silence. Blackness turned to white.

THIRTY-TWO

The plans were finished. Maxim, Anthony and Tom prepared to leave for the journey to the dimensional accelerator, while Medrar said his goodbyes and headed for his post at the bell. He had barely climbed the pole when Hector and Recce appeared, as if on cue.

"Medrar ... Medrar, it's been too long since our last hellos," taunted Hector. The diminutive scout chose to appear as a menacing looking medieval warrior in full black armor replete with gauntlets, gorget, greaves and a breastplate with spikes.

Medrar wasn't impressed. "Looking particularly dangerous today, Hector."

"I think he looks ridiculous," added Recce.

"Bite your tongue, if you had one," barked Hector.

There's no love lost between these two, thought Medrar, ready to hatch the plan.

"We heard there were intruders in Sector 8 and that you may have seen them ... even spoken to them." Hector stared deeply into Medrar's eyes looking for any signs of deceit or weakness. "Of course this couldn't be true. That would be treason."

Medrar got right to the point. "No, I haven't seen anyone, but I thought I heard some commotion near the old temple about three blocks away." He pointed in the opposite direction of where Maxim had headed with Anthony and Tom.

Lost in Plain Sight

Obviously caught off-guard, Hector dispatched Recce to investigate some nearby alleyways and abandoned streets in an attempt to conduct a quick search.

"If they're still there, I'm sure you'll find them and haul them off to the authorities," coaxed Medrar.

"That we will," hissed Hector. He continued to examine the bell-ringer for any sign he was lying. Not completely satisfied, he called out to Recce. "I will inspect the temple and surrounding area. Watch him closely until I return."

"With pleasure." Recce sat on a nearby rock to keep watch over Medrar while Hector lumbered off, armor rattling with every step.

Medrar took advantage of the opportunity. "How is Drakar? He's done a fine job rounding up the useless inhabitants of Sector 8."

"What do you care?" spat Recce. "It is by the grace of Mandible you are still alive to ring that bell."

"I don't disagree." Medrar changed the subject. "I've heard from some of the rank and file that Hector has done well on his missions. Drakar may be considering a promotion."

Recce became enraged. "Lies! He has done no such thing. Without my presence much would be missed." The scout began fidgeting uncomfortably.

"No truer words have been spoken," lied Medrar. "I don't trust him with good information. He only uses it to further his own cause." He noticed Recce's mood change from indignation to interest.

"What you say is true," responded Recce, staring at the ground in obvious anger ... even if it comes from a lowly bell-ringer."

Medrar ignored the comment. "I didn't want to say anything with Hector present, but I have some news ... it may be a rumor, he cautioned." He paused momentarily to draw the scout's attention.

Recce stood and came closer to Medrar, whispering. "If you are lying, you will be killed. Now, what is this rumor?"

"I've heard there may be an attempt to escape."

Recce's eyes widened. "Where?" He surveyed the surrounding streets, suddenly fearful.

"Not here," Medrar continued. "The rumor was vague, but I heard it might be Sector 4." He purposely chose an area far from the Sector 8 accelerator. "This is very sensitive information. I heard it from one of the Argons."

"They are foul beasts but never tell untruths. Loyal to Butu they are," Recce pondered.

"It is true that we have felt something amiss in the energy fields of the outlying regions but the commanders haven't uncovered the source. Most of the citizens of this city have been captured, but I am sure there are some still at large." Recce spoke to himself as much as to Medrar.

The wheels in his mind were turning, Medrar noticed ... no doubt to the accolades he would receive for uncovering such a plot. A look of affirmation, as if Recce had made his decision, was reflected in a wide grin. Medrar knew he had made up his mind.

"If what you say is true, you will be rewarded when I am promoted." Recce shot Medrar a sinister smile.

If Recce was able to plant the rumor before a successful escape through the accelerator, Medrar knew all hell would break lose ... literally.

Hector came sauntering back with a look of disgust. "You idiot bell-ringer. There was no such breach at the temple. Recce, we waste our time conversing with this sorry excuse for a watchman. If it was up to me, I'd have the Argons suck the life-force from his deformed head. Let's go."

Recce stayed silent. Before the scouts departed back to headquarters, he looked back at Medrar suspiciously. The bell-ringer just nodded back in encouragement.

#

The trio's journey was relatively uneventful. The streets were deserted and the buildings abandoned. Only an occasional flounder-like beast about the size of a small dog could be seen slithering across the road. Its strange squared-off snout sucked the road like a miniature street sweeper.

"Maxim, what is that thing?" Anthony wasn't sure if he should stay away from it.

"Is it dangerous?" asked Tom as he ducked behind a damaged wall.

"It's only a Calluna. An unpleasant looking but harmless beast that ingests minute particles that gather in the streets and ditches, anywhere there is little activity."

They moved out again and surveyed the desolate section of the city, draped in the dimness of a perpetual twilight. As they continued up the road, they heard the sound of a siren in the distance. Anthony and Tom stopped where they stood and listened.

"It means that we are nearing the forbidden region," warned Maxim. "It is a sign of impending danger for those who might be tempted to locate the accelerator. There will be no communicating except for hand signals from here on out."

The landscape was something out of a futuristic horror movie, thought Anthony. He glanced over at Tom who was putting on a brave face. An intense fire could be seen in the distance. At first it looked like a bonfire, but as they moved closer they realized it was a large, round torch sitting on a square stone pedestal. It reminded Anthony of an enormous concrete bird feeder. The siren blared nearby.

Anthony experienced a strong sense of déjà vu and shuddered as he remembered the nightmare that had triggered it. This was the place he had dreamed of! A feeling of dread entered into his mind. He couldn't shake the thought that he was walking toward his ultimate doom. He concentrated on the steady movement of Maxim, just ahead, to keep from contemplating what they were about to attempt. He was anything but confident he would live to tell the story. No one would believe him anyway, he thought grimly.

Maxim stopped short and held up his hand. He quickly motioned them to hide behind a massive light fountain that had long been extinguished. It stood dark and foreboding, a monolith to Nefar's cruelty.

As they hid behind the base of the fountain, two Argon demons appeared from nowhere, sniffing the area like jackals searching for carrion. Their grotesque snouts expanded and contracted like bellows fanning a flame as they frantically sought new victims to satisfy their hunger, satiated only with the extraction of their prey's essence. They were parasites, vampires of the death-realms. Silvery saliva-like material dribbled limply from the sides of their mouths. As the demons jerked their heads sideways in an attempt to spot their prey, gobs of the spittle splattered against the base of the fountain, inches from Anthony's head. They pulled back into the shadows.

In a frenzy, the demons searched every crevice. Then Anthony lost his focus and allowed an errant thought to be telepathically broadcast while the demons were distracted with something on the other side of the courtyard. They stopped dead and quickly turned their heads in his direction.

Anthony and Tom searched Maxim's eyes in a panic. The demons slowly approached the fountain; their blank stares fixed and unblinking on the spot where they hid. Maxim quickly moved around Anthony to act as a shield as demons prepared to pounce.

The Argons stopped when Maxim appeared and seemed confused as what to do next. Then they carefully inched closer as Maxim moved in a semi-circle to his right, away from the fountain. In a deathly dance, the demons and the lone guide circled each other looking for an opportunity to attack.

Anthony was paralyzed with indecision. He huddled in a corner with Tom, unsure whether to stay hidden or run. Then he heard a faint voice inside his head. It was Maxim! He glanced at Tom and could tell he had heard it too.

"Your only chance is to teleport to a place nearby that you can visualize clearly." Maxim kept his gaze on the demons as he spoke.

How do the Argons not hear him? Anthony thought. But there was no time to wonder.

"You did it once when you escaped the cave. You can do it again. The nearest location to visualize is the plasma bubble near the accelerator in Sector 8." Maxim jumped back as one of demons lurched forward. Then they continued to circle each other. "When you materialize, find a place to hide and keep out of sight. Do it now!"

Anthony turned to Tom. They both tried to calm their minds and visualize the clear bubble they had seen on the map. Fear, once again helped them focus. Almost instantly geometric shapes began to swirl around them and they were gone.

The Argons felt the disruption in the energy field as the spirit bodies dematerialized, and turned to the spot behind the fountain.

Lost in Plain Sight

Maxim used their momentary distraction to force an intense burst of light into their personal force fields. He only had a moment. Even with his strength, it was virtually impossible to penetrate an Argon shield when they were focused on their enemy.

It worked. The light penetrated their hard, black, shell-like bodies like a laser. They screamed in pain, clutching at their chests and bellowing like lions. The horrific sound reverberated throughout the entire sector, alerting the sentries, so Maxim quickly teleported to an area near Retarius and the accelerator. The demons slithered on the ground in agony, unaware he had disappeared.

Anthony and Tom appeared behind the plasma bubble. The clear prison cell encased a huge artificial landscape of rolling hills, woods, meadows and a stream. It was somehow lit from within and reminded Anthony of a huge snow globe, without the falling snow.

Viewing from the relative darkness of the surrounding countryside, Retarius could be clearly seen strolling along the banks of a stream meandering through the center of the massive bubble. Anthony wondered how many of these cells, masquerading as idyllic scenes and memories from the past, dotted the territory of Tambora. Could they all be this large and elaborate? It was an enormous undertaking and underscored how much Nefar wanted to control the Fourth Realm. He shook his head in disgust.

They observed the odd scene from behind a large rock ledge that jutted-out from a hill leading to a forest of scrub-brush behind them. Strange looking trees with leaves shaped like giant flint arrowheads dotted the landscape. The sector was still ... almost claustrophobic, thought Anthony. He searched the area near the guard station for any sign of Maxim but saw nothing.

He turned his attention back to Retarius, trapped amongst beautiful trees with spring blossoms, gently rolling hills and meadows filled with colorful wildflowers dancing playfully in an artificial breeze. The sterile setting seemed obscene in its beauty; its prisoner unaware his city was being stolen from underneath him.

THIRTY-THREE

Retarius, the massive warrior and leader of Tambora wandered aimlessly among the rises and depressions of a meadow admiring the wildflowers. Their sweet scent permeated the valley. An errant breeze brushed his cheek as a sense of familiarity overcame his awareness.

I've been here before, he thought. Maybe I never left. For a moment he questioned his presence in the field, but the notion escaped him as quickly as it had appeared in his mind. He continued his stroll through the landscape of his youth as if time stood still.

A deep voice shouted a command to one of the guards. "I told you to monitor his thoughts. He almost broke through the hypnosis. Have you forgotten he was leader of this city … that his mind never rests from seeking escape?"

"No sir," the guard responded hesitantly.

"He is strong. No more lapses!"

"Yes sir," the guard snarled under his breath as the commander turned his attention to the accelerator.

#

Maxim had taken the shape of a tree just off to the side of the plasma bubble but within sight of the accelerator and the entrance to the central square. He needed to be close enough to Retarius to

Lost in Plain Sight

break through to the deepest recesses of his mind, yet unobtrusive enough not to be noticed. Although he was an expert shape-shifter, any guard paying attention might notice the tree had moved from its former location, just moments earlier. Fortunately, the heated exchange between the local commander and the guard responsible for watching Retarius had distracted them from any changes to the surrounding landscape.

Maxim projected his essence into the clear surface of the bubble. Only the most subtle energy of an advanced soul could penetrate the force field and communicate with the prisoner. Even at that, he knew he had to be very close to make it work and not be detected.

Gradually, he tapped into the highest frequencies of his personal energy field. His essence gently floated from the tree and, in the stillness, invisibly pierced the top of the plasma bubble. Using his intention, he guided his awareness down through the branches of a beautiful white birch tree, settling in a small tidal pool created from a tiny tributary that branched off a stream.

Retarius was sitting in the grass staring blankly into the stillness of the pool. Maxim decided to appear as a reflection in the pool so Retarius would recognize him. He stared back at the warrior, as if a water spirit, and gently prodded his mind.

"Retarius, leader of Tambora. This is your friend, Maxim. Wake-up."

Retarius continued to stare into the pool, as though unaware.

Maxim continued. "You have been put to sleep by Nefar. Your city has been attacked and is under his control. Wake-up, my friend."

This time Retarius moved slightly and his eyes tried to focus. Maxim could tell his subconscious was beginning to stir. He reminded his friend of the laughter they had shared over many lives, the battles they fought together and the families they had once loved. Then he broke through with the suggestion to let his mind breathe.

"Retarius, spiritus ... spiritus!"

Retarius' body jerked suddenly, and Maxim quickly calmed his mind. From the pool, he set his eyes on the leader and welcomed him back to reality.

"You are free, my friend."

Retarius began to rise, but Maxim sent a warning. "No sudden moves. You are being watched by Nefar's guards."

Slowly, Retarius became more aware; all the while Maxim soothed his confused mind, blocking any thoughts from escaping and alerting the guards. He explained what had happened to Tambora and how he and the souls who inhabited the realm had been captured. He told him of Nefar's evil plans and how, at this very moment, the ancient destiny was being fulfilled. He instructed Retarius to get up and walk to the stream but keep his mind quiet so as not to bring himself unwanted attention. Finally, he warned him that chaos was about to explode around him but to pretend he was unaware. Help would be on the way. When Maxim had finished he knew that Retarius was fully in the present. The leader's eyes reflected gratitude and understanding.

Privately, even Maxim had his doubts that all the pieces of the plan would all fall into place. It was a lot to ask of two inexperienced souls.

#

Anthony and Tom turned their attention back to the guard station and the accelerator. Two sentries marched back and forth across the front of the portal, inspecting the surrounding area for any suspicious movement. From Anthony's vantage point only the rear of the accelerator could be seen; a black hood-like appendage thrust up through the uneven ground below. An acid-green light projected out from the portal onto the road, forming undulating patterns, as if it were alive.

Across the street, dilapidated buildings and deserted homes stood barricaded, as if someone was trying to silence them from telling their story to whomever would listen. Front yards and empty lots were replaced with freshly dug ditches and temporary structures that looked like shiny black pyramids, the size of mobile homes back on Earth.

Anthony was sure they must be some type of barracks. Did they sleep in these realms, he wondered? Dozens of these strange buildings dotted a huge central square that the citizens of Tambora must have frequented before they were taken away.

They looked for signs of the army, but all they could see were the two sentries dutifully completing their rounds.

"You know this place is crawling with Nefar's spies, demons and every sort of miscreant." Anthony surveyed the scene with disgust.

Tom agreed. "How do we get close to Retarius to let him know we are here to help?" He was clearly agitated and unclear about the plan.

"We don't … leave that to Maxim. Just be ready to enter the accelerator when we see the sign."

"What sign? He never told us exactly what he would do."

"Oh, you'll know." Anthony smiled. "He was never one for unassuming entrances. Just be ready to run."

Tom gave him a look of consternation, which Anthony ignored. They stayed hidden and kept their minds focused by observing the great warrior, who by now hadn't moved for some time. He sat staring down at something they couldn't see. Slowly, he rose, walked over to the stream and kneeled down to wash his face. From Anthony's position, he seemed oblivious to the world just outside his sterile prison. Then, suddenly Retarius looked-up with surprise.

A loud "crack!" startled Anthony and Tom from their observations. They noticed a blue-white flash of light appear at the entrance to the square. Maxim had appeared from nowhere and stood, hands outstretched. A blue stream of light shot from his hands to the tip of each black pyramid in the pattern of a grid.

Anthony heard Maxim in his mind. "Run to the accelerator now!" He could tell from Tom's expression that he had heard it too.

The two sentries had, by now, run toward Maxim, leaving the accelerator unattended. The distraction seemed to be going according to plan. Anthony knew they would realize their mistake and be back in no time. Demons were now streaming out of their shiny black barracks like ants pouring out from a nest.

"There's no time. You must go now!" Maxim pleaded.

The two men jumped out from behind the rocks and made the distance to the accelerator in about ten seconds. Anthony noticed Retarius watching them curiously. He made brief eye contact with the leader and thought he saw a moment of realization cross his face. Did he understand the gravity of the moment?

In the confusion, all eyes were on Maxim. The demon army seemed paralyzed by the mesh of light he had spread over the command post. It was as if he had trapped them in a net made from beams of light.

Anthony and Tom faced the dimensional accelerator. It loomed over them like a giant archway. Tom seemed overwhelmed by the power of the vibrations emanating from the portal. He stepped away, gazing with terror at the undulating swirls of light colliding in an angry storm of acid-green clouds and what seemed to be electrical flashes of light.

"We'll die if we enter that void!" he screamed.

"We'll die if we don't!" Anthony yelled over the noise of the accelerator. They held out their hands, palms-up, closed their eyes and became one with the vibrations. As their spirit bodies became more in tune, the vibrations became less violent and began to smooth out. Then suddenly, both their frequencies matched the vibration of the portal and all sound ceased, with the exception of a beautiful deep musical tone.

Anthony noticed that the swirling clouds had vanished into a clear blue sky. He turned to Tom. He was calm, all fear erased from his face. The hint of a smile reflected a sense of peace.

Anthony began to feel something pulling him toward the accelerator like a magnet. He went with it. No more fighting, he thought. A sense of tranquility and exhilaration, surpassing even that of his out-of-body travels, coursed through him in an instant. The last image he saw was an angry Argon demon rushing toward them as they were pulled instantly into the endless blue void.

THIRTY-FOUR

Everything became clear. There was no time, only the present moment containing pure thought, pure light, pure being ... the seat of consciousness. All was unified as it had always been and always will be ... he had transcended physical life.

Whoosh! Anthony stood in a great hall. Large, white marble tiles stretched as far as the eye could see. Overcome by dizziness, he fell to the floor. From transcendence to reality, just like that, he thought. Except reality was now located in dimensions he didn't understand. It felt like spiritual whiplash, and he wasn't happy about it. Maybe he was dead. This couldn't be a dream. It was too real. He felt as if he would never see the Earth again. For the first time in his travels to the other side he longed for his physical home.

Nothing was in his control.

Pop! Tom appeared about thirty yards away, disoriented. He fell to the floor in a daze.

"Tom! Over here. Are you alright?" Anthony rushed over to his friend.

"Yeah, I'm groggy but fine. Where are we?"

"I don't know. According to Maxim the accelerator was supposed to take us to the Seventh Dimension but it looks deserted."

They looked around what appeared to be a great hall. Marble pedestals with strange looking sculptures were scattered about as

Lost in Plain Sight

far as they could see. Each occupied an area the size of half a city block with nothing in between them except an endless expanse of polished marble tiles.

They decided to inspect the nearest of the sculptures. As they moved closer, it was obvious they were enormous. They stood at least ten feet tall and almost as wide.

Anthony marveled at its strange beauty. They felt its power radiate outward, blocking them from getting any closer. It vibrated, emitting a deep, powerful hum, like a neon sign. Energy seemed to emanate from the inanimate object like an electrical field.

Anthony didn't want to touch it and neither did Tom, judging by the distance he was keeping from the monument. Anthony studied the design. He had seen this shape before, but where?

"A symbol!" he jumped back, startling Tom.

"Why'd you have to do that?" Tom croaked as he got up off the floor. "Scared me half to death."

"Sorry. We ended up in the right place, alright. This is it!"

"What are you saying?"

"The Realm of Symbols. Don't you see? This is one of them ... for real." Anthony slowly moved closer to the sculpture, awed by the sight.

"Okay. It's a symbol. They're all over the place. So now what?"

Anthony ignored his friend as he contemplated what the symbol might represent. He stared deeply at the center of the design and then outward to the edges. It was round, ringed in a beautiful deep yellow-gold about ten inches wide. He looked as closely as he could at undecipherable markings etched into the outer band ... almost like hieroglyphics or ancient runes. But he couldn't understand what they meant. Four wavy lines originated at the border of the band from different points on the perimeter and met within a circle in the center. Yet these lines seemed to be suspended with nothing to hold them up. Without thinking, he reached out to touch them but jumped back, repelled by some kind of force field. The disturbance seemed to have woken the symbol. It stretched like a rubber-band and then peered down at them. Anthony and Tom stared at the living symbol, dumbfounded and ready to run.

The circle in the middle of the ring had become a large pupil that stared at them with an occasional blink. Anthony felt as if he'd been thrust into a living cartoon. He couldn't take his eyes off the thing. Tom lay next to him staring into the enormous eye as he slowly crawled backward on his rear-end.

"Don't be afraid." Its voice echoed throughout the endless chamber. "We will not hurt you." It leaned closer to the floor for a better look at the two travelers. Anthony and Tom slid back and away from the enormous blinking eye.

Anthony spoke first. "Who are you?"

"I am the Symbol of Unity. These lines represent the different pathways we can take in life toward our ultimate goal. Because we are all imperfect beings with free will, the pathways meander. I am a reflection of the unevenness and fragmented nature of life but also an affirmation that no matter which paths we choose we all arrive at the center ... the circle of unity. May I ask why have you come?"

"We have been sent here by my guide to ask for help. Tambora has been taken over by Nefar's army of the damned," Anthony explained.

The symbol pulled back quickly, as if taken by surprise. "If what you say is true, the Fourth Realm could be lost and the middle realms in danger." The symbol let out a loud metallic call that shook the floor of the great hall.

Slowly, one by one, the symbols that had stood silent throughout the chamber came to life. They stretched and turned toward the two travelers with expressions of curiosity, then stepped down off their pedestals and moved toward them. Some merely lifted off their bases and floated over like a bizarre army of cartoon characters. Their movement was so freakish that Tom sat frozen to the floor, staring in disbelief.

Anthony tried to calm him down. "It's okay. They're here to help. Maxim wouldn't have sent us here if there was a chance they would harm us." This seemed to relax Tom. He picked himself off the floor to cautiously greet the symbols face-to-face.

The first to approach was another circular symbol with the same curious markings etched into a gold band around its perimeter. It seemed to be the leader. Anthony noticed that the design, suspended in the middle of the circle, differed from the first symbol. Rather than four wavy lines meeting in the middle, this one had a large swirl. The giant symbol stopped not ten feet in front

Lost in Plain Sight

of them. The rest stayed behind, standing or suspended in silence. Then it spoke.

"Welcome to the Seventh Realm, where the universal symbols of life reside. I am the Symbol of Consciousness, also known as the life-force and spiritual protector. What brings you here, travelers?"

Tom gestured for Anthony to speak. "I'm Anthony and this is Tom. My guide, Maxim—"

"Maxim?" interrupted the symbol. The other symbols began to chatter among themselves. "Quiet, my friends," he commanded. "If Maxim sent you, we are at your service. He has assisted this realm on many occasions. Tell us what he needs." The symbol moved closer with obvious interest in what Anthony had to say next.

Anthony and Tom took a step back. "He ... we need your help to free Retarius, the leader—"

"We know of Retarius," interrupted the symbol a second time. "Continue."

"He is trapped, as are most of the citizens of Tambora. They have been imprisoned by Nefar. We are no match for his army of demons. Retarius must be released so he can help us free the city. By now, our escape is known to Nefar and his commanders. Maxim cannot continue to hold them back on his own, and they will surely retaliate!" Anthony could feel the panic rising in his voice.

"Be calm, Anthony ... or should I say Tabor." The swirls in the great symbol formed a smile.

"How did you—" Anthony began.

"I am the Symbol of Consciousness. I recognize all energy, all awareness, no matter how unique. You are no different. Nor are you, Rad." The symbol turned to Tom.

"Of course you would know," acknowledged Tom.

"You were born from the spirit world," continued the Symbol of Consciousness. "As are all humans. You spiral outward as you live your lives and develop as souls. Ultimately, you return to your source, your origins. There are no exceptions."

"Is that what you represent?" asked Tom.

"It is," responded the symbol. "However, before we can help you we must seek the assistance of the Realm of Music. Only the notes have the high frequencies needed to break the force fields that trap Retarius and—"

Anthony heard a commotion at the far end of the chamber. Everyone turned in the direction of the noise but could see nothing. They all rushed to the spot and peered downward through what looked like a large glass window to a courtyard below. It was dotted with whimsical looking trees, straight out of a Dr. Seuss book, and white benches placed around beautiful multicolored light fountains. There, standing amongst an army of musical notes milling about the courtyard was Daniel, looking directly up at them.

THIRTY-FIVE

Anthony couldn't believe his eyes. He turned to Tom. "It's my son!"

Tom's eyes widened and the biggest smile Anthony had seen yet from his friend, lit-up his face. "What are you waiting for … go see him."

The symbols chimed-in. "Yes, go to him!"

Anthony's desire to see Daniel was so great that he teleported to his side immediately without another thought. For a moment, they stared at each other in amazement before throwing their arms around each other. Anthony couldn't help himself and cried like a baby. The courtyard became silent as Tom, the symbols and the notes witnessed the emotional scene.

Anthony stepped back to look Daniel, relieved he was safe. "You look well."

"So do you, Dad," Daniel laughed. "You don't look much older than me. Go to the pool at the base of that fountain and look at your reflection."

Anthony hadn't much thought of what he looked like in his spirit body but remembered how young and beautiful Diane appeared when he saw her after the accident. He approached the pool and peered over the edge. A wave of surprise came over him. He looked twenty years younger!

A voice bellowed behind him. "Your spirit body is a reflection of your human form at its best," the Symbol of Consciousness explained.

Anthony noticed again how acute his eyesight had become. He could see every minute detail of the courtyard, symbol and note. His distance vision was astounding. He surveyed the massive buildings that made up the complex where the symbols lived. After having a moment to think, he turned to Daniel with an urgent question. "How did you arrive here?" Had Daniel died? Fear suddenly coursed through him in anticipation of the answer.

"No, Dad. Professor Ross warned us you were in trouble."

"How did he know?"

"In his dreams ... he saw you. He came to me and Emily and led us to a secret place. There was a rock—"

"A gateway," answered a symbol with the head of an eagle. "I am the Symbol of Courage. You soared above your fears and crossed the veil from the physical world you knew to the after-death dimensions you had forgotten, to find and save your father. It was your intention that brought you to the place you desired to be."

"And now that I'm here we can return," Daniel replied.

Anthony desperately wanted to go back home with his son, but the symbols and notes had done so much for them already. Tom had become a true friend through all the danger. He thought of Retarius, alone and trapped, of Maxim holding off a legion of demons, and of Medrar distracting the scouts so they could make their escape. So much had been sacrificed by so many to help him. How could he just leave?

"Daniel, the professor was correct. I was ... am in trouble. But there are others in more danger at this very moment. They are relying on us to return and help them."

"I don't understand. What can you do for them?"

Anthony explained how he had been taken prisoner by the demon, Maloda; the same entity that had attacked Daniel ... how he met Tom, their escape to the city of Tambora, of Medrar, Maxim and Retarius and the consequences of a victory by Nefar.

As he spoke, Anthony noticed that Daniel's expression became thoughtful, as if he was beginning to understand. The symbols and notes listened intently, gasping as he described the dangerous encounters and the fate of Retarius and Tambora. When he was done, there was silence. Only the sound of the light-fountain spraying droplets of light into the pools nearby could be heard.

"Then we must help Retarius and defeat Nefar. Tambora and the Fourth Realm must be freed," Daniel agreed.

The notes rose up and sounded a powerful symphonic battle hymn in support of the decision, and the symbols all agreed they would help. The Symbol of Consciousness stepped forward and asked for calm.

"We all agree that we must help Maxim and Retarius," he bellowed, "but it is not as simple as one would hope. The same fate awaits us if we do not plan carefully. Bass Clef, are you here?" Everyone turned toward the notes.

From the rear, a bass clef floated over the notes, past Daniel and stopped in front of Anthony and the symbols. It turned on its side so that the two dots became eyes and the C shape became a thick mustache that moved up and down as it spoke. "Symbol of Consciousness, how may I help?" it boomed.

"I believe you are familiar with the plasma bubbles that Nefar uses to trap his victims?"

"I am. We once freed a soul group that became lost traveling through the Third Realm. They were intercepted in the swamp lands and imprisoned within the plasma bubbles of which you speak."

"How was this accomplished?" asked the symbol.

"With a combination of very low frequencies to make the force field unstable. That was followed by an attack from hundreds of our sixteenth and thirty-second notes at very high frequencies to burst open the force field from all sides."

"And it worked?"

"Yes, with great effort. You describe an entire city blanketed with these cells. It would take a massive army of notes attacking simultaneously to defeat them."

"Can this be accomplished?" The Symbol of Consciousness became extremely serious in his tone.

"It is possible but only with permission from the Council of Elders. We would need to call notes away from their duties in several dimensions and assemble within striking distance in the Fifth Realm."

"I will speak with them," spoke a symbol in the back of the group. It was shaped like a torch and emanated a beautiful white halo. "I will seek permission from the Elders."

"Thank you, Symbol of Light. We will discuss a plan of attack while you speak with the council in hopes of their permission. You are free to go." The Symbol of Light zoomed off like a slingshot as the Symbol of Consciousness turned to Anthony, Daniel and Tom.

"Some of us can accompany you, others must stay. We will allow you, Tabor, to choose ten among us, representing the ten dimensions that may help you the most." Then, the symbol proceeded to explain what each symbol represented.

Anthony considered his choices. "First, I choose the Symbol of Consciousness. You came to us first." The symbol nodded respectfully. "Without consciousness, we don't exist. Next, the Symbol of Light, Love, Belief, Hope, Humanity, Humility, Courage, Responsibility and Action."

Each symbol respectfully stepped forward, with the exception of the Symol of Light who was already on its way to the Council of Elders.

"Everyone gather around me," the Symbol of Consciousness gently commanded.

Anthony, Daniel and Tom stepped closer to the massive symbol as the notes surrounded them.

"Many souls, many consciousnesses from countless dimensions and realms within are sacrificing themselves to assist you." The symbol looked at each of them. "Tabor, by choosing to return to Tambora, you may forfeit your return back to physical reality. Do you understand this?" He searched Anthony's eyes for acknowledgement.

"Yes, I understand."

"Dad!" Daniel protested, but Anthony raised his hand for him to stop.

"You have a destiny that is strong, but the future is never certain. If the fates are on your side and you are able to re-enter the physical plane again, then we ask for something in return; something unselfish and of immense value to your fellow humans experiencing the trials of physical reality."

"What is it that you wish me to do?"

"We will infuse your mind with the ancient, universal truths that early humans knew and understood. Humankind has separated themselves from nature and their spiritual source. This separation has caused devastating destruction to your planet, your relationships between peoples and nations, your very psyche. The joy of existence has been lost. Touch the human spirit. They will know you speak the truth. We will give you the gift of reaching that dormant portion of their awareness that allows them to awaken."

"I will be honored, but what are these truths?"

"They are simple, as are all the great truths."

Everyone leaned in a little closer to the great Symbol of Consciousness.

"Consciousness exists in the present moment. In that moment, each of you creates your own reality through your beliefs, thoughts and actions. Every human, no matter their condition has that ability. There are no exceptions. That is all."

The symbol paused to allow Anthony and his friends to absorb what had just been imparted to them. He had heard it before from Maxim, but somehow coming from the Symbol of Consciousness, it radiated a force that he had not expected.

The symbol continued. "The power of truth is undeniable. Feel it in your heart ... in the deepest recesses of your soul—that knowing part of you. Heed that intuition. It is the wisest part of your spirit."

"If I'm able to return to Earth, I'll pass the knowledge on to all who will listen."

"A word of caution. Nefar, Butu and Maloda are aware of your destiny. They know that if you are successful in making even a handful of humans aware of these basic truths, buried in the sub-conscious for hundreds of generations, their power to rule the physical and after-death realms through fear will be diminished. They won't allow it. You are Enemy Number 1."

THIRTY-SIX

The Symbol of Light appeared unannounced before the Council of Elders, interrupting an important debate regarding the life selection staging areas. It stood alone in the large circular auditorium facing the twelve sacred ones. The space seemed immense and was capped by an ornate domed ceiling. Beautiful white light streamed in from all directions.

An Elder wearing a deep purple robe and a beautiful golden medallion rose to greet the symbol with a warm smile. His medallion reflected the meaning of those souls that stood before him. For the Symbol of Light it carried the sign of the Sun's rays; straight lines beginning at the perimeter of the circle like spokes on a wheel and coming to a point in the center. The symbol understood that the sign represented universal support from all the Elders on the council for its actions.

"Welcome, symbol," spoke the Elder in the center of the twelve council members. "What brings you to the council? This is most unusual."

"Sacred ones. I have the most urgent of news."

"Does it have any connection to the disturbance we are sensing in the Fourth Realm?" answered the Elder.

The others ceased their conversations and took their seats at the long table.

"Indeed it does." The symbol told the council about the visit from Tabor, Cometes and Rad, the takeover of Tambora by Nefar and the imprisonment of Retarius. "The symbols and notes seek permission to confront Nefar's army before Tambora and the Fourth Realm are lost." The symbol waited for a response as the council whispered amongst each other. Finally, the leader of the council rose again to address the symbol.

"The time of change and the time to act are upon Tabor. His mission is of great importance to all in these realms, to humans on Earth and to the progression of his soul as he overcomes the obstacles set down in the Sphere of Destiny. Go forth with our blessing."

"I will pass the word and we will embark immediately. Thank you, wise ones." The members of the council watched the symbol disappear down the hallway leading out of the chamber.

The Symbol of Light returned to the courtyard to report to the Symbol of Consciousness as the notes were arranging themselves into a formidable percussive notation. Booming whole and half-notes supported eighth and sixteenth notes to create sharp and powerful military marches. The Treble and Bass Clefs had suspended themselves over the throngs of notes as they formed the dissonant melodies and chords that would be necessary to burst open the plasma bubbles. The cacophony of sound permeated every corner of the expansive courtyard as well as the interior of the great hall.

After being briefed, the Symbol of Consciousness stood on a nearby pedestal, his voice booming over the sounds of music interspersed with excited chatter. "My friends ... we have word from The Council." The courtyard quieted as everyone focused their attention on the symbol, his swirls moving like lips. "The Council of Elders has approved our plan." The courtyard exploded with cheers. "Quiet! Please. This battle is fraught with danger. Many will not return." A hush came over the notes. "Some will be ingested into the evil energy of the demons and trapped as if their souls were truly extinguished. Others will be taken away to the lower realms where escape may not be possible and many will be put through unimaginable pain ... but we fight for the light and All That Is! Their power is strong but we must be stronger. Are you prepared for the battle that will reverberate across the universe?"

"Yes!" Anthony, Tom, Daniel, the notes and symbols all rose as one.

In the distance, the sound of a magnificent symphony could be heard. Anthony turned and looked past the courtyard into the vastness of the Seventh Realm and saw movement. At first, it appeared as a long horizontal black line on the horizon. As it drew closer, it grew in size and the sound became louder. He began to make out what looked like a gigantic sheet of music spread out to the horizon. It rose up from the ground to one hundred feet, filled with musical parts for every type of instrument. All the notes expanded and contracted as they played themselves in a wonderfully coordinated piece that Anthony had never heard before. He glanced over at Tom and Daniel who seemed equally fascinated by the performance. The multitude of notes floated over to the courtyard as a unit, became silent and paused in front of Anthony and the symbols.

The notes who had accompanied Daniel to the Realm of Symbols were also silent for a moment before bursting out of the courtyard to greet their long-lost friends from the other dimensions. The Symbol of Consciousness allowed them to finish their joyous reunion and then spoke.

"My friends, we thank you for joining with us to defeat the evil that has engulfed our cousins in the Fourth Realm. Your family of notes from the Seventh Dimension will brief you on our strategy to free Tambora. The time to act is upon us. Let us be one in spirit!"

A huge roar filled the Realm of Symbols as everyone took their places and prepared to leave for the mission.

#

Recce and Hector teleported back to Sector 8 headquarters to report to Drakar. They rushed through the pyramid shaped barracks, passing by countless entities from the lower realms that had been drawn into the conflict.

"It looks like Butu dragged-out every demon he could find. This place is choking with them," snarled Hector.

Recce was half-listening, intent on getting the news of a possible escape to Drakar. He would surely be rewarded for his information with a promotion and finally overshadow his undeserving partner. He laughed to himself as he glanced at Hector in disgust.

"What are you looking at?" growled Hector, catching Recce's eye.

"Oh nothing. Absolutely nothing," Recce grumbled.

They came to the largest structure in the encampment, an enormous black pyramid with a triangular entry. It was large enough to easily allow an eight-foot Argon demon to pass through. Two silent guards stood at either side of the door with force-field cannons at the ready for anyone attempting to enter uninvited. A green light, also in the shape of triangle, threw out a beam of light which was directed at matching emblems on the chests of the two scouts. The light switched off, and the door rose silently into the pyramid wall.

They entered the darkness and stepped onto two disks of light that were illuminated from underneath the floor. Six other disks were scattered about the interior but nothing else was visible in the blackness. As soon as they took their positions, a green cylinder of light rose from the perimeter of the disks, engulfing them. Once it had risen above their heads, the light began to swirl clockwise around them, slowly at first but increasing in speed, until the two scouts had disappeared.

Just as quickly, they arrived, standing on two similar light disks at Drakar's headquarters. The commander was waiting. His yellow eyes bore into the pair like a drill.

"Well, you both finally decided to return. I almost sent my sentries after you. Why the delay?"

"That bell-ringer sent us looking for nothing but a couple of pitiful Callunas scraping the alleyways in Sector 4," barked Hector. "The entire area was deserted."

"I'm surprised at you, Hector. We felt a disturbance in that quadrant and you found nothing?" Drakar spat.

Hector backed off. "No sir. I searched it thoroughly."

"Get out of my sight, you useless shape shifter."

Hector bowed respectfully and left the room, stone-faced. Drakar shifted his attention to Recce. "You seem strangely silent, Recce."

Recce smiled sinisterly. "I have information." He could barely hold his excitement and anticipation.

"Really? Well, tell me then." Drakar moved uncomfortably close to the diminutive scout.

Recce leaned in hesitantly toward the imposing commander. "The bell-ringer confided in me."

"Oh did he? And what did he say?"

"He said there was a rumor going around of an escape from—"

"Escape!" Drakar screamed. "Impossible! No one has escaped from Tambora." His snout was inches from Recce's face. "And no one will," he whispered. "Ugh!" he scoffed at the surprised scout, but his eyes reflected worry. He began to pace back and forth, deep in thought, while Recce crept backwards.

"Where do you think you're going, you sniveling little—?"

"Nowhere sir. I'm just telling you what he said."

The commander began muttering to himself. "I'll have to tell Mandible. Butu and Maloda will know in no time. Complications!" He ripped a holographic projector off the wall and threw it across the room. Then, he turned to Recce and sneered. "Get out!" Recce stared blankly at the commander. "Get out, now!"

Recce skulked out of the commander's office, mumbling under his breath.

There's no choice in the matter, thought Drakar. I must tell Mandible. If it turns out to be false, we'll dispose of Recce. "He is useless anyway," he hissed. If it's true, he thought, better that I get to him before something happens on my watch. He held his talon-like hands over the dashboard that gave him direct communication with the mid-level commander. He liked the device. No errant thoughts could be intercepted by traitors and spies. The place is teeming with them now, he thought suspiciously.

Almost immediately, a holographic heads-up display appeared suspended before him. He placed a long fingernail over a red light located on the bottom-center of the three dimensional light beam, and Mandible's dog-like face filled the large screen.

"What is the meaning of this? I told you never to use this channel unless there was a true emergency. There has been no such breach detected," snarled the commander.

"I am aware of this, sir. However, I received news from one of my scouts that there may be an escape attempt, possibly from Sector 4."

Lost in Plain Sight

Mandible's image formed into an ugly scowl. "I have heard of no such thing. All the quadrants are secured. Every accelerator is guarded. There have been no reports—"

Suddenly, Mandible turned away as if someone had entered his headquarters. After a moment, he turned back to Drakar, the slits of his golden eyes reflecting a worried expression.

"I must go. Create a perimeter around Sector 8. Your warning has come to pass." The screen went dark.

Drakar stared into the blank screen in shock. How could it be? Every square inch of Tambora was being watched. "In *my* sector!" he screamed. He teleported immediately to the Sector 8 accelerator to interrogate the sentries in charge.

THIRTY-SEVEN

Maxim released the web of light he was maintaining over the barracks. He had successfully prevented the soldiers and demons from reaching Anthony and Tom during their escape, but now he was exhausted. He vanished as the sentries charged the spot where he had been standing.

By this time, Retarius was fully aware of the situation but pretended not to notice the pandemonium that had broken-out around his prison cell.

The two sentries who had guarded the accelerator were stunned and taken away. Nefar's infantry poured through the gates onto the main road and fanned-out over the surrounding countryside in search of other intruders. Flashes of light burst out across the massive central square as reinforcements from other parts of the city teleported to the scene to assist.

Three green shock waves sounded in the middle of the square in front of Drakar's headquarters as Nefar, Maloda and Butu appeared to survey the commotion.

"Silence!!" screamed Butu.

Almost instantly, the throngs of Nefar's army stopped in their tracks and became silent. All eyes turned toward Nefar and his two lieutenants.

"Drakar!" snarled Maloda. "Step forward." Her black eyes were set on the commander as he stood before his superiors.

"Tell me what happened," Nefar inquired, almost gently.

Drakar knew his fate hung in the balance. "I had received word of a possible escape plot and reported it immediately to Commander Mandible," he responded nervously.

"And who told you about this plot?"

"My scout, Recce."

"Step forward, Recce!" yelled Butu.

The diminutive scout appeared from out of the crowd, shaking with fear. Nearby, Hector chuckled at his partner's predicament.

Nefar continued. "Is this true?"

"Yes ... sir," he squeaked.

"And where did *you* come by this information?"

Recce answered without hesitation. "The bell-ringer, Medrar."

Nefar turned to Maloda. "Find this bell-ringer and bring him to me now!" His voice echoed throughout the central square.

"Gladly, Master Nefar," she growled, disappearing into the twilight.

The soldiers filling the great square stirred and began conversing among themselves as Butu stepped forward. "Silence!" he screamed a second time.

All became still again. Only the thrashing sound of the accelerator could be heard from across the main road. The angry green clouds reflected off the shiny black walls of the pyramid behind Nefar and Butu. The two leaders stared menacingly into the crowd as the reflection of the portal danced like leaping flames in their jet-black eyes.

"We will wait," commanded Nefar. "It won't take long for Maloda to find this bell-ringer you speak of, Recce. We'll get to the bottom of this treason."

Recce trembled as two Argon demons stood on either side of him.

"Just in case you have any ideas of escape," Nefar sneered. He turned away to discuss something with Butu.

At that moment, Maloda reappeared with Medrar who was restrained by two of her elite warriors. A deafening roar filled the square as the legions of soldiers demanded that he be executed.

"Traitor! Throw him into the River of Sorrows for all eternity!"

Nefar raised his hands and the crowd fell silent. He turned to Medrar. "Does Recce speak the truth about you, bell-ringer? Did you warn him of the escape?" He looked directly into Medrar's eyes.

"Yes—"

The warriors raised their weapons as one. "Traitor! Give him to the Argons!!" Two fearsome demons stepped forward, silver saliva dripping from their jaws, eager to do their bidding.

"And how did you know of this escape when not even the local commander was aware?" He shot a nasty glance at Drakar, who diverted his eyes.

"A rumor—"

"Lies!" He struck Medrar across the face and knocked him to the ground. He turned to Maloda. "It matters not. Impale him on the tip of this pyramid and allow the Argons to rip him apart and remove his essence. Make it slow and painful."

#

Maxim reappeared behind the plasma bubble. He watched Medrar courageously stand his ground, only to be attacked and dragged away to be executed. For the first time, he was worried. He couldn't fight them all himself, he thought. Had Tabor been able to get help?

He saw movement from inside the bubble. Retarius had spotted him and seemed to be trying to communicate through the force field. Maxim could tell by his expression that he had seen the dramatic capture of Medrar. He also knew that Nefar allowed the prisoners to selectively hear what was going on outside their cells because there was nothing they could do to help. It was a mind game to demoralize them. It proved to be especially effective against a proud leader like Retarius.

He tried to signal that help was on the way but Retarius seemed in a panic and had begun pacing and banging against the force field in frustration. Maxim was hopeful the symbols and notes would be on their way but when? He tried to calm his mind and renewed his faith in Tabor's destiny.

Lost in Plain Sight

At that moment, an energy wave burst from the accelerator. Thousands of musical notes streamed across the main road into the huge square. They began their attack on Nefar's warriors like a swarm of hungry mosquitoes. A majestic symphony underscored the moment, becoming the sound track for the battle. The music perfectly reflected the dramatic scene as fights began to break out amongst the barracks.

By themselves, the notes couldn't defeat the powerful army, but they created the diversion the whole and half-notes needed to surround the plasma bubble and attempt to free Retarius, who was now cheering them on. They had already released an entire battalion of his soldiers imprisoned outside the city limits. Hundreds approached the great square as Nefar's army took their positions.

Nefar, Maloda and Butu scrambled up a nearby hill for a better look at the battle that had suddenly erupted.

"The great fight for Tambora has begun!" Nefar screamed. "Not since the dark days before the Christ when the middle realms were at our mercy, has so much been at stake." He raised both arms high in the air as he continued his rant. "That time is at hand again!!" He pointed to his fighting masses attacking Retarius's returning soldiers. "The Fourth Realm is within our grasp! We will rise!!" he shouted gleefully.

Meanwhile, an Argon demon spotted Maxim and rushed over to slash him to pieces with a spirit mangler. Maxim recognized the weapon at once and ducked as it swooshed over his head. Even he could be hurt by the mangler, designed to scatter a spirit body into fragments. He held the Argon at bay using his light energy but was nearly depleted. The imposing demon was dangerously close to overtaking him.

He glanced back to the plasma bubble to catch the attention of the notes, but they were busy building-up low frequencies to blast open the transparent prison cell that held Retarius. As he fought on, thousands of notes waited silently behind a nearby hill for the sign to attack the force field, now surrounded by battle.

In the chaos, more notes spewed through the portal as if shot from a fire hose. They were followed by Anthony, Tom, Daniel and the symbols as they burst through the opening and were thrown onto the main road. A sentry shot at them with a force field cannon. It missed hitting them directly and destroyed one of the guard stations. The shock wave knocked them down a hill and into a ravine.

In the confusion, Medrar managed to get free and steal a photon generator from one of the distracted Argons. It was a devastating weapon. He aimed it at the two demons that had forced him to the tip of the pyramid and blew them to pieces. Their bodies exploded into a million tiny particles that rained over the fighting masses below.

He spotted Anthony, Tom and a young man he didn't recognize as they reappeared over the ridge next to the accelerator looking dazed. He slid down the pyramid, fighting off soldiers as he ran toward his friends. A demon noticed him running out of the square and jumped in front of the surprised bell-ringer. Medrar skidded to a stop as it lunged toward him. He had just enough time to pull out the photon generator, obliterating the beast where it stood.

By this time, he had lost sight of Anthony and Tom. He decided to fight his way through the masses to get a better view while newly freed reinforcements clashed in a ghastly dance of destruction with Nefar's warriors.

Anthony, Tom and Daniel searched up and down the main road, looking for an opportunity to join the fight, but the area was so thick with flailing limbs and exploding bodies that entering into the fray was nearly impossible. They jumped behind a large boulder and watched Retarius to see how he was doing.

The noise was deafening. A battle hymn sounded throughout the square, intermingled with scattered high frequency bursts as the notes attacked groups of the most dangerous demons. The whole and half notes had positioned themselves just outside the plasma bubble and sounded an impossibly low frequency that could be heard, or rather felt, throughout the valley. The plasma bubble began to shake, as did the ground beneath it.

The notes that had been positioned on a nearby hillside, waited for the frequencies to hit a certain pitch. They were ready to rush forth en-mass to break open the force field and free Retarius. Anthony spotted him crouching behind a tree, sword at the ready.

A huge explosion rattled the barracks in the great square, as an entire battalion of demons were blown into tiny black spheres by the ultra-high frequencies of the notes.

Others stood stunned, unable to think as their minds filled with numbing white noise.

On cue, the sixteenth and thirty-second notes launched out from the hillside and commenced a withering attack on the force field bubble that had sealed Retarius inside. The high-pitched frequencies increased in intensity until the force field weakened and finally exploded with a tremendous boom. Notes flew in every direction from the blast.

Retarius, who had found refuge in a cave, emerged and stood in the meadow a free man. He raised his golden sword high over his head and let out a triumphant cry, jumping into the fray and disappearing amongst the masses of fighters.

Four demons spotted Anthony, Tom and Daniel behind the boulder. They approached rapidly, carrying long poles tipped on both ends with large claw-like hooks. The trio was surrounded. Anthony shouted at Daniel to run, but Maxim appeared from nowhere and whisked him away from the raging battle before the demons could react.

Anthony and Tom turned their attention back to the attackers who were moving together as one. They raised the weapons over their ghastly heads, spinning them as they moved-in on the defenseless men. Anthony quickly nodded to Tom, indicating he should take the two demons to his right. He would take on the other two.

One of the beasts dove forward toward Anthony and brought the deadly weapon straight down over him as if it was wielding an axe. He quickly moved to his left, side-stepped the attacker and thrust the heel of his hand into its soft underbelly, just below the hard shell of its chest. The creature groaned in pain as one of the claws at the end of the pole came swooshing down over his right shoulder and gouged a hole on the ground.

The second demon swung the pole directly at his head, but Anthony ducked again. The claw found the belly of the first demon. It collapsed to the ground.

Enraged, the second demon tried to hit Anthony square on the crown of his head but he jumped backwards and the weapon crashed into the dirt on the main road. Rocks scattered in every direction. Sensing an opportunity, Anthony jumped onto the pole before the creature had a chance to raise it again and used it as leverage to kick the monster directly in the eyes. It immediately dropped the weapon, covering its face in pain. Anthony grabbed the pole and brought it down on the demon's neck. It doubled over and dropped like a sandbag.

He briefly felt a sense of regret for having killed the beast, but quickly refocused on helping Tom who was still battling both his demons. Anthony raised the pole over his right shoulder. With all his strength, he cut down one of the demons from behind, hitting it on one of its grotesque rear-pointing knees. It made a sickly crunch as the creature screamed and fell backward onto the road. The other demon turned around and let out a deafening roar. Ignoring Tom, it jumped over its wounded comrade, now thrashing about on the ground, and pointed the claw-tipped pole directly at Anthony's chest. He was caught off-guard by the demon's speed and froze. Time stood still and death seemed inevitable. A loud "crack" broke through his stupor and the demon crashed to the ground in front of him.

There, standing with a hammer in his massive right hand, was Medrar, smiling. Tom jumped up and patted him on the back while Anthony, exhausted and on one knee, gazed up at his friend and shouted, "Thank you!"

"My friends, we've far more problems than these two creatures!" Medrar yelled over the din of battle. "Look around you. Maxim asked me to take you to safety while Retarius and his army finish the job. Come with me!"

Medrar ran ahead. A tall, heavy-set soldier wearing black armor noticed him and raised a photon cannon in his direction. Before he could pull the trigger, Medrar threw his hammer and hit the warrior square in the face. He fell to the ground in a heap. Anthony and Tom watched, stunned at his speed and accuracy.

"What are you two waiting for? You look like demons thrust into the light of day. I can take care of myself. Come ... quickly!"

They caught up with Medrar, dashing urgently away from the main road. Exhausted, they followed him up the hillside to their original lookout position where they saw Daniel surveying the battle. After a brief reunion, the four comrades crouched behind a large rock. From this vantage point they could see the entire city.

"Everyone ... look over there." Anthony pointed to explosions in the distance. The notes had spread-out over the landscape, releasing the citizens and soldiers of Tambora from their prisons.

Force fields burst open one-by-one like glass bubbles spewing multicolored rays of light into the dusky sky. The horizon lit-up like a fireworks display. Hundreds of soldiers joined thousands of musical notes and continued their attack on Nefar's army across the entire city. They formed massive groups and then split-off in every direction, pounding enemy battalions attempting to send their own reinforcements to the plasma bubbles that had been breached in every part of Tambora. But it was too late for Nefar's legions. The tide was turning and Retarius's newly freed army had gained the advantage.

Maloda and Butu regrouped in a panic as the battle raged on, but Nefar calmly surveyed the chaos. He raised his hand and ordered them to stop their bickering.

"Our forces will prevail!" he shouted.

The green clouds of the accelerator collided in an angry soup of magnetic energy, lapping outward like talons grasping for a nearby victim, while Nefar's unblinking eyes surveyed the carnage spread out before him.

Retarius had joined with the symbols as they fought their way through the great square toward the leaders now perched on top of the largest pyramid. The symbols of light, love, humanity and courage turned their attention to the damned that had been forced by Nefar to fight the great battle or be thrown into the River of Sorrows for eternity. The symbols were able to identify them by the auras that projected around their spirit bodies. They faced the warriors individually, infusing their tortured souls with the best attributes inherent in each of them. One-by-one they awoke from their condemned state and accepted the invitation to change their beliefs and ultimately their realities.

Nefar now watched in horror as the transformed souls of the damned joined Retarius's newly freed soldiers and turned on his conscripted legions. Slowly, they began to beat them back. Maloda snarled at the scene while Butu blamed her for their predicament.

"It's all your fault. This was your plan!" he spat.

"Despicable idiot! These are your regiments," she replied with disgust. "They cannot fight a ragtag army and a handful of symbols and notes?!"

"Enough!!" raged Nefar. His voice echoed throughout the city.

Thousands of warriors turned to listen to their leader, and the fighting gradually ceased.

"The stench of Tambora would fill our senses without pause if we had to embrace it into our pure dimensions. Let us leave this foul place at once!"

Retarius and the Symbol of Consciousness came before the three leaders. "A wise choice, Nefar. You were well on your way to defeat," spoke Retarius defiantly. His powerful voice matched the now silent Lord of the Dark Realms. The symbols continued to wake the souls of the damned, and the square became quiet.

In the distance, a great horn sounded, filling the city with its fearsome call.

"We will return ... and sooner than you think," warned Nefar as he, Maloda and Butu faded away.

Slowly, the demons and warriors that hadn't been slaughtered vanished from the great square along with the pyramids and the remnants of the prisons that had dotted the landscape. The swirling green clouds that had filled the dimensional accelerators turned a clear blue-white, and the twilight that had smothered the Fourth Realm gradually gave way to the comfortable yellow hue that marked the City of Hope.

THIRTY-EIGHT

Anthony, Medrar, Tom and Daniel stepped-out from behind the rock outcropping to view the valley and the outskirts of the city. Anthony took in the atmosphere that had suddenly become lighter. Despite the fact that there was no air in these realms, he could feel the sensation of breathing as if he was back in his physical body. He could smell the flowers, hear the nearby streams and feel a breeze on his face. The barren landscape had been transformed in the blink of an eye.

"Anthony."

He recognized the voice at once and turned to see Diane standing near a small pond. Her familiar energy radiated toward him. After a moment of hesitation, he ran over to embrace her.

Medrar, Tom and Daniel looked on as Retarius and the symbols left the great square and came up the hill toward them. The notes brought up the rear playing an exultant symphony.

Anthony was in ecstasy as his spirit merged with Diane's. After a few moments, he stepped back to look at her. She was radiant.

"You have shown great courage. Many are grateful. Look around you." She gestured to his friends filling the hillside. Even Maxim had come to share the moment. He stood with Daniel who was sobbing with joy at the sight of his mother.

Lost in Plain Sight

"Daniel ... come to me," she whispered.

He ran over and threw his arms around her. Even the fierce warrior Retarius pushed back a tear.

All became quiet.

Diane gestured for Anthony and Daniel to follow her to the other side of the pond for a private conversation. "Anthony, the Council of Elders has offered a gift for your courage. The one you most wanted, but knew you could never have," she told him gently.

His face brightened for a brief moment. Then he turned to Daniel and to all of his new friends standing on the hillside. The one thing he wanted more than anything else would have to wait. He took Diane's hands and gazed deeply into her eyes.

"I ... can't." He could barely utter the words. "I can't leave Daniel without a father and I made a promise to a good friend." He acknowledged the Symbol of Consciousness, who nodded back respectfully. "My work is unfinished."

"I know." She smiled. "That is why I did not ask you to cross the white veil myself. I'm so proud of you." She embraced him once more and motioned Daniel over. "Take care of your father. I will always be thinking of you and never far away."

Daniel began to cry. "But I'll miss you, Mom." He hugged her tightly as she whispered softly in his ear.

"When the leaves fall gently in autumn and the snowflakes drop silently in the hush of a winter day, I will be with you. When the rain taps gently on your windowpane in springtime ... when a lonely summer breeze ruffles your hair and caresses your cheek, it is my kiss until we meet again." She gently stroked Daniel's cheek and faded away.

Not a sound could be heard.

Maxim stepped forward to address the crowd. "I have spoken with the Council of Elders and have a decree. Retarius has been restored as the leader of Tambora!"

A joyful roar burst forth from the crowd as Retarius smiled and waved to the masses that continued to assemble on the hillside.

Maxim raised his hand to quiet the crowd. "There is more. For his bravery, Medrar has been granted Governorship of the West Quadrant of the Fourth Realm! He will oversee the very sector where he was enslaved!" Maxim bowed to an utterly surprised and ecstatic Medrar, who turned to the cheering crowd sporting the biggest smile Anthony had ever seen from the ex bell-ringer. Retarius grabbed Medrar's wrist and raised his arm in victory.

Maxim stood before Tom. "You traveled to these realms a boy and will leave them a man. You will be granted safe passage back to your time and given the gift of insight and remembrance of your experience here. Go forth and awaken those that will listen about the ancient truths. Clear the way for Anthony so that he may continue those good works in his time." Maxim nodded to Anthony as the crowd cheered again.

Maxim turned to Daniel. "Your love, Emily, is worried and waits for you. The symbols will escort you to the Realm of Dreams. Meet with her there and assure her of your safe return to the physical."

"Thank you, Maxim."

"And finally—"

The crowd erupted with the loudest cheers yet for Anthony. Maxim waited for them to quiet. He put his hand on Anthony's shoulder. "The Council is eternally in your debt as are the spirits of the Fourth Realm. You have fulfilled your destiny and saved countless souls from the oblivion of hopelessness." The crowd roared again. Maxim raised his hands. "Your work is not complete but such selflessness and courage deserves a gift of equal value. The Council and I have agreed to bestow upon you the gift of channeling ... yours truly." Maxim laughed and bowed to Anthony as the crowd applauded and roared with approval.

"While on Earth, you will be given the ability to go into a trance and allow me to speak through you to all who will listen to their hearts and find their personal truths."

"I don't know what to say ..." Anthony was overwhelmed by Maxim's gesture.

"And lastly, Tabor." Maxim purposefully used Anthony's spiritual name in front of the crowded gathering. "There is someone waiting for you at the Temple Portal. You have known each other throughout many lives."

"Who would that be?"

Maxim playfully ignored him as Medrar and Retarius sniggered. "Say goodbye to your friends for now." He gestured to the crowd as Anthony said goodbye to Tom.

"All the best to you, my friend."

"And to you as well. Maybe someday, we'll meet again on Earth," he said hopefully.

"Maybe." Anthony patted him on the back. "Make my job easier, if you can," he joked to relieve some of the sadness of the goodbye.

Tom smiled through tears and nodded, *yes*.

Anthony turned to Retarius who bowed and wished him a safe journey. He thanked each of the symbols and especially the Symbol of Consciousness. The symbol's swirl formed a great smile. Then, he faced the multitude of notes and thanked them for their kindness and courage, receiving a triumphant trumpet cadenza in return. He saved a hug for his friend, Medrar, who seemed sad to see him go.

Finally, he stood before Daniel. "Safe travels, son. Tell Emily I'm safe and will see her again soon. I love you."

"I love you too, Dad."

Maxim waved his hands slowly over their faces. Within moments, they were on their way to their destinations and had vanished to all those left behind in Tambora.

THIRTY-NINE

Anthony appeared at the steps to the Temple Portal and was greeted by Jaster, whom he was actually glad to see. "Hello, my friend. It's been a while."

"Greetings, Tabor. Time has barely taken a step forward during your absence." The diminutive man grinned. "It is your perception."

"Maybe," Anthony laughed. "I was told someone is waiting for me here."

"This is true. Follow me inside."

The great doors opened and Jaster hopped over the threshold excitedly. "Come, come … follow me." He waved Anthony on impatiently as he bounded down the rows of massive columns toward the rotunda in the middle of the temple.

Anthony followed as quickly as he could but could not keep up with the energetic Jaster. The rotunda came into view and he saw the silhouette of a woman. Something seemed familiar about her. As he moved closer, she turned to face him. He stopped in his tracks as their eyes met. Memories came flooding into his mind from the after-death dimensions and his past lives. She had been with him always.

"Candra!" In an instant, he had wrapped his arms around her waist and lifted her off her feet. They twirled like dancers over the brilliant mosaic floor. "My God, how could I have forgotten again? I missed you," he cried through both laughter and tears.

"You say that after every life on Earth, Tabor," she laughed. "You *are* courageous to accept so many physical lives." She gazed deeply into his eyes and kissed him passionately. "I've missed you too."

#

Elizabeth woke-up and looked about her room.

"No ... go back to sleep," she told herself. She closed her eyes and tried mightily to hold on to the feeling but it began to fade. No, she told herself. Go back to the beautiful temple ... Tabor, she sighed half-asleep, attempting to keep his image in her mind.

"Anthony!" she sat-up in bed. "Oh-My-God. It's him!" She swung her legs over the side of the bed to think. It seemed so real, she thought. Something deep inside her understood they had known each other all along.

Then, an idea popped into her mind. If it's true, he'll know. "Maybe he had the same dream," she giggled out loud.

She quickly cleaned-up, got dressed and poked her head into Abby's room. Good, she's still asleep, she thought happily. She quietly closed the door, tip-toed down the stairs and gently locked the front door. When she turned around, she saw Anthony coming down the pathway. He stopped and gave her the most beautiful smile she had ever seen. She knew immediately it was true. He ran to her. It was as if they had never been apart.

ONE YEAR LATER
In Anthony's Time

Mom told me that someday a lot of people would be coming to you for help but if you didn't get started soon the only one getting help would be Max. What did she mean?"

Anthony laughed out loud as Liz stood in the background holding back her own laughter.

"You know, she's right," Anthony agreed, glancing playfully at Liz. I might as well start with you, Abby. Why don't you sit down and give me a minute to get ready.

"Okay, Dad."

TWENTY-EIGHT YEARS LATER

In Tom's Time

Tom played around with his new Wi-Fi enabled laptop, sifting through the stock images of desktop backgrounds. One in particular caught his eye. A mountain stream cut through a beautiful meadow that ran up a hillside filled with spring flowers. It reminded him of his travels to Tambora so many years ago. He took a sip of his cappuccino and closed his eyes as the delicious concoction soothed his caffeine craving.

Twenty-eight years had passed since his miraculous return home. What was it about that number twenty-eight, he wondered. It seemed to stick in his mind for some reason.

He was now in his mid-forties and not sure where to go next with his career. He had been in media sales for twenty-four years and was tired of the grind. The digital space had been good to him until 2000, but it had been struggle ever since. Now it was 2004 and he was just beginning to make some headway. He loved his part-time gig as a life-coach and wished he could do it full-time but couldn't afford it. So many people seemed to be looking for a second career or some meaning in their life. He was grateful for the gift of remembrance bestowed so many years ago on that distant hillside. He had told no one where he had gained his knowledge, but he had helped many. There was no doubt about that, he acknowledged privately.

Lost in Plain Sight

He looked around the cafe and wondered how many of these people felt they needed a change in their lives as they munched on donuts and bagels and downed their supersized coffees.

He set his new background and launched his browser to check-out the markets which defaulted to the CNBC web site. He was in one of a very few experimental Wi-Fi locations in the country and he loved the convenience. Being an early adopter has its advantages, he thought with a smile.

The main headline was an IPO for the search engine, Google, which seemed to be growing pretty rapidly. However, it had a long way to go before catching-up to the success of Yahoo! He had kicked himself for not buying Yahoo! back in 1998 or Cisco a couple of years earlier. So many tech companies have failed in the last few years, he reminded himself.

Just for fun, he checked out the IPO price ... $85.00 a share. Kinda rich, he thought. One hundred shares would cost me $8,500.00 ... "Yikes!" His WorldCom and Enron stock were doing great, and he owned a lot of shares of each. He'd have to sell them and add cash. I don't know, he thought.

He glanced at his watch. He had a meeting to catch and didn't have time to play around with the market. He clicked on Google to search the company web site and pin point the meeting location and it suddenly hit him. "Google!" He slammed the table and laughed, launching curious stares from the other patrons. "Thank you, my friend," he said to no one in particular.

Printed in Great Britain
by Amazon.co.uk, Ltd.,
Marston Gate.